NEW YORK

A NOVEL

Ca
cha

IF WE MEET AGAIN

Nicole Spencer-Skillen

FROM BEST-SELLING LESBIAN ROMANCE AUTHOR

ALSO BY NICOLE SPENCER-SKILLEN

Choose Me

Are You Still Mine

Nicole Spencer-Skillen

IF WE MEET AGAIN

First Edition: November 2021
Edited by Hayley Ramsey
Cover by @bookcoversonline

For all the hopeless romantics that believe in the power of a single moment.

1

June 2014
Ashley

Ashley looked towards the hectic bar area. The chances of getting served were slim to none. That was unless you knew the bar manager—having friends in the hospitality industry had its perks. Jason had been trying so desperately to acquire her services in recent months, but the tips at her current place of work were the only reason she could afford to live in Manhattan at all.

Jason nodded in her direction, a signal that meant *I will have someone with you shortly*. It was a Saturday and a rarity that Ashley was not working herself. The tips were substantial on a weekend, so rarely would she take time off. It was the first weekend she had booked off in almost six months.

Within minutes, Jason appeared with a pitcher of beer in one hand and a tray of shots in the other. His dark brown skin looked flawless as always, Ashley was instantly jealous. His curly hair was slightly shorter than when she'd last seen him, but the half-grown beard and his lanky frame would never change. He insisted his beard was his most attractive feature, so Ashley dare not disagree, despite the fact it didn't quite join up, which she often teased him about.

"Girls, this one's on me."

They had an enviable position, the glares from the bustling bar area came one after another. Ashley looked enthusiastically towards her friends—it's not what you know, it's who you know. That was more apparent in the state of New York than anywhere else in the world.

"Jason, you're the best. I owe you one."

"Darling, please. What are friends for? You know I would love to stop and chat, but I am slammed tonight. If you're still around later, let's catch up."

"Sure, sounds great. Thank you so much for the drinks."

Jason had already made his way speedily towards the bar, collecting glasses and bottles as he went. It was only her second night off and she already missed the fast-paced buzz that came with the job. Regardless of the fact it was only a stepping stone until she became a fully fledged writer, she had surprisingly grown to love the job as she entered her third year in the industry.

Midtown 101 had been in business for ten years. A bar accustomed to regulars with the occasional tourist. It was seen as a hidden gem by many who lived in the area and often the spot that Ashley and her friends found themselves frequenting whenever they had the time. Ashley scanned the bar; she noticed one or two familiar faces. The DJ nervously tugged at the wires of his equipment, preparing for his set that was due to start in less than five minutes; being unprepared would be an instant calamity. The people of New York liked to voice their opinion—it was eat or be eaten. A new server dropped an empty glass, the bar exploded with cheers. Panic overwhelmed her, causing a further glass to fall. Jason rolled his eyes; another one bites the dust.

Ashley's attention was drawn to a familiar stature, a figure that her eyes had observed the night before. She was there again, the girl with no name. The occupier of her dreams the previous night. There was something different about the way she looked this time. Her long brown hair was down as opposed to up and she wore a tight, white dress that proudly displayed her figure, complemented by a pair of low, black kitten heels and a matching bag—an outfit choice unbefitting the dingy bar they found themselves in. Opting for the low heels had been a solid choice, the extra height wasn't something she needed. She had donned a more casual outfit the previous evening. The same group from the night before crowded her. They moved in and out with the rhythm of the music, partially blocking the mystery girl from view.

Ashley watched in awe; discretion was altogether lost on her. The one dominant intention she had went against every characteristic she usually possessed—*make her notice me.*

The unknown figure spun to the left, briefly removing her from the blockade her friends had inconveniently created. It put her in plain sight and within seconds, they caught one another's stare. Ashley smiled uncontrollably and was met with the ultimate reciprocation. Mystery girl's eyes crinkled; the corners of her mouth grew wider, exposing an almost perfect set of teeth. Her grin caused small dimples in her cheeks; the smile was infectious and captured the moment perfectly. Ashley could only assume that the girl in white had likewise felt the connection the night before.

The opportunity she had previously missed presented itself once again. The thrill proving more powerful than either could have anticipated. *Was this really happening? What are the odds?* Ashley thought. The smile they shared lasted until the DJ introduced the next track and the spell broke all at once. Ashley turned back towards her friends. Unbeknownst to her, they had both witnessed her trance-like state.

"She's still looking at you."

Ashley could now only rely on her friends' interpretation of the scenario that played out behind her.

"Shit, really? What do I do?"

Emily handed Ashley a shot of tequila to calm the nerves, which she didn't hesitate to accept. Emily Baker was a couple of years older than Ashley, a blonde-haired, green-eyed PA from The Big Apple. She met Ashley at the bar she worked in three years prior; they instantly hit it off. Emily's refusal to settle down left a string of broken-hearted women wherever they went, which meant she was more comfortable and accustomed to the dating scene.

"She keeps glancing over. She 100% wants your attention." Emily grinned.

The excitement was building. Emily couldn't hide her approval of the situation. The group of friends immediately became aware that the connection in the room was unique and thrilling.

"Shall I go over? Or is that a bad idea?"

Ashley looked to her friends for assurance. The thought of approaching the girl made her stomach churn. Even more so than the time she ate eight doughnuts and rode The Cyclone at Coney Island.

"You have to go over, Ash!"

Emily jumped up and down like an excitable child. Madison took a calmer approach, as she often did; observing the scene as it unfolded. Madison Roberts was the same age as Ashley, with cropped blonde hair and blue eyes. They had grown up together, living in the same neighbourhood in Jericho, Long Island for ten years before taking the plunge from suburban to city life at the age of twenty-two. A year later, they met Emily. The three were now inseparable.

"I'm nervous. Have you seen her? She's insanely attractive."

"She's probably thinking the same about you. The smile was mutual." Madison pointed out.

"If you don't go over to her, I will. Connection or not." Emily winked.

That was the push Ashley needed. She wasn't about to let her best friend speak to the girl she had been so eager to make contact with.

"Don't you dare."

"Girls like that don't just sit around and smile forever."

"It was obvious, wasn't it? The way she smiled at me? I didn't dream that, did I?"

Ashley glanced over her right shoulder. The mystery girl was swaying side to side with the music—she wanted to dance, but she wasn't intoxicated enough to let loose.

"It was so obvious. She is into you."

Madison removed the drink from Ashley's hand; there was no time like the present.

"Seriously, go over there now. You'll regret it tomorrow if you don't."

The peer pressure mounting caused the nerves to set in. After another minute of tough persuasion from her friends, Ashley plucked up the courage to approach the girl in white. It was a moment of rare confidence that stemmed from the electrifying smile aimed directly at her.

Ashley sauntered through the crowd of people. As she got closer, the girl appeared unaware of her approach, which made Ashley agitated. *What if she didn't reciprocate her advances?* The alcohol levels in her system were not high enough to warrant such a confident exterior; inside she was crumbling, but the urge to try far outweighed the fear of the outcome.

Ashley was now face-to-face with the girl whose name she was yet to discover. Despite the precarious looks from her friends flanked on all sides, Ashley kept her composure and leaned in towards her left ear, placing one hand gently at the base of her back. The noise in the bar amplified as the DJ warmed up, making the intimacy of the communication between them a necessity.

"Can I buy you a drink?"

The girl looked surprised at the request. Ashley found it hard to believe that this wasn't a regular occurrence for someone as beautiful as her. She smiled graciously before responding.

"Maybe later?"

She gestured towards her already full glass. The response was kind and promising, which gave Ashley some hope that eased the discomfort of complete rejection.

"Okay, sure."

Ashley retreated to her friends as swiftly as she had approached. She could feel the eyes burning in the back of her head as she walked away. The confusion of the mystery girl's friends was evident. The excitement radiated from Emily and Madison, both were qualified enough to be the ultimate wing woman and Ashley was fortunate to have both.

Despite the outcome being somewhat of an anti-climax, Ashley, for the first time in a long time, felt alive.

"So? What did she say?" Emily probed.

"You came back quick! Did she say no?" Madison followed.

"She said, 'maybe later'. Is that a blow-off?"

A chorus of laughs erupted; Ashley's included.

"Maybe she was looking over at me instead?" Madison teased.

"Or maybe it was me? We were all standing pretty close. Should I go over and see if she lets me buy her a drink?" Emily rose from the bar stool, poised and ready to make her advances toward the unknown girl. She took two steps forward before spinning and playfully embracing Ashley.

"I'm kidding. Believe me, she was staring at you."

Ashley felt relief. They continued to make light of the situation over the next two hours. Emily became preoccupied with her phone—girl trouble—while Madison and Ashley danced the night away. On several occasions, Ashley surveyed the bar looking for the girl. Their eyes locked once and a small smile crept up on their faces as if they anticipated it would happen.

"How long is acceptable to wait? Like, what does 'maybe later' even mean? Twenty minutes? An hour? Three hours?"

Madison shouted above the blur of the music, "Does she still have a full drink?"

Emily looked up from her phone for the first time in fifteen minutes. "Does it really matter? If you keep waiting for her drink to be empty, you'll never go over."

The evening drew closer to last orders. Midtown 101 was due to shut in less than an hour. Ashley's time was running out.

"Shall I go over now?"

"Yes, 100%," Emily vocalised. Madison nodded in agreement.

"What's the worst that could happen? She rejects you and you go home with a bruised ego. At least you tried," Madison advised.

Ashley tipped her glass up towards her mouth, the remainder of the gin and soda went down easily. Jason had continued to supply them with drinks up until the end of his shift. Ashley now had a reason to approach the bar; in order to get there, she would have to weave through several tables, the hectic dancefloor and by the mystery girl who stood directly in front of the bar twenty metres away.

"Okay," Ashley confirmed, "I can do this."

Madison placed a reassuring hand on Ashley's arm and pulled her in close so her words could be heard clearly.

"Ash, some girls just feel a bit uncomfortable with being approached. Especially when they're out with their friends. So maybe just ask her for her number then you can continue the conversation tomorrow."

"Okay. You're right."

Ashley glanced towards the bar. It was now or never; she took off.

"Ash, get me another beer please." Emily yelled.

How best to approach the situation had been eating her alive all night. As soon as Ashley saw her, she had become her primary focus. She had to know who the mystery girl was at any cost. If that meant facing the fear of humiliation head-on then that's exactly what she was going to do.

"Hello, again." Ashley stiffened.

The girl laughed awkwardly.

"Hello." Her voice was drowned out by the roar of the DJ as he made everyone aware that the countdown of the final ten songs was now underway. Ashley leaned in closer.

"What's your name?"

The girl looked towards her friends and then back at Ashley, who had relaxed her shoulders and placed one hand in her pocket.

"It's Megan. What about you?"

The girl in white finally had a name. Megan.

"I'm Ashley."

Ashley kept her eyes firmly focused on Megan. The calming aura she tried to emit to hide her nerves was being put to the test by the intimidation of Megan's friends. Two of them turned away, minding their own business, but one was firmly watching the exchange unfold.

"I see your drink is full—again. Asking to buy you another is pointless, isn't it?"

Megan laughed and gestured towards a group of men at the bar.

"They beat you to it," she revealed.

Ashley rolled her eyes blatantly and laughed. Megan wasn't from New York; from the little she could make out of her accent, it sounded almost English, but with a slight American twang. Ashley was all the more intrigued.

"Do you want to have a chat? I need a refill. Join me at the bar?"

Megan looked cautiously toward the friend immediately to her left. *Was she looking for approval?* Ashley was unsure of the friend's significance. Megan leaned in closer towards Ashley's right ear, leaving her friend unaware of what was said next.

"Sorry, I can't leave my friends. This is the first time I have seen them in over a year."

"How about I just take your number instead? We can talk tomorrow?"

Madison would be proud. Megan pulled her phone from the black clutch under her arm, typed in Ashley under 'create contact' and handed the phone over.

"Here, put your digits in."

The screen was severely cracked, but Ashley managed to punch her number directly into the keypad with no mistakes.

"I guess I will hear from you soon then?"

"You bet."

2

Ashley

The following morning, Ashley poured herself a cup of coffee and walked up onto the roof of her fifth-floor apartment. Ashley and Madison had been lucky enough to find a pre-war loft space to rent that had the added benefit of a rooftop deck with views across the city. The loft had become available for the first time in a decade when a friend recommended it to Ashley. Twenty-four hours later, it was theirs. The bills had been over budget at first; they both worked every hour imaginable to pay the rent, but that was a price they were willing to pay to live in New York City. The two-bed apartment had the authenticity and charm they had been looking for, with stunning iron columns and exposed brick. It had been a no-brainer.

After six months, they both agreed it was time to find a lodger. The open-plan living area was extensive enough to create a third bedroom. It wouldn't be as private, but they agreed that for the right person, it would be appealing. Emily immediately made her interest known—having recently broken up with her girlfriend of two years, she was looking for somewhere to live. The timing had been impeccable.

Ashley raised the cup to her lips, admiring the view as she took a sip of her freshly ground coffee—Italian Roast. A new blend that was recommended by a customer; she wasn't disappointed. The gentle summer breeze rippled through her t-shirt. The plants on the rooftop emitted a ruffle as the wind swept through their leaves. She made a mental note to water the peace lily; the leaves had drooped and it required some attention. It had been Madison's idea to purchase plants. Three years later, it was only Ashley that attempted to keep them alive, but they added some colour to an otherwise dull rooftop.

Ashley would undergo the same routine every single day. Wake up, make a coffee of choice, sit on the roof. She fast became accustomed to living in the city and she had no plans to retreat to her mundane life in the suburbs.

Ashley was twenty-five years old, with blonde hair and brown eyes. She was of slim build and above average height at 5'7", her features—ordinary. She would often describe herself as plain. Her features were not unusual; she didn't stand out from the crowd, unlike her roommates. She aspired to be a writer—like almost everyone in NYC—but she was different, at least that's what she told herself. The passion she possessed from a young age was even more formidable now than it had ever been. There was a deep-seated determination within her to one day become a writer for one of the city's top magazines—even if that meant grinding away in a bar for ten years. She would do whatever it took to prove that it wasn't just a pipe dream.

Ashley pulled her phone from her pocket as she took a seat on the bench, placing her cup on the large coffee-stained wooden table. Flashbacks of all three of them trying to get the table onto the roof came flooding back. The sheer entertainment value made it an unforgettable memory. The table was severely battered and bruised by the time it reached the rooftop, but despite the turbulent

New York weather, it had stayed faithful for almost three years.

There was still no message from Megan. It was almost lunchtime and the suspense she felt unkindly woke her up four hours earlier than her planned alarm. Emily and Madison would be dead to the world until at least three in the afternoon. Ashley placed the phone on the table and recalled the first night she'd seen her.

Mystery girl, now known as Megan, had arrived at Midtown 101 almost an hour after Ashley. The group entered extravagantly, bought two trays of shots, and congregated directly in front of Ashley and Madison. It was hard not to notice them, or her. The infectious laugh, the picture-perfect smile and flawless skin. The beauty she possessed was unusual in bars like 101; it was often locals, regulars or people looking to blow off some steam after a long day at work. The friends that surrounded her were at ease. They said hello to the occasional passer-by and ordered drinks without hesitation, but Megan seemed out of place. Potentially more suited to the Upper West Side of Manhattan. *That must be where she's from*, Ashley considered.

Megan didn't only catch the eye of Ashley that night.

"Have you seen the girl in the white shirt?" Madison asked.

"I noticed her as soon as they walked in. I don't recognise her, do you?"

"No, she must be from out of town. If a girl like that came in here often, I would have seen her."

Madison frequented Midtown 101 regularly, so Ashley trusted her observations. Emily arrived shortly after and just in time to solve the dilemma.

"She has glanced over a few times. She's definitely looking in my direction." Madison proclaimed.

Confident and pleased that she appealed to the mystery girl.

"You're dreaming. You wish she was looking at you!" Ashley challenged.

The two would often fight over the attention of women. They had been the same ever since Madison came out as gay two years earlier, but Ashley regularly had the upper hand.

"Emily, who is she looking at?"

Ashley turned towards Emily, with one hand typing away on her laptop and the other cradling a Moscow Mule. Emily often found herself in the middle of the bickering. Friday nights were always spent dealing with the accumulation of emails she had tried to avoid all week long. Emily glanced towards the group at the bar, her focus on the girl and the way her eyes flickered between her friends and the table she occupied every thirty seconds. The conclusion was swift.

"She is 100% looking at Ashley. Now, can I finish these emails?"

Emily buried her head in her laptop once again, determined to enjoy her friends' company at some point that evening. Ashley smirked as Madison slouched back in her chair, visibly unhappy with the verdict.

"Better luck next time, Mads." Ashley grinned from ear to ear.

The jiving continued, but it was all in good spirit, as Ashley reminded Madison—if your best friend can't knock you down a peg or two, then who can? Three gay women living together came with its challenges. Female drama holding the number one spot on that list.

Madison pushed her bruised ego aside, allowing for the conversation to continue. They discussed, in-depth, their workdays and their weekend plans, but Ashley couldn't shake the presence of the mystery girl all evening.

"I'm out. Do you guys want another drink?" Ashley gestured towards the empty glass in her hand where the last remnants of her third beer lingered.

"Sure, I'll take another beer. Get a pitcher? Let me pay though, it's my round."

Madison pulled out a wad of tips from the zip conveniently placed on the inside of her leather jacket. The better service she gave to the customers buying beer in her bar, the more drinks she purchased in others. It was the circle of life, only in beer form. Ashley waved off Madison's effort to pay for the drinks, took one look at Emily, who was still engrossed in her emails, and then headed to the bar.

Ashley found herself in close proximity to the girl she now knew as Megan. There was a moment of manoeuvring required to allow Ashley access to the bar, located inconveniently behind the crowd of people. That was standard for a bar of 101's size. Ashley considered taking the longer route and accessing the bar from the south side, but the opportunity to see the mystery girl up close prevented her from changing direction.

The tall, shabby wooden table they congregated around only had two chairs; both seats were taken, so said girl stood directly to the right, closest to the bar area. Ashley observed the girl, who was blissfully unaware of her approach until the very last second. Then, as if the collision was somehow deliberate, they found themselves face-to-face. At the moment Ashley politely excused herself through the crowd, Megan had turned towards her friend, who she must have assumed was still standing directly behind her. The timing was perfect. Ashley was now within arm's length of the girl who had consumed her thoughts all night long and, for a concise moment, time stood still.

They were almost perfectly matched in height. Naturally, their eyes locked. They say that a person's eyes are the window to their soul. The true meaning of that was perceptible at that moment when they communicated without words at all. The connection so powerful that Ashley forgot to breathe—a quick gasp for air brought her back to a somewhat normal rhythm.

Confusion clouded Megan's eyes as she became the first to lose her nerve and drop her gaze to the floor. Ashley glanced towards the bar and then back at Megan once she'd safely found a spot to order.

"One pitcher of Black Forest, please."

The encounter lasted less than thirty seconds—that's all it took for Ashley to be consumed by the connection between them. After she gathered the drinks, she returned to her table, eyes focused on Megan for the rest of the evening. As she sat in awe of the girl she so desperately wanted to know, she asked herself; *how does such a connection form without communication or touch?*

***

Ashley came back to reality—her coffee was almost empty and she found herself wondering whether it was normal to connect with someone purely through body language and eye contact. *Had the atmosphere been as electric as she perceived it to be that first night? Or the second?* She awaited communication from Megan for clarification.

The way the wind whipped back and forth required more than the t-shirt Ashley donned. She swiftly headed

back down to her apartment, made another coffee—
PERU medium roast this time—and perched herself on
the couch.

Ashley was fully engrossed in a new thriller Emily
had recommended when her phone lit up. She scrambled
for the remote to pause the TV. The number on the screen
appeared unknown. Her fingers went to work on the
security pin, accessing the message in seconds. The
message read;

Hey, it's Megan.

Ashley burst upright from her reclined position.
There was a breakthrough. She waited no time at all to
compose a reply.

Hi, Megan. How's your head today?

The response was lacking wit and somewhat
cautious. Ashley, unsure how the conversation would
play out, wanted to make sure she didn't come on too
strong.

*On a scale of 1 to 10, I would say it's a solid 7.
Nothing I can't handle. How about you? Did you have a
good night?*

The keypad went to work as Ashley tapped away, the
response sincere, but too forward. She realised fast
before her fingers hit send and abruptly deleted the
message. The composition of another message, more
casual, better suited the conversation.

Nothing a few cups of coffee can't fix. It was a fun night, the first weekend I have had off in a long time, so it was a welcomed rarity. You?

There was no response immediately. Ashley reverted to her sprawled position on the couch, left with a sense of satisfaction from the night before. She knew her friends would quiz her intensely when they woke, and the embarrassment of not getting a reply would be mortifying.

After noting a third cup of coffee before lunch would be unacceptable, she opted for a refreshing glass of pineapple juice and some vitamin C instead. The second she placed her glass down on the hardwood floor, her phone sprang to life. It was Megan. She gripped the phone in one hand, with her finger poised and ready to hit the green symbol. *Why was she calling?* Ashley was unprepared for a phone conversation; she jumped up and down before irreversibly taking the plunge.

"Hello?"

"Hey. I thought I would just call. I hope that's okay?"

Ashley stuttered, "Sure, of course."

The pause on the line emphasised her quick, uneasy breathing. Nervous, she recalled what she had wanted to ask the night before. "So, are you from New York?"

"Do I sound like I'm from New York?" Megan laughed.

"No, not in the slightest. I honestly couldn't even take a guess at where you're from—no offence."

"None taken. I am originally from New York, believe it or not, but I moved to England when I was six. So the accent is a little bit of a mixture."

"That's so cool. Why England?"

"My dad was a professional basketball player. He got offered a contract in the British league when he was twenty-five and he took it."

"I bet that was interesting, growing up in a different country?"

"It was different for sure. I was so young though I didn't really miss New York, not until I started visiting in my teens."

"What brings you back to New York now?"

"I actually came back to America four years ago when I was eighteen. I got offered a scholarship programme to play basketball at Stanford University and I just graduated."

"Stanford as in, California?" Ashley queried.

"That's the one."

"And that would make you…" Ashley totted up the years in her head, "…twenty-two?"

"Correct. Just turned last month. How old are you?"

"Twenty-five." Ashley considered the information just divulged. "So, you're from New York, you moved to England, then to California, and now you're in New York again?"

Megan chuckled. "You got it in one."

"How long are you staying in New York?"

Sounding less than enthusiastic, Megan responded. "That I don't know. It all depends on whether I get signed. It's complicated and stressful." Megan sighed. "I am just here to enjoy myself for now."

Ashley wanted to know where she might go if she didn't stay. Would she go back to England? Not wanting to pry, she moved swiftly off the subject.

"Where are you staying whilst you're here?"

"On the Upper West Side. My aunt has lived here most of her adult life, so I'm staying with her."

Ashley's prediction had been correct.

"You look like an Upper West Side kind of girl," Ashley joked.

"What does that mean?" Megan laughed nervously.

"Nothing. Does your aunt live in a condo overlooking Central Park with marble floors and a doorman that greets you by name?" Ashley teased, hoping her sarcasm would be well received.

"Actually, the doorman doesn't know my name yet, but I have only been there a week, so I will give him the benefit of the doubt."

"Just a week? How is the Big Apple treating you? Have you been back often since you moved away?"

The questions came out in a flurry, the conversation unforced.

"I have been back at least once a year since we left. It still feels like home, even though I remember little about being here when I was younger. My family is here though, so it's nice to come back." Megan paused. There was a conversation going on in the background that she had a brief input in before returning to her explanation. "It's been years since I went up the Empire State Building, so I did that on Wednesday last week. I met up with friends and family, did a bit of shopping, nothing out of the ordinary. The food in New York is what I miss the most, so I have been indulging at every opportunity."

"Where have you been eating? I could recommend a few spots. I like to think of myself as a food connoisseur."

Speaking of food, Ashley headed to the kitchen to see what was available. They hadn't bought any groceries in over a week, so the options were slim. An out of date carton of eggs and two day old left over lasagne didn't appeal. Thankfully, the food truck directly outside their apartment served the best cinnamon pastries. Ashley, now on a first-name basis with Howard (the food truck owner), would often receive a discount for her loyal service. At the end of the day, if Howard had any leftover pastries, he would ring up to their apartment to see if they wanted some—that was an easy decision every single time.

"A food connoisseur is a big title to acquire. I hope you can live up to that kind of expectation," Megan laughed. "My friends know all the good spots. We went to a little place called Joe's Pizza on the corner of 21st and 8th in Chelsea. Have you been?"

"I have, quite a lot actually, it's not too far from me. The pizza is out of this world. The question is, what's your flavour?"

"Pepperoni every time. How about you?"

"I think you and I will get along just fine." Ashley's go-to pizza was pepperoni. It irritated her beyond belief that Emily and Madison both hated it. On the plus side, there was always enough leftover pizza for breakfast.

"Well, that's good to know. So, do you always go to Midtown 101?"

"Not particularly. My best friend Madison goes a lot more than I do. We just fancied a chilled vibe this weekend, and 101 is perfect for that. Was it your first time?"

"Yes, could you tell?"

"Not at all," Ashley expressed her amusement.

"You're taunting me, aren't you? What about me wasn't stereotypical enough for you?" Megan quizzed.

"I could just tell, that's all. You were too well-groomed, shall we say."

Ashley had already gauged Megan's sense of humour from the brief phone call and assumed she'd appreciate the banter.

"Groomed? What am I? A poodle?"

"If we are speaking in dog terms, you were a poodle in a bar full of Rottweilers." Megan burst out laughing. *The analogy hits the nail on the head*, Ashley thought.

"Well, that's a new one!" Megan pondered. "So, if I go again, how do I make myself look less like a poodle?"

Ashley considered the question thoroughly.

"That's easy. You don't brush your hair, turn up wearing a coffee-stained shirt and order a beer. If you want to be extremely convincing, you could even hurl abuse at the bartender for not putting the basketball game on."

Creating a picture of an unruly Midtown customer proved unproblematic for Ashley; she only had to picture the masses of people she dealt with daily.

"Well, I will bear that in mind. I suppose I should take it as a compliment then, being a poodle?"

"It's definitely not an insult," Ashley confirmed.

She heard Megan open her mouth to respond, but the hesitancy in her reply shut down the words before they formed. Ashley slouched back deep into the beige two-seater sofa, placing her feet on the solid oak coffee table in front. She sensed Megan's reluctance.

"What is it?" Ashley probed.

"What do you mean?"

"You were going to say something."

"I don't know," Megan paused, "I was just curious about something I guess."

"Curious about what?" Ashley sat upright, unable to keep the same position for longer than a minute. The intrigue was too intense to relax.

"What made you come and speak to me?"

"Honestly?" Ashley stood up and paced the room. The fifth-floor loft had a balconette window that looked out over a busy Manhattan street. It was a Sunday, but the New York rush never stopped. She pictured Megan walking along the street—what she would give to see her again.

"Yes, honestly."

"I thought you were the most attractive girl I had ever seen." Ashley pinched the bridge of her nose and squeezed her eyes shut, apprehensive and afraid that she would make a fool of herself.

Megan chuckled. "You liar."

"Why would I be lying?"

"I'm flattered obviously, but I still don't believe you."

"Don't believe me, but it's true. There was just something about you that captured me instantly. I imagine you have that effect on a lot of people."

Megan was too modest to admit it, but Ashley knew from her own experience that Megan was a rarity that men and women alike became easily drawn towards.

"Stop it, you're making me shy. Besides, if I had that effect on a lot of people, I wouldn't still be single," Megan jested.

"That is very true. There must be some deep-rooted problem I am yet to discover," Ashley teased.

"Charming."

"What made you look in my direction, anyway? Was it the creepy way in which I refused to look away?"

"You'll be glad to know I didn't find you creepy in the slightest. You are obviously attractive, so that appealed to me, but..." Ashley waited in anticipation, "...you just have this charming, engaging persona. I watched you laugh and I couldn't look away. It was strange. Anyway, I'll shut up now."

Ashley punched the air with a sense of pure elation.

"So attractive and charming that you rejected me the first time?" Ashley joked.

"That is not true."

"You reluctantly took my number the second time I came over, so I'll let it slide."

"Reluctantly? I was more than willing to take your number. In fact, I would have asked you first if the circumstances had been different," Megan declared.

"What do you mean?" Ashley heard the bathroom door close. Madison had arisen earlier than expected.

"The group of friends I was with didn't know I was gay. So, it put me in a strange position when you walked over because I really wanted to talk to you."

"Didn't know?"

"They do now. I told them shortly after you left. I wasn't hiding it from them through fear they'd not be okay with it, I was just waiting for the right moment. It was the first time I'd seen them in almost two years, so it wasn't the first thing on my mind."

"One brief encounter and you're already coming out to your friends. I must have made a good impression." Ashley smirked. The conversation felt abnormally comfortable, which baffled her.

"You're hilarious," Megan mocked. "In all seriousness, they're not stupid. I think they could tell from the energy between us."

The immediate chemistry had been clear to not only Ashley, but Megan and her friends as well. That discovery alone settled Ashley's nerves.

"I am glad I could be of assistance."

Megan responded quietly to a mystery voice in the background.

"I need to go. My aunt is taking me for lunch, but maybe I can call you tomorrow?" The request filled Ashley with welcome anticipation.

"Sure, I'd like that."

"Enjoy the rest of your day."

"You too. Goodbye, Megan."

Ashley pressed the end call button, threw her phone onto the couch and ran towards Madison's bedroom at the far end of the apartment, narrowly avoiding the iron column that stood between the kitchen worktop and the corridor that led to the bedrooms. She couldn't contain her excitement, and whether Madison liked it or not, she was about to hear word-for-word the entire conversation.

3

Megan

Megan Davis pulled the curtains open in the expansive corner bedroom of the 21st-floor condo. Two separate floor-to-ceiling windows overlooked one of the largest and most recognised parks in the world, Central Park. The grand and iconic views that she had become so accustomed to over the years never failed to amaze her.

After graduating from Stanford, she had arrived in New York with no plan other than to see her family and explore the city she loved. Gaining a scholarship to Stanford to play NCAA Division 1 basketball was a dream come true. With over 400,000 high school basketball players in the USA and a 1.2% chance of making it to play D1 basketball, the chances were slim. When the head of recruitment called in the summer of 2010, it was an easy decision to make. The ticket to California was booked the following day.

Megan opened her suitcase at the foot of the bed and pulled out her shorts, a WNBA hoodie and her latest sneaker purchase—the Nike Kobe 9 Elite in white. The orange basketball sat out of place at the foot of the large grey bed, flanked by two mirrored bedside tables and a desk to match. Megan's aunt had never had children or pets, so the condo was always show-home ready.

"Megan, I'm going to work. Will I be seeing you at dinner?"

Julie Davis popped her luxurious brown bob around the solid oak door.

"Sure, I'll be here. Have a nice day at work."

"Thanks, sweety, see you later."

The summer sun shone through the condo. FOX 5 New York predicted a heatwave that was likely to challenge the hottest on record, with temperatures reaching a soaring 104 degrees over a five-day period. Megan had purposefully set her alarm for eight o'clock in the morning; she had to shoot her daily hoops before the weather became unbearable, then she could retreat to the comfort of the air-conditioned condo.

Megan entered the grand open-plan living and dining area, with dark hardwood floors and soaring ceilings. It reminded her of her home in England. The decor was similar to that of her parents' contemporary barn conversion that was set on seven acres of land; it was a place she adored. The similarities between New York, USA and York, England stopped at the name. The bustling city of New York differed tremendously from the calm, tranquil countryside of York, but Megan was grateful for the opportunity to experience both.

To quench her thirst, a fresh smoothie was in order. The large glass fruit bowl sat delicately on the white marble kitchen surface, housing an array of fruits. This morning, she opted for raspberry, rhubarb, apple and pomegranate—a new concoction. Within minutes, she had a glass full of a pink, fruity blend that pleased her tastebuds.

Like clockwork, her mobile phone rang. It would only be one person at that time in the morning. A phone call from her father was an expectation on a daily basis. England had a time difference of five hours, so they often planned phone calls for a time that suited everyone.

"Hi, Dad."

Michael Davis was forty-one years old, with brown eyes, a 6'7" athletic frame and a head of grey hair. Often referred to as the 'silver fox' by his family and friends, he had gone prematurely grey at twenty-nine.

"Hi, Meg. I wasn't sure if you'd be awake."

"The idea of sleeping in did appeal to me, but do you know how hot it's going to be today? I'll pass out if I try to work out in that heat."

"Your mother mentioned it actually, it's not quite the same here. I think we will be lucky to hit 17 degrees today."

Megan often found herself confused between the two; degrees Celsius was used in England to determine the heat, whereas Fahrenheit was used more predominantly in America.

"I don't miss the English weather. California has spoilt me."

"Have you heard anything from Cheryl yet?"

Cheryl Eagan was a former Division 1 head-coach-turned-agent and Megan's current representation.

"Not yet. She had those few offers we discussed, so she's been trying to work out the best deal."

"Is it still between Lyon and the Mystics?"

Numerous scenarios had unfolded after an unsuccessful WNBA draft in April of that year. Megan was a 5'8" guard. The league had been looking for more height, which immediately ruled her out. Cheryl had suggested playing in Europe to gain some vital professional experience, which she could then hopefully, one day, take back to the USA. There had been several teams interested after submitting contract demands; the two teams remaining were Lyon or The Mystics—she would be heading to France or returning to England.

"Pretty much, there was a couple of teams in Germany interested, but they fell through."

"Are you still leaning more towards Lyon?" Megan's conversations with her dad always started and ended the same way—basketball.

"I think so, but at this point, I just want to be able to play the sport I love at a high level. Whichever team I go to, I'll give it 110%," Megan stated with confidence.

"I know you will. It would be nice to have you back with us. We miss you so much, but I know all about doing what's best for your career, so I'll support you no matter what."

The familiar feeling of nausea returned. Conversations with her family brought to the forefront the homesick feeling she tried so hard to bury. The four years spent at college meant she only saw her family once or twice a year. It was tough, but she became accustomed to the lifestyle; her dream of playing professional basketball required that of her.

"Thanks, Dad. As soon as I know what's happening, you and Mom will know."

"How's Aunt Julie?"

"She's Aunt Julie. No change really. She gets up every day at five in the morning to run on the treadmill for an hour. Spends her evenings responding to emails with a glass of wine. Makes a killer dinner, but rarely ever eats it warm because her phone never stops ringing. You know how she is. We went for lunch yesterday though, that was nice."

Julie had always been the perfect career role model to Megan. She was successful and driven, but never to the detriment of others. She possessed an overbearing passion to help those in need, which now made her one of the most sought-after therapists in NYC, treating well-known celebrities she couldn't name for legal reasons. It took up a large part of her life. One day, Megan asked her if she would ever have a work/life balance, to which she replied, *'There is no such thing as a work/life balance. If you love what you do, then your work becomes your mission in life and the two become combined.'* That statement alone made Megan more determined to play professional basketball; it was her mission in life, her calling, and she would stop at nothing to achieve it.

"That's nice. I'm glad you're spending some time together; she loves having you there."

"I love being here. I miss New York, it's always nice to be back. Will you be coming over at any point this summer?" Megan hoped she could see her parents sooner rather than later.

"We will see. I have a lot of work on at the moment, but maybe sometime in August. It depends where you are, doesn't it? I might be flying out to Lyon."

"Or driving down the M62 to Manchester," Megan laughed, optimistic for the former.

"I hope you're working on that mid-range, that's what will get you into Lyon. They're missing some mid-range magic."

"Every day, it's not like I can dunk, Michael. I wasn't graced with your height. My jump shot is all I've got."

Michael Davis chuckled. "Okay, smart ass. You're right. You can blame your mother for that. She brought you down a few inches."

They both laughed in unison. Amanda Davis' 5'4" frame was often blamed.

"I don't think that will ever get old. Where is mom, anyway?"

"She's with the developers at the new plot."

"How's it coming along?"

"Better than expected. We're ahead of schedule by a week or so. We should be able to get them on the market soon."

"That's great, Dad, I can't wait to see some photos." Megan drank the last of her smoothie, disposing of the remains down the drain.

"Where have you been playing ball, anyway?"

"Down on 46th and 9th, it's the closest one, otherwise I would have to go all the way over to Hudson River."

"I know the one."

"It's decent, not quite Stanford levels, but it'll do the job."

"I'll let you get to it then, sweetheart. Call me when you hear from Cheryl, okay?"

"Okay, Dad, I will."

***

Megan collected her basketball, a bottle of water from the fridge, and headed for the door. The usual elevator routine commenced—twenty-one floors—the timing was terrible; everyone would be leaving for work. The alternative of taking the stairs was something she regretted the day before. Regardless of her athletic nature, it took a mere five floors before she gave up and opted for the elevator.

The elevator doors opened up to the ground floor, the classic brown marble flooring was polished to perfection. The concierge smiled as Megan passed by, a friendly chap with a full head of grey hair, brown square rimmed glasses and a brown suit, he fitted in superbly with the surroundings. Despite the forty-one floors and 200+ apartments, the building never felt overcrowded.

The black revolving doors stopped directly in her path, the transition from inside the lobby to the sunlit street outside swift. The heat was already notably hotter than yesterday morning, Megan noticed.

The same doorman stood to the right of the door in his crisp white shirt and gold-buttoned black suit, eagerly awaiting to greet her as she left. The gold name tag read, Alberto.

"Good morning, Miss Davis."

Megan chuckled internally to herself, remembering briefly the conversation with Ashley. The urge to speak to her had been present since the day before, and she made a mental note to tell her about the doorman who now knew her by name—she would find that amusing.

"Good morning. Don't you ever take a day off?"

"It would seem as though I don't, but someone needs to be here to watch the door." Alberto shrugged and smiled politely.

"How long have you worked here?"

"Ten years, Miss Davis."

Megan took a guess that he must be in his late forties. She thought he was handsome for his age; the military crew cut and wrinkle-free complexion helped his cause.

"You must have seen a lot of things, huh?"

"I have enough stories to last a lifetime, but I don't like to gossip." Alberto winked playfully; his smile was infectious.

"I bet! Anyway, I must go."

"Adios, Miss Davis."

"Bye, Alberto."

Megan walked down Central Park West. The sun remained hidden behind the skyscrapers of New York for the time being. She had been to the same basketball court four times in the past week. The leisurely stroll lasted forty minutes; it was a pleasant one and also qualified as her warm-up.

After five minutes, she turned onto 69th, detouring away from Central Park and towards the rows of brownstone apartments. The streets around Central Park reminded her of a small suburb in the middle of a big city. Megan noted how the quiet serenity was unusual for New York; the birds chirping in the tree-lined streets filled with friendly neighbours exchanging pleasantries—it was postcard-worthy.

Ashley had crossed her mind on multiple occasions since their telephone conversation, but to her disappointment, there had been no attempt to reach out. That made Megan curious to know; *what was she doing? Did she think about her too?* Their brief conversation had been effortless, or at least she thought so. The ease with which they conversed had surprised Megan and made her eager to get to know Ashley more. There was no time like the present.

Megan pulled her phone from her pocket, clicked on the message icon and within seconds, she sent the message—no hesitation.

Hey! Are you at work?

The answer was immediate.

Hi! Not until later this afternoon. Why?

That was the answer Megan had hoped for. While the courage still surged through her body, she hit the call button.

"Hello?"

"Hey, can you talk?"

"Sure. I get the feeling you don't like texting."

"Not if I can help it."

"How come?" Ashley probed.

"It's boring, don't you think? I will text if I have to, but I much prefer to call someone. Besides, I can hear how hilarious you think I am down the phone, not so much on a message. *'Lol'* just doesn't cut it for me."

Ashley laughed; Megan's point proven.

"See, you find me hilarious. How would I know that through a message?"

"I agree, you are funny. Hilarious might be a stretch, but there is time to be convinced."

"I'll take that challenge. What are you doing? I didn't disturb your morning meditation, did I?"

"What makes you think I meditate?"

"I don't know. Most people in New York meditate or do yoga, I figured you'd fit into one of the two. Is that too stereotypical?"

"Very, but I'll let you off. I fit into neither actually, I like to do my own thing."

Megan grinned. "And what does that involve?"

"Drinking a selection of the finest coffees whilst watching re-runs of F.R.I.E.N.D.S. If I'm feeling really adventurous I'll sometimes go for a jog."

"I see, you're that type," Megan sniggered. "Speaking of stereotypical, my interaction with the doorman this morning made me think of you."

"Oh, really?"

"Yeah, turns out he does know my name and I now know his; he's called Alberto. Seems like a nice guy."

"So, I was right. I have my stereotypes down, you on the other hand, need to work on yours."

"Okay, I'll take that feedback on board." Megan wiped at her damp forehead; the humidity barely tolerable. "What is your day off this week?"

"Thursday. Why? Are you free?"

Megan bounced the basketball at her feet twice before gathering the ball under her arm again.

"I can be free."

"So, if I said I'd like to take you out, would that be something you'd be interested in?"

Megan beamed, "Sure, I'd like that. Do you have any ideas?"

"Leave it with me; I'll think of something. It will probably involve food."

"Well, yesterday you confirmed you are, in fact, a food connoisseur, so I'll be expecting big things."

"I won't disappoint you."

"How about you choose the food and I will choose the activity after the food?" Megan glanced across the street; it didn't look familiar. *Perhaps a wrong turn,* she thought.

"You are assuming we will make it past the food? That's presumptuous, don't you think?"

"You're right, but just in case."

The sound of Ashley's hoarse laugh on the other end of the phone left Megan unable to control the smile on her face.

"Okay, well I will look forward to food and maybe something after that."

"Me too."

After walking a block further than intended, Megan turned back. The welcome distraction on the other end of the line filled her with excitement that consumed her focus.

"Where are you heading?"

"Just to get some practice in. I need to stay sharp, so I go for an hour or two every day."

"Which courts?"

"The ones on West 46th."

"I know the ones, there's a really nice Korean place just up from there, on the corner of 10th avenue. I would recommend it. Providing you like Korean food."

Megan's eyes lit up at the prospect. "I love Korean food. Do they serve Kimchi Stew?"

"They do the best Kimchi Stew, trust me."

"You've sold it to me. I'll grab a dish on the way home." Megan's mouth watered at the thought. "Did you say you lived in Midtown?"

"Yes, I live in Chelsea and I work in West Village."

"Where do you work?"

"A bar called Analogue."

"Do you like working there?"

"It's not what I aspire to do, but it pays the bills. The tips are great, a hell of a lot better than the last place I worked so I can hardly complain."

"And what is it you aspire to do?"

"I want to be a writer."

"What kind of writer?"

"I'd love to write for a magazine like Reader's Digest, or *The New York Times* would be the dream, but my lack of experience makes it tough."

"My cousin is an associate editor for NBC and she loves it, but it took her years before she got the job." Megan rounded the corner near the basketball courts, hoping they would be empty. "What about writing books, has that never appealed to you?"

"The editing process appeals to me; my dream job would probably be editor-in-chief for a magazine or publishing company. I have written a few short stories, but I prefer to write articles."

"Well, if you want it enough, you'll make it a reality."

"Very philosophical."

"Not quite Gandhi." Megan laughed.

"Are you almost there?"

She stood directly outside the gates to the court. One solitary child, roughly twelve years old, attempted a long-range jump shot that rattled the rim.

"I am, there is only one kid playing. I can deal with that."

"Do you want me to come and remove him?"

"Nah, I'll just embarrass him with a quick 1 on 1. He'll soon leave."

"I like your style."

"Thank you."

"I'll have a think about Thursday and maybe let you know tomorrow?"

"That sounds great, I'm looking forward to it."

"Me too. Enjoy your basketball."

"Thanks. Bye, Ashley."

"Goodbye, Megan."

There was an unexpected comfort in talking to Ashley, Megan realised. After two phone conversations, she had barely scratched the surface, and the insight gained into Ashley Stewart's life was minimal. The prospect of meeting her face to face again brought a wave of anxiety, but she was hopeful of a spark if the first encounter was anything to go by.

Suddenly, the prospect of being in New York longer than planned brought enormous anticipation.

4

Ashley

Thursday morning arrived; the vast and cloudless blue sky had remained clear for the fourth day in a row. The temperature had dropped to 85 degrees, still too hot for some, but it was bearable due to the gentle breeze.

Ashley scrutinised herself in the mirror of her en-suite bathroom. Her eyes looked tired. Her shift the night before had been due to finish at eleven, but in true fashion, the pre-midnight rush kept her until close to one in the morning. On the plus side, the tip jar in her bedside table was growing considerably; she almost had enough money to afford the new laptop she so desperately needed. The sun had blessed Ashley with a radiant glow; two mornings basking in Central Park was all it took. She pulled her hair back into a bun, leaving some rogue parts to fall out at the front for a more relaxed look.

The smell of roasted coffee lured her to the kitchen and, without delay, Madison handed her a beige coffee mug, boiling to the brim.

"I need this, thank you."

"You're welcome. Did you sleep okay?"

"Average, you?"

"Same. Are you excited for today?"

Ashley brushed the loose hair from her eyes before placing the mug to her lips, taking the time to contemplate her feelings.

"I am, but I'm also a bit nervous."

"That's understandable though." Madison stretched over the reclaimed wooden breakfast bar, all ears. "Have you decided on your plans for the day?"

"When I spoke to her yesterday, she told me her favourite style of food was Mexican. So, I have booked us in at Dos Caminos."

"The one on Broadway?"

"No, the one in Soho—it's quieter there."

"Okay, definitely a good choice. What about dessert?"

"Ansel Bakery, of course, for a famous Cronut."

"Nice choice. I'm impressed. I haven't had a Cronut in so long. What's their flavour this month?"

The half-croissant, half-doughnut pastry was a creation Ashley had stumbled upon two years prior when she stopped at Dominique Ansel's bakery for a coffee. There she discovered just how in-demand they were— she grabbed the final available Cronut that day and swears, to this day, that there is no other pastry like it. The flavour changed monthly, and no two were ever the same.

"It's apricot jam with caramelised milk chocolate."

"What if they have none left? You know what it's like."

"I pre-ordered. So, they'll be ready to collect after lunch."

Madison nodded her head in approval. "Good thinking." She made her way to the fridge and returned with a fresh carton of blueberries. "Has Megan given you any idea what she has planned after? Providing you get that far." Madison playfully threw a blueberry, which inadvertently said she meant no real offence.

She had only briefly spoken to Megan the day before; her reluctance to share the plan intrigued Ashley even more.

"I have no idea. It's exciting though. I don't do this kind of thing, do I? So I don't know what to expect."

"No, I suppose your experience is rather limited. Maybe you should be taking tips from Emily."

Ashley laughed. "You're right. She is the queen of dating."

"Speak of the devil." Madison glanced towards the door as Emily sauntered in. The usual glam appearance she worked hard to maintain was tarnished. A mascara-streaked left eye and heels in hand indicated a heavy night.

"Aspirin, please." No hello.

"Coming right up, your majesty," Madison chuckled. "Coffee? It's a fresh pot."

Emily put her hand up, retching at the thought, "No, I can't stomach that yet."

"Heavy night, Em?" Ashley watched as Emily clawed off her denim jacket and flopped onto the sofa.

"You could say that." She placed her hand over her eyes to block out the light streaming through the balconette window. "Why do I do this to myself?"

Ashley and Madison took one look at each other, the temptation to say *I told you so* a hard one to turn down.

"Where did you stay last night?" Ashley enquired.

"At Caroline's."

"Who is Caroline?" Ashley and Madison uttered at precisely the same time.

"Just a girl from work."

Ashley rolled her eyes. "Care to elaborate?"

"There is nothing to elaborate on. I thought she was straight." Emily gladly accepted the aspirin and water provided.

"And?"

"Turns out, she's not."

Ashley almost choked on her coffee. "Oh, I see."

"That could get awkward. What does she do?" queried Madison.

"She works as a receptionist on the same floor as me." Emily took a big gulp of the ice-cold water. "Why would you assume it'll get awkward?"

"Because it's you," Ashley chimed.

"You always do this," Madison agreed.

"Do what?"

"Do we have to spell it out for you again? You find a straight girl, you sleep with her, she falls in love with you, you tell her you're not looking for a relationship and move on to the next poor unsuspecting girl."

"Why do you two always make out like I am so promiscuous?"

"Because you are!" Ashley and Madison screeched.

"Tell me how you really feel why don't you..."

Ashley savoured the last taste of coffee before joining Emily on the sofa. Madison made herself comfortable on the opposite side, so Emily was firmly sandwiched between them.

"Oh, come on, we're only playing. Aside from the devastating hangover, did you have a good night?"

"From what I can remember, it was really good. Enough about me though, don't you have your date today?"

"Yes, I was just telling Mads. I'm so nervous."

"Why?"

"You saw her. How could I not be?"

"You have no reason to be nervous. She will love you."

"You think?"

"I know she will." Emily smiled sincerely. "I would normally get my kicks out of winding you up, but the truth is you're amazing. You just need to be yourself."

"Thank you."

Ashley could recall a time when she thought Emily liked her as more than a friend. There had been rumours flying around for the first few months of their friendship, but Ashley downplayed them every time. The relationship was purely platonic on her part and she made sure to never blur the lines, which ultimately led to them having a once-in-a-lifetime friendship. Ashley relaxed back, admiring her two best friends and the ease with which they cohabited with one another—three years of memories she would cherish forever and so many more to come.

***

The morning passed by steadily. It was a rarity that all three of them had the same day off together. When the opportunity to sit, drink coffee and watch daytime re-runs arose, they jumped at the chance.

"What time did you say you were meeting Megan?" Madison enquired.

"Why, what time is it?"

"Almost twelve."

"What? Shit..." Ashley jumped up, almost knocking a half-asleep Emily to the floor. "How did I not realise the time? I said I'd meet her at two."

"Take it easy, you've got two hours to get ready."

"I don't even know what to wear. I need your help."

Ashley ran the length of the corridor from the living room to her bedroom, skidding smoothly to a halt outside her door. Once inside, she freshened up, applying an array of moisturisers and eye creams. Deodorant, followed by a body mist spray, set the tone; she would decide on the perfume of choice once she was dressed.

Ashley's closet, although stuffed full of clothes, rarely inspired her. If she required anything of colour, Madison's wardrobe was the place to go and if she required anything super-tight-fitting and sexy, then it was Emily's. The casual style she often donned would fit the bill for today's date, she thought, but there had to be something she could wear that would add the extra special *'oomph'* she was looking for.

"MADISON!" Ashley bellowed.

Madison appeared at the door moments later. "What's up, Ash?"

"I honestly have no idea what to wear. I can't wear this..." Ashley waved the black denim shirt from side to side, "...because I wore that the night I met Megan. I can't have her thinking I have nothing else to wear. I also can't wear this..." Ashley waved a tight-fitted grey sweater next, "...because it has a hole on the arm."

One by one, items of clothing spilled onto the floor at Ashley's feet.

"Wait, what about that one?" Madison pointed towards a navy blue t-shirt.

"Isn't that a bit boring?"

"You are boring. Your wardrobe consists of black, white, grey and navy. You can't get much more boring than that."

"Charming. Some of us just don't have the ability to pull off that much colour." Ashley pointed towards

Madison's attire, which included bright green sweatpants and a vintage red sweater.

"I know, it's a gift."

"I don't have time for this. If I go with the navy top, what about bottoms?"

Items of clothing flew like projectiles across the bedroom while Ashley searched for a suitable pair of jeans.

"Got them." Black jeans, simple and stylish. "What do you think?"

"I think that will look great. It's simple, understated, doesn't look like you've tried too hard."

"That is exactly the look I was going for. I have one favour to ask."

"Nope."

"What do you mean, 'nope'?" Ashley batted her eyelashes and chewed on her bottom lip.

"Stop trying to be cute. I know exactly what you're going to say."

"Please?"

"Ashley, you have worn those trainers more than I have. I didn't pay $800 for you to wear them all the time."

Madison rarely purchased designer clothing, but a shopping spree on Fifth Avenue two months prior had turned out to be her most expensive one yet. The tips at work paid for a new pair of Dior trainers and an LV handbag. Items she cherished and begrudgingly let her friends borrow.

"But they would look so good with this outfit."

"Fine, I'll add it to the list of things you owe me a favour for. It's mounting up."

"Thank you, thank you, thank you," Ashley squealed, launching herself toward her best friend to plant a kiss on her lips. A gesture often shared between the two.

"Get off me." Madison wiped at her lips dramatically. "I will leave you to get ready."

Ashley was left alone with just her reflection, one she hoped would be pleasing to the eye—Megan's eye, in particular.

***

One hour later, Ashley emerged from her now dishevelled bedroom. She found Madison and Emily sprawled on the sofa.

"So, do I look okay?" She feared the response. Her friends had always been brutally honest. A trait she admired, but equally dreaded at the same time.

"You look perfect."

"Yes, like so hot. Love the hair."

They both beamed. She opted for a half-up-half-down combination, the pieces of hair that fell over her face shaping her features like a dream.

"Thanks, guys."

Ashley fidgeted with her phone, glancing repeatedly at the locked screen. The light remained dull, no sign of activity—it made her nervous. When she'd spoken with Megan that morning, it had been brief. Since then, not a word. They'd agreed the time the day before, but the lack of response made her uneasy.

"Why are you still standing there?" Emily challenged.

"She hasn't replied to my last message."

Emily sat upright. "When did you message her?"

"About two hours ago."

The time was 1:30 p.m. It would take less than twenty minutes to walk to Dos Camino's.

"That's strange."

"That's what I thought. Should I be worried that she'll stand me up?"

Madison shook her head, "I'm sure there's an explanation." She pulled her brown headband down and proceeded to run her fingers through her brown cropped wavy hair; the new style took some getting used to. "You'll be fine, Ash, but you need to go. You don't want to keep the girl waiting."

"Good luck!" Emily chimed.

Ashley exited her apartment through the large wooden door. Howard waved from his truck.

"Bagel, Ashley?" he called above the queue of customers.

"No thanks, Howard! I'm going on a date."

"Very exciting, have fun."

The stern woman awaiting her order glared in Ashley's direction.

Conscious of the fact she hadn't heard from Megan, she took her time, stalling at the entrance to James J. Walker Park on the corner of Hudson Street. A solitary bench sat underneath a Norway maple tree with a vast circumference that shaded the surrounding area. Ashley took a seat and removed her phone from her pocket for the tenth time in ten minutes. A message appeared.

I am so sorry I haven't replied sooner. I wanted to get my head down for an hour after my workout this morning, but I didn't set my alarm. What an idiot! I will quickly get ready and be with you as soon as I can!

Ashley exhaled a sigh of relief. The fear of being stood up was replaced by an ever-growing nervousness. Ashley's dating resume was slim-to-none. During her time at Long Island University, she dated two different women, the second for almost two years, but she wanted to pursue her dreams in New York and Grace had other ideas. That soon ended when Ashley left. Since moving to New York, there had been a brief fling or two, but nothing that had the potential to be the real deal. Ashley and Grace remained somewhat friends after the break-up. There had been little choice in the matter because of Grace's friendship with Samantha Stewart—Ashley's younger sister.

The pang of guilt returned whenever she thought about Samantha. It had been almost six months since their last phone conversation. After her move to the west coast two years earlier, their contact had diminished. Samantha had become so self-absorbed, a trait she had in common with one member of the Stewart family in particular, and the reason her parents were no longer married. It was not the time to be rehashing bad memories, so Ashley gathered herself and continued towards her destination.

The time was 2:20 p.m. Megan had informed Ashley that she was on her way. Other than asking Megan to meet her on the corner where West Broadway meets West Houston St, she had disclosed no other details. The front of the restaurant had recently been painted a teal colour; black railings surrounded the outside dining area to the left and a large red neon sign flashed above the door. It wasn't a 5* decorated building, but what the restaurant lacked in glamour, it made up for in quality. It was the only place Ashley would go for Mexican food.

Her phone beeped.

I'm here. I can't see you.

Ashley spun around, her eyes rotating in every direction, looking for undoubtedly the most beautiful girl in the neighbourhood. Her gaze locked on a figure across the street. She looked sporty in a pair of black gym leggings, a black t-shirt and some white running shoes. Ashley removed the sunglasses from her face to get a better look; her long brown hair was tied tightly into a hair band. Her casual attire made Ashley feel overdressed in her jeans and expensive trainers. The glare of the sun meant she couldn't be 100% sure it was Megan, but she waved anyway, hopeful the figure would return the gesture. She did—it was her.

Ashley shifted her weight from one foot to the other as she watched Megan approach. The butterflies in her stomach caused such a flutter that she was thankful such a thing was not visible. Megan placed one foot in front of the other as confidently as anyone, strutting her way across the street as if she belonged. Intentional or not, it caused Ashley to feel inadequate. The beaming smile never once left Megan's face, a kindness radiated that made Ashley feel more at ease.

"Hello."

"Hey. Thank you for coming."

"I am so sorry I'm late."

"Don't worry, at least you're here." Ashley smiled sweetly.

"Did you think I wouldn't show?"

"It crossed my mind."

"That's ridiculous. I have been looking forward to this all week," Megan made brief eye contact, her emerald green eyes wide and captivating, "the food I mean."

"I agree, just the food." Ashley winked playfully.

"Speaking of food, what are we having?"

Ashley turned and pointed towards Dos Caminos. "You like Mexican, right?"

"I love Mexican."

"Have you ever been here?"

"I may have done when I was a kid, but I can't remember."

"You'll love it. Shall we head inside?" Ashley gestured towards the door, holding it open as Megan passed through. A server directed them towards the back of the restaurant to a nice, quiet corner.

"Can I get you any drinks?" The polite young male server enquired.

"I will have a Mojito please."

"Make that two," confirmed Megan.

The server nodded and returned to the bar. Ashley glanced at the menu; she already knew her order, but the alternative meant looking directly at Megan and the thought alone made her incredibly nervous.

"So, you like Mojitos? I didn't think athletes were allowed to drink?"

"Normally, if I was in the middle of a season, I would probably opt for water, but I'm not, so what the hell." Megan removed the phone from her pocket and hit reject before placing it back. "Besides, I assume they're really good if you're ordering one? I am completely trusting your judgment today."

"They're the best." Ashley signalled towards the phone. "You can answer that if you need to."

"No, it's fine don't worry. It's just my dad. He likes to check in most days. It can be a bit much. I'll call him back later."

"At least he cares."

"That's true. What about your parents?"

"Divorced." There was an awkward pause.

"I'm sorry."

"Don't be, they're better off that way."

"Do you have any brothers or sisters?"

"One, a younger sister called Samantha. What about you?"

"Only child." Megan shrugged her shoulders. "It has its advantages and disadvantages."

"Would you have wanted a sibling?"

The server returned with two Mojitos swaying on a large silver tray.

"Have you decided what you would like to eat?" he asked.

Ashley looked at Megan for approval. "I always get the same thing. Do you know what you want?"

"I'll have the sizzling steak fajitas, please." Megan closed her menu, seemingly happy with her choice.

"Same for me please," Ashley grinned, "I swear I'm not copying you."

Megan took a sip of her Mojito. "That is incredible." Savouring the taste on the tip of her tongue. "So, you get a tick for the drink. Let's see what the food is like."

"Do you always order steak?"

"100% if steak is on the menu, it's the first thing I look for."

"Then you won't be disappointed, I promise. I have had the steak fajitas more times than I can count and every time I swear they get better."

"I trust you." Megan giggled.

The sound was a rare thing, so pure and genuine that it made Ashley determined to hear it more.

"What were we talking about?...Oh yes, the sibling thing. I think if I had the choice, I would have had a little sister. I always wanted someone to play with growing up; I was so jealous of all my friends. You must have had a lot of fun with your sister? How much younger is she?"

"She's three years younger than me. We had some good times, always up to no good. We drove our parents insane," Ashley said, holding the Mojito to her lips before swiftly changing the subject. "I'm looking forward to your part of the date."

Megan briefly raised an eyebrow, acknowledging the change in conversation, but Ashley hoped she would oblige.

"Is that what this is? A date?" Megan's grin was partly concealed by the large glass.

"Would you prefer me to call it something else?" Ashley questioned.

"No."

"Well then, it's a date."

Megan nodded. "Will there be a date number two, that is the question?"

"What are the terms?"

"I think it all depends on this food."

Ashley smiled confidently, "If the food is what gets me a second date, then the dessert will 100% get me a third."

The Cronut would impress, Ashley had no doubt about that.

"I hope you're right."

"You'll see." Ashley winked.

The conversation was natural and unforced. The initial jitters had been present, but in Megan's company, she felt more alive than expected. Every time there was a brief pause, Ashley searched frantically for the next conversation starter, worried that silence would be met with awkwardness and the date would be ruined, but much to her surprise, eye contact or a simple smile filled the momentary gaps in conversation.

Ashley asked Megan about her family and what it was like growing up in England. She soon came to realise that it was as cold and wet as the movies made out, but the intrigue she'd always possessed to visit London grew far greater throughout the conversation. They spoke about animals; living on seven acres of land meant Megan had grown up surrounded by an array of animals, including chickens and goats, but she lit up when she spoke about Fred—her shire horse. She rode him every day up until she was fifteen years old, and then the fear of falling off and potentially damaging her basketball dreams became the focal point in her decision to stop riding altogether.

The conversation switched fleetingly to previous relationships. Megan had dated two women casually whilst at Stanford, but neither developed enough to consider them serious. Ashley found that hard to believe; from the moment Megan walked into the bar she had been in awe of her beauty, which made her wonder how someone so beautiful and kind-hearted wouldn't have people falling at her feet.

The generic icebreakers gave way to more in-depth intelligent conversation. They argued over which classic book they favoured, *The Great Gatsby* was Ashley's choice whilst *Pride and Prejudice* was Megan's. After much debate, eventually, they agreed to disagree. The topic of art arose, Ashley's passion for The Met was obvious in her ramblings; one of the world's greatest art collections was something to be admired. Megan listened intently, propping her head up in her hands as Ashley discussed her favourite paintings.

The conversation naturally switched to basketball, the subject in which they shared the most common ground. Typically, Ashley supported the team she had been surrounded by her whole life, the New York Knicks—a family tradition. Despite Megan's father supporting the Knicks, she grew up watching the Lakers, with the move to Stanford cementing her love for the Californian coast and arguably the greatest basketball team of all time.

There was no subject off-limits, the way in which they developed a knowledgeable foundation in a mere two hours was effortless, similar to that of two people who had known each other for many years. There was still so much to learn, a depth in which Ashley hoped she would have the chance to explore.

Ashley watched the animated girl before her so passionately describe her goals in life, the girl who had been a complete mystery less than a week ago. Megan could have been describing a piece of fruit, and Ashley would still be admiring her so intently. The fluid way in which she moved as she gestured was captivating, the athlete within so obvious to even the untrained eye. The blend of English and American in her accent had been hard to understand the first time they spoke, but now Ashley found it fascinating.

5

Ashley

"Well?" Ashley watched as Megan licked the remainder of sugar from her lips, eagerly awaiting the verdict.

"I think…" Megan used the napkin to wipe her hands, "…that might be the most incredible pastry I've ever tasted."

"Seriously?"

"No joke, that was amazing."

"I told you, didn't I? You were unsure about the combination, but do you understand it now?"

"I get it. I can't believe I have never had one before."

"It was only created a couple of years ago. It just absolutely blew up all over New York." Ashley signalled towards the queue of people outside the bakery, "You've seen the people waiting, it's like this every day."

"Well, firstly, I am extremely grateful you pre-ordered, and secondly, I am glad you pre-ordered four because I have absolutely no shame in admitting I'll be eating the rest later."

The combination of croissant and fried dough covered in sugar, filled with cream and topped with glaze, was a sensation for the mouth. The pride radiated from Ashley—lunch and dessert had both been certified winners.

"Both? Do I not get one?"

"We can eat them together if you like?"

Ashley smirked, "I like the sound of that."

"Thank you again for two amazing choices. You lived up to the hype after all."

"You doubted me, didn't you?"

"Not at all." Megan winked.

"Hmmm…all I will say is, after that 5-star performance you have a lot to live up to."

"I accept the challenge. Are you ready to go?"

"Lead the way."

***

They took a cab and within half an hour, they had arrived on the west side of Central Park.

"This is our first stop."

"Central Park? You know I live in New York and I pass through here almost every day?"

Megan nudged Ashley with her elbow. "Stop jumping to conclusions." She scowled.

They walked a familiar route, past Umpire Rock, on to Cherry Hill Fountain and then over Bow Bridge, before stopping to the right of the Lake. Central Park on a summer's day was the perfect shady escape. With over 840 acres of green space, there was no place quite like it. Ashley frequented the most iconic park in the world three or four times a week, but it never failed to amaze her.

"Are we jumping in the lake?"

"No, but if you carry on, I'll push you in." Megan searched the benches one by one. "It should be around here somewhere."

"If you tell me what you're looking for I can help?" Ashley trailed behind, confused. Megan rounded a large bush onto a small patch of soil at the lake's edge. There sat a solitary rustic bench.

"Here it is." Megan dusted off the silver plaque with her finger until the inscription became clear.

"What does it say?" Ashley said.

"After all these years, I still hope for your return. This bench signifies my ever-lasting love for you. Always yours, Christopher."

"Who's Christopher?"

"I'm glad you asked. Take a seat with me, I'll tell you the story."

The bench had seen better days. Ashley guessed it must have been one of the oldest, but it was sturdy. The view across the lake was the perfect setting for a story.

"In 1958, a man called Christopher was set up on a blind date by his friends. They arranged to go to a local drive-in cinema—that's where he met Nancy. She was a senior in high school; he was in his first year of college. He initially thought he would find her immature, but on meeting her he couldn't have been more wrong." Megan turned towards Ashley. "Do you believe in love at first sight?"

"No, I think the idea is nice, but it's not realistic."

"Well, this meeting, in Christopher's eyes, was love at first sight. The feeling was exquisite, electrifying, and simply magical. After that first date, they spent every waking minute together. Nancy fell behind on her studies because she was so obsessed with him, she couldn't concentrate or focus on anything other than him. The months passed by and Nancy finally introduced Christopher to her parents. They were devout Catholics, attended church every Sunday, and lived their life through the eyes of God. Christopher was the opposite, he was the son of a construction worker, he didn't believe in any religion, he was seen as a bit of a bad boy, he never got in trouble with the law, but in his neighbourhood, he had a reputation for being good with his fists."

Megan glanced to check Ashley was still listening and then turned back towards the water.

"In other words, he was quite the opposite of what Nancy's parents wanted for her. That didn't stop them. Even after her parents discovered Christopher's lifestyle and grounded Nancy, she would sneak out every night to see him. They continued that way for almost a year. Then one day, Nancy got home from school and her parents told her they were sending her away to live with her grandparents in Charlotte, North Carolina. They'd known all along what she was doing and when she didn't stop seeing him, they saw no other choice," Megan paused.

"Surely she didn't go?" Ashley probed.

"She had no choice. It was different back then."

Ashley swung her right leg up onto the bench in an attempt to get more comfortable. "Carry on, please."

"The next day, Nancy moved away. She didn't even get the chance to say goodbye. She wrote a note before she left and handed it to her best friend, who lived next door to Christopher. The letter never made it. He thought Nancy had up and left without any attempt to contact him."

"Why didn't he get the letter? What happened?"

Megan smiled, "Why don't you let me finish the story and then you'll find out."

Ashley held her hands up, apologising. "Please, continue."

"Christopher, now heartbroken, tried to find out her new address, but her parents refused to give any information despite his pleas. Eventually, he had no choice but to move on with his life. He met someone else three years later and got married. As the years passed by, he thought about Nancy often. It wasn't until a high school reunion twenty-five years later that he saw her again. It was 1983, and Christopher was pulling out of the local gas station when he caught sight of a woman getting out of her car in his rear-view mirror. He slammed on the brakes, the car screeched, causing the woman to look his way. It was Nancy. He couldn't believe his eyes; they spoke briefly about why she was in town and he asked if she would have coffee with him."

"She said yes, right? Is he still married? Is she married?"

Megan playfully hit Ashley on the right knee. Instinctively, she tried to stop it, catching Megan's hand in hers. The accidental touch was the first form of intimacy between the pair. Ashley welcomed the feel and Megan, in return, didn't pull her hand away.

"Christopher was still married and so was Nancy. On their coffee date, he found out she had been married for twenty years and had two children. They exchanged pleasantries, but it wasn't until the end of the conversation, when Christopher asked why she didn't try to contact him, that he discovered Nancy did write him a letter. The best friend I told you she gave it to? Well, that was now Christopher's wife of twenty-two years."

"YOU ARE JOKING?!" Ashley yelled.

"Nope. She never gave him the letter because she'd always had a crush on him and saw her opportunity once Nancy left. Scandalous, right?"

Ashley nodded in agreement, "What a shitty best friend she was."

"So, after the reunion, Nancy went back to her life in Charlotte. Christopher eventually split from his wife after the revelation. They'd never had children because

Kathy had never been able to. At the age of forty-four, he took his half of the money from the house sale and opened a bar in Midtown Manhattan; he called it Nancy's."

"He named the bar after her? Wow."

"Yep, even after all those years, he still loved her. Another five years passed—that's around the time they started allowing people to buy plaques for the benches here. The money you pay for the bench goes to preserving the park. At the time, the park had seen better days and there were signs all over asking people to donate money or to volunteer to help clean it up. The bar was doing exceptionally well; it became a hotspot for the locals. So, Christopher decided to buy a bench. He spent a long time wondering what to write on the plaque. Then it seemed most natural to write about Nancy. After all, she still consumed his mind after all those years."

Ashley held onto Megan's hand, slowly caressing the edge of her thumb. "That's incredible."

"Fast forward to 1993 and guess who turns up at his bar?"

"I really hope it's Nancy, otherwise this story is going to really disappoint me."

"Of course, it's Nancy. She comes to New York on vacation with her oldest daughter, who was twenty-eight at the time. They stumble across a bar in Midtown that just happens to be named after her, so she feels obliged to go inside and have a drink. She sits down at the bar and Christopher walks out. Their eyes meet and all of sudden, it makes sense—she drops the glass in her hand, obviously in utter shock. They talk for a while, Christopher invites her out to dinner, her daughter insists she should catch up with her old friend. They spent the next three days together; her daughter had friends in New

York so she was occupied. They couldn't believe how easy it was. Even after thirty-five years, they still had a connection that was undeniable. Nancy was still married, being born into a family of devout Catholics meant the divorce rate was 0%. She was married to a nice man; they had built a nice life together and she would never regret the two children he gave her, but there'd always been something missing. The more time she spent with Christopher, the more she realised *he* was that something."

Ashley looked directly into the piercing green eyes that had consumed her afternoon, "I swear, if this story doesn't end the way I hope it does, I will never allow you to tell me a story again."

Megan laughed, the small creases in her nose adorable—Ashley found it difficult to look away. The manner in which she told the story with such conviction made Ashley feel as though she had been a part of it. The sentimentality of the story was yet to be revealed, but she was hooked.

"Nancy had no choice but to go back to her life; she wasn't sure what to do. She couldn't help but feel selfish at the prospect of leaving her family behind at fifty-three to be with someone she hadn't known properly for over thirty years. Two more years passed and Christopher had lost hope. It wasn't until the Christmas of 1995 that everything fell into place. She turned up at his bar once again, this time with a suitcase in her hand. Presumptuous, but of course he welcomed her with open arms. It was as if no time had passed. Their hair had gone grey and their bodies had become weaker, but what remained was the love they shared for each other. Despite thirty-seven long years, that never faded. Christopher had always hoped that one day she would find her way back to him. He didn't show her the bench until six months later and she couldn't believe it. A lot of people would see it as a waste, all those years apart, but they just saw the blessing that brought them back together."

"So, they ended up together? Where are they now?" Ashley eagerly awaited Megan's response.

"They still live here in New York City. Nancy's children are all grown up. Her son moved away and her daughter stayed here in New York, but Christopher and Nancy started their own life together. They got married two years later. They travelled the world, neither of them had ever left America, so they wanted to experience something new together. I guess you could say they now live happily ever after."

Ashley had a tear in her eye. "How old are they?"

"Christopher is 76 and Nancy is 75."

"How do you even know this story? You tell it as though you know them."

"I do know them. Nancy is my grandma," Megan revealed.

Ashley's eyes widened. "Your grandma?"

"What a story, right?"

"It's an incredible story." Ashley paused and readjusted her place on the bench. "I guess I'm just a bit confused as to why you told me?"

"You told me the other day that if you were to become a writer for a magazine that you would want to write stories that mean something, real-life stories that will give people hope or something to believe in. There's your first story. I asked my grandma's permission to share it with you. If you want to write it, then the story is there for you to write. That was the watered-down version. When you meet my grandma, she will explain it all."

"When I meet your grandma?"

"Sure, this was part one of the date."

"What's part two?"

Megan grinned, "We go to Nancy's."

***

On the corner of Lexington Avenue and East 27th Street was Nancy's. Christopher had originally opened it as a sports bar, but once Nancy arrived in 1995, she had another vision—it soon became a cocktail bar. Not wanting to lose the original custom, they agreed to keep the sports bar title, but made it a more sophisticated atmosphere. The outside was black with a gold sign, polished to perfection. Upon entering, Ashley was immediately drawn to wooden panelling on the wall—it was unique, accompanied by large, flamboyant paintings, each with its own unique, colourful design. Along one wall sat a long olive-green sofa, with circular brown tables and accompanying brown leather chairs. Across the other wall were more intimate two-seater tables, with navy blue tub chairs. The bar felt contemporary—recently updated, it would seem—and everything was immaculate. Behind the bar area housed several large-screen TVs, with tall leather bar stools; that was the place to sit and watch sports whilst the rest of the bar enjoyed cocktails. It had been set up in such a way to please all customers; Ashley liked that.

"This place is amazing."

"It's perfect, isn't it? They recently had it re-decorated, my aunt Julie helped them modernise it."

"I just love the whole atmosphere. I can't believe I've never been here before."

"It is now, before it was a little outdated and very much an old-fashioned bar that wouldn't attract the younger generation, but since the revamp, that seems to have changed."

"I bet."

Megan placed the palm of her hand on Ashley's back and edged her towards two stools at the end of the bar. "Can I get you a drink?"

"What do you recommend?"

"The 1995."

"What's in it?"

"Vodka, strawberry, mint, lemon, rhubarb and soda. It has a similar taste to a Mojito, but the strawberry and rhubarb make it fruitier. It's my favourite."

"The 1995 sounds perfect to me."

A bartender with dark brown, slicked-back hair and a shirt that was three sizes too small approached. "What can I get for you, Meg?"

"Two '95s please, Alec."

He smiled eagerly. "Coming right up."

Ashley swivelled to the right to face Megan, "Thank you."

"For what?"

"Telling me the story. Allowing me to be a part of that; it's quite the tale."

"Will you write about it?"

"Yes, I would love to."

Megan placed her hand on Ashley's arm. "I can't wait to read it. I hope I did it justice."

"You did. I am excited to hear more."

"I'm guessing my part of the date isn't what you imagined it would be?"

"Not at all. It's better."

"Really? I wasn't sure if you'd find it lame."

The sarcastic response was her first, "I can't say anyone else has ever taken me to see their grandma on a first date," Ashley laughed. "That being said, it is the most unique date I have ever been on."

"And it's not even over yet," Megan teased.

"There's more?"

"Well, I thought we were eating Cronuts together and watching TV?" Megan raised a quizzing eyebrow.

"How could I forget?"

Ashley raised her drink; the clink of the glass on Megan's signified a successful date. Nancy appeared ten minutes later with the details of her life in tow. She was a fascinating woman. Despite being seventy-five years old, she moved with a spring in her step, one she assured was down to the new lease of life she found when she returned to Christopher. The grey hair and thick-rimmed glasses aged her appearance slightly, but her slim build was that of someone thirty years younger. Ashley found it hard to imagine her as the centre of an epic love story. She shared pictures of her younger self in high school and the most recent photo of her and Christopher. The years had been kind to them. She shared the details of her split from Megan's grandfather, the effect it had on the children and ultimately the aftermath of a divorce that shook Nancy's parents to the core. It was the hardest decision she had ever had to make, but the alternative was far worse in her eyes.

The conversation lasted almost an hour before Nancy left for the evening. "Make sure you take full advantage of the bar girls." They both nodded obediently. "It's been great talking to you, Ashley. I will look forward to reading your take on my life."

"I hope I do it justice."

"I'm sure you will, sweetheart."

The bar became busier the closer it got to tip-off. 8 NBA games were due to begin, and Megan felt underdressed to still be out, so they made their way back to Ashley's apartment. The warm summer nights made for a pleasant stroll back to Chelsea.

Ashley pulled her phone from her jeans pocket. The urge to warn her friends of their arrival had been playing on her mind since they left Nancy's.

Megan is coming back with me. Be on your best behaviour. Don't embarrass me...or else.

Ashley knew introducing Megan to her friends on a first date was precarious. They loved to wind her up, last year she'd been dating a girl for all of five minutes when they went to the coffee shop she worked in disguised in sunglasses and hats to make sure she wasn't a 'catfish' – Ashley had already met her in person at this point, but they insisted they were just doing some *background* checks. If only they'd act like they worked for the FBI when it actually mattered like the time she lost her watch for three days. Despite this, the desire to spend more time with Megan far outweighed the potential risk of embarrassment.

They were only five minutes away from Ashley's fifth-floor Chelsea apartment. Megan wrapped her arms around herself; the breeze making it too chilly for just a t-shirt.

"Are you cold?"

"Yes, aren't you?"

"Not so much, I'm warm-blooded."

Megan rolled her eyes. "What are you, a werewolf?"

"Maybe." Ashley grinned, showing her pearly whites, "You better be careful, it's a full moon tonight."

"I'll take my chances," Megan admitted.

Ashley shifted the bag of Cronuts into the opposite hand and outstretched her left arm, "Come here, I'll warm you up."

Megan didn't hesitate; she fully embraced the invitation to get closer to Ashley. She wrapped one arm around her back and the other around her front, clinching her hands together in a delicate bear-like hold. Megan had to slouch slightly due to the one-inch height difference, but that didn't stop her. There was absolutely no benefit to the embrace; there would be no sudden rush of warmth, Ashley knew that, but it was an opportunity to feel her touch that she couldn't pass up.

The search throughout the day for an opportunity to kiss her had gone amiss. She thought the intertwined hands on the bench in Central Park could have been the moment, but it didn't materialise. The nerves were still present. Despite feeling comfortable in her presence there was still a perception that she needed to impress— that she couldn't quite let her guard down. The prospect of Megan spending the night had not occurred until they were four drinks in at Nancy's. Those exact words had not been said, but Ashley assumed that was the plan.

"What did you say your friends are called again?"

"Madison and Emily."

"Okay."

"Why?"

"Just want to make sure I get it right."

"Don't worry about them, just ignore anything they say unless it's 'hello', we don't need to stop and chat, we can head straight to my room."

"Are you scared they might say something that'll embarrass you?" Megan teased.

"Something like that."

"Don't worry, I'll stick my fingers in my ears."

"That would be great," Ashley laughed.

The chemistry between them was unmistakable. They strolled toward her apartment entwined as one, as though they were doing something they did daily. To anyone else in the street, they looked as though they knew each other deeply, the way they embraced, the way they laughed and poked fun at each other so effortlessly.

The night ending at that moment filled Ashley with a sense of wrongdoing, just the mere thought brought about a sadness she couldn't understand. All she could hope was that Megan felt the same.

They stopped at the foot of some sandstone steps; a brown, wooden door awaited at the top with two large glass panes and an intercom to the right with the numbers 1–12. Within minutes, they stood in the corridor of the fifth-floor apartment that Ashley called home.

"Here we go," Ashley muttered under her breath.

Upon entering, the apartment was silent. No sign of Madison or Emily, "That's weird."

Ashley removed her shoes at the door, prompting Megan to do the same.

"Guys?" Ashley approached the kitchen with caution. "Hello?"

The Cronuts made their safe arrival on the countertop before she made her way around the kitchen towards the fridge. From behind the counter, out of nowhere, jumped Madison and Emily.

"Boo!" they screamed.

Ashley dropped her phone; heart racing. Megan staggered backwards, the sheer panic fast-diminished and was replaced by amusement. The girls leant over the counter in hysterics.

"Honestly, I hate you both." Ashley glared at her so-called best friends. "How long have you been hiding down there?"

Madison shrugged, "Maybe twenty minutes."

"We were very dedicated to the cause," Emily chirped.

When everyone's breathing returned to a normal rhythm, their attentions soon turned towards Megan, who had openly found the prank hilarious.

"Nice to meet you, Megan," Madison grinned; a smile that made anyone feel welcome. Emily had always been more reserved. She proceeded with caution whenever a new friend or partner was introduced. The bond she had created with Ashley over the three years they had known each other was the singular most important thing in her life and she feared that would one day be taken away from her. Emily's face was less inviting, a forced smile appeared as she greeted Megan.

"Hi, Megan."

"Hello, it's nice to meet you both."

"Sorry about that, we are normally on our best behaviour, but we couldn't resist."

Ashley scoffed, "They are absolutely never on their best behaviour." She winked at Megan to make her feel more at ease. The discomfort of meeting best friends was always unnerving in any situation.

"I actually found it hilarious."

"See Ash, we are hilarious." Madison grinned.

Emily eyed up the bag on the counter. "Are those Cronuts?"

Ashley swiped them away before she had the chance to explore the contents, "They're not for you."

"Please, it's been ages since I had one."

Ashley rolled her eyes, unimpressed by the child-like whining coming from her best friend.

Megan politely intervened. "You can have mine."

"Seriously?" Emily questioned.

"Sure. I'll share Ashley's." Megan winked playfully.

"I like her." Emily snatched the bag from Ashley's hand and proceeded to unwrap the precious pastry. "You can come again."

Ashley's eyebrow furrowed, confused but also amazed at the way in which Emily interacted with Megan; it was notably more than the last girl she dated.

"Did you have a nice time anyway?" Madison enquired.

"It was really good. I'll tell you about it in the morning because we're going to watch a movie." Ashley glanced towards Megan reassuringly. She smiled, seemingly happy with the plan. "With our one Cronut." She glared towards Emily who was now completely oblivious, face filled with cream.

"What? They're just so good," she said in a stifled voice.

"Anyway, night. Love you both."

A chorus of good nights echoed back and forth as Ashley made her way down the corridor to her room.

"So, this is my room. As you can see, I wasn't sure what to wear this morning." She scurried from one side to the other, gathering items of clothing from the floor and abruptly hurling them into the open wardrobe. There was no organisation involved, she would deal with that another day. On the occasions that her bedroom was in an orderly fashion, she loved it. The exposed brick walls and large, black-framed windows made for a quirky space. The king-size bed floated alone in the middle of the room underneath a large abstract grey rug that gave the room a stylish touch, whilst adding the warmth it needed. The closet sat on the back wall; two grey, up-cycled bookcases filled with trinkets and pictures sat to the left. A matching TV unit placed at the foot of the bed with a large flat-screen TV finished off the room. The exposed brick walls were filled with artwork—one in particular caught Megan's eye.

"Who painted this?"

"Madison did."

"You're kidding? It's incredible."

"I know, she's been painting all her life."

"Does she have any commissioned artwork?"

"Not yet, she's hoping to one day have her own gallery. That would be the dream."

They both stood and admired the large oil painting; the abstract movement of city lines created a gold and green version of New York.

"It goes really well in here."

"I asked her to paint it for me to go with the theme. She did an amazing job. So many of our friends want the same thing, but she likes to be unique, so she won't ever paint the same thing twice."

"That's so cool." Megan admired the painting for a while before she wandered over to the bookcase on the opposite side of the room. Ashley found her inquisitive state humorous.

"Let's see what we have here then." She flicked through the large selection of books, stopping immediately at *Pride and Prejudice*. She held the book up in surprise.

"I said I preferred *The Great Gatsby*. I never said I didn't like *Pride and Prejudice*."

"I see. Well, you have gained some points back with that."

Megan settled next on a black, leather-bound version of *Wuthering Heights*. The intricate silver detailing on the front cover and the spine made for an interesting edition; one which Ashley adored.

"How old is this?"

She stood directly behind Megan now, close enough that her voice could be heard as a whisper in her ear. The intimacy was sudden and unexpected.

"It's from the '60s."

Megan froze in place. "It's in perfect condition."

"My mom gave it to me. It's beautiful, isn't it? The bookshop down the road actually has an original from 1848."

"Seriously? I would love to see that!"

"It's more valuable than mine though," Ashley sniggered. "I enquired once, and he said it cost him $10,000 at auction."

Megan looked over her left shoulder and directly into Ashley's eyes, shocked. "Seriously? Wow."

"Have you read it?"

"Once, about four years ago. My aunt has all the classics, so I tend to indulge when I come to visit."

"What did you think?"

"I think Catherine should have run away with Heathcliff. I expected a Romeo-and-Juliet-type love, but I actually think the story was more about Heathcliff's revenge."

Ashley reached her hand around Megan to grasp the book, flicking knowingly to chapter nine.

"This is my favourite quote. It's so well known now, but I think it's just the perfect way of saying that you love someone without actually saying it." Ashley pointed at the two lines in question, and to her surprise, Megan read them aloud perfectly.

"*He's more myself than I am. Whatever our souls are made out of, his and mine are the same.*" Megan smiled softly. "It's beautiful."

The proximity between them was minuscule. The book pressed up against Ashley's torso was now the only thing separating them. Almost evenly matched in height, their eyes searched each other's for a sign. Ashley's breathing quickened; the nerves causing her stomach to do somersaults. Megan reached to tuck a strand of hair behind Ashley's ear before dropping her gaze, seemingly embarrassed by the uncharacteristic boldness.

Ashley placed the book back on the shelf and lifted Megan's chin with the tips of her fingers; she moved a step closer, closing the gap further. Megan's fingers brushed the length of her arm. Neither one of them was entirely sure who made the final step towards the other, but their lips parted just enough, brushing together for the first time. It was as though they didn't intend to kiss at first. The rhythm was off—Ashley's mouth hard and inflexible on Megan's. Until Megan placed her arms around Ashley's waist and their lips softened, easing into the kiss. The warmth consumed her as she leaned further in, embracing the beautiful girl before her in all her glory; she was perfection and her lips matched that perfection.

Ashley retreated slightly, taken back by the depth in which Megan used her tongue. Ashley, reluctant to delve in, preferred a passionate kiss without the use of tongues—a topic that had not been broached throughout the day.

"Less tongue," Ashley muttered.

Megan pulled away ever so slightly. "What?"

"Less tongue. I'm not a huge fan," Ashley repeated.

Megan's face flushed. Embarrassed, but she didn't pull away. "So you're basically saying I'm a bad kisser?" Her breath was on Ashley's lips, teasing as she nibbled on her bottom lip. The sensation sent shockwaves throughout her body.

"I never said that," she whispered, her heart rate increasing with every word.

Megan smirked, "I'm not offended, let me try this again."

The confidence aroused Ashley. The initial kiss was always a risk; she had been too intimidated in the past by the intensity of the situation to say anything of the sort, but Ashley had learnt biting her tongue (mind the pun) got her absolutely nowhere in her past relationships. The kiss was the single most important thing at the start of any relationship. It builds chemistry, passion and desire; three things Ashley felt an abundance of in that moment.

Megan's hand grasped the nape of her neck. That was all the encouragement she needed. They stumbled towards the bed; Ashley fell backwards, pulling Megan on top of her flailing body. The inelegant way in which they fell caused a fit of laughter, easing any remaining tension.

Ashley felt all the emotions she expected when kissing Megan for the first time—desire, excitement, nerves—but what she didn't expect to feel was familiarity. She hated a cliché, whether that be love at first sight or love conquers all, to name a few. It didn't conquer all, otherwise, her past relationships would have worked. Despite her previous scoffs at the concept, she found herself wondering if it was a cliche to feel you'd known/met someone before? Maybe in a previous life—

if you believe in that sort of thing. Ashley was sceptical, but open to being persuaded.

Trying to avoid the disruption in her head, she continued to explore Megan's lips. Her hands roamed under her t-shirt, edging it closer to being removed.

"Ash..." There was a brief knock at the door, the kind of knock someone does whilst opening the door, defeating the object completely, "...Jason's here, he wants the jacket back you borrowed."

Madison barged in, unaccustomed to the word privacy, "Whoops."

"Madison, seriously?"

Megan rotated and removed herself from the straddled position, hastily tugging at her unkempt hair.

"Sorry, you know what he's like. Where is it?" Madison preceded to rummage through her closet. Ashley's position on the bed didn't change; she lay propped up on her elbows, awaiting Madison's swift exit.

"Ash...girl...where you at?" a voice called from down the corridor, growing louder as it closed in. Disturbance number 2—Jason—the timing of her friends was outrageous, as always.

"There you are, girl. I need the denim jacket I let you borrow. I have a date tomorrow and it will go perfectly with my outfit."

Jason was a close friend of Ashley's, going back to her first bar job in New York. They had only worked together for three months, but they hit it off instantly. He was the only gay man in her life and he was quick to remind her that was all she needed.

"Damn, have I interrupted something?" The 'damn' was drawn out for dramatic effect; he stood in the doorway with one hand on his hip.

"No, Madison kindly interrupted on your behalf!" Ashley launched the closest thing she could find at her best friend, who was still buried in her closet.

"Jason, this is Megan."

"Hey, sweetie, it's great to meet you." He marched across the room and extended his hand.

"Nice to meet you too, Jason. I recognise you actually."

"You'll have seen him at Midtown 101. He's the manager there."

Megan nodded, "That's right."

"Honey, I'm the manager unless you're complaining, then I like to pass people on to my superior, Mr. Bird." Jason showed the back of his hand with just the middle finger extended upwards, followed by a mischievous wink. Megan found the gesture hilarious.

"You're the cute one that ordered an Appletini?" Jason raised his eyebrow.

"An Appletini? At 101?" Ashley taunted.

"Give me a break. How was I to know that wasn't a thing here?"

"Sweety, an Appletini is like asking for Caviar at Wendy's." Ashley laughed uncontrollably, whilst Jason remained as straight-faced as ever. Megan was the butt of the joke, but she didn't care. She embraced it and Ashley admired that.

Madison emerged from the closet moments later. "Where is the damn jacket, Ash?"

Ashley pointed towards the back of the door. "Underneath my leather jacket, I think."

"Seriously?" She stomped over to the door—if looks could kill. "You couldn't have told me that 5 minutes ago?"

Madison hurled the jacket at Jason before making a swift exit.

"Thank you for letting me borrow that."

"You're always welcome. Just next time, give it back sooner so I don't have to come and hunt you down whilst you're making out with gorgeous foreign girls." He winked in Megan's direction, causing her to blush.

"You can leave now." Ashley stood, edging him towards the door.

"I see when I'm not wanted. Call me tomorrow." He slung the garish denim jacket over his shoulder. "Actually no, call me Saturday because tomorrow I have a date and you know I'll be preoccupied all evening." He glanced back at Megan, "Bye, honey."

They were finally alone again.

"I'm sorry about that."

"Don't worry, your friends seem great. It must be nice to have close relationships like that."

"It has its pros and cons, like anything."

She lay back on the bed, her arm outstretched, Megan tucked in beside her. The moment had passed. Maybe she should have been more disappointed in the unsolicited appearance of her friends; they had ruined the moment after all. Instead, she found herself holding a girl she had known for less than a week in her arms as though it was a regular occurrence, a habitual embrace. What did that mean? That part she hadn't figured out.

"Can we watch something on TV?"

"Sure, you can choose."

They searched for a movie, instead settling on a highly anticipated series titled *Orange Is the New Black*—a choice they were both happy with.

There was a brief chatter around what Megan could wear to bed, the spare toothbrush that Ashley would provide and the quick text to her aunt to let her know she would be staying out. The sleepover had been unforeseen, therefore the preparation was poor. It left Ashley unprepared, in more ways than one, if anything was to happen between them. To get a shower would have been too presumptuous, so she opted for a more virgin-like experience.

Megan, now firmly snuggled under Ashley's arm, moved into a more comfortable position, placing her right hand on Ashley's chest and overlapping their legs. The manner in which they lay together made Ashley question again the differences between the encounters. She vividly remembered the first dates of previous partners and they were nothing in comparison. They had been awkward at times, intimidating and nerve-wracking. The date with Megan had been none of the above, at least, not to the extent they should be.

She felt Megan's breathing slow, the movement in her chest coming to a steady rhythm. That indicated sleep, but Ashley had never been more awake.

Sparks didn't fly; there was no initial thrilling experience, but it was entirely different somehow. Ashley struggled to gather her thoughts, to make sense of the feelings deep inside. There was attraction definitely, but there was also a connection, an emotional bond created in such a short period of time. *How was that possible?* she asked herself. *How was it possible to feel as though you had known someone your whole life? To be content in their presence, as if that very presence was always going to present itself to you?*

6

Ashley

The morning sun peeked through Ashley's window, creating a stream of light in a perfect line across the bed where they both lay. Half-conscious, she attempted to wriggle her arm free from underneath Megan. The position they had maintained for the whole night had caused the numb, tingling sensation in her arm that she now found distressing.

Megan rolled to the right, reaching out her clenched fist in a punch-like motion as she stretched, almost catching Ashley on the chin.

"Woah, easy tiger."

Megan peered through her partly exposed left eye, "Sorry."

"I didn't mean to wake you. I just couldn't feel my arm." She prodded and poked at the dull limb without sensation.

"I'm sorry."

"Stop saying sorry," Ashley laughed.

"Okay, sorry."

"How did you sleep?"

"Really good, did you?"

"Apart from being drooled on and the dead arm, it was perfect."

Megan looked mortified. "I don't drool!" She turned to the pillow, looking for evidence before wiping at her face frantically.

"I'm joking."

"Are you always this much of a wind-up?"

"Yes."

"I may have to re-think date number two then."

Ashley pulled Megan in close. "I'd be really upset if you did that." She lowered her bottom lip, eyelashes fluttering.

"What is that face?" Megan teased.

"It's my unhappy face."

"Well, it's making me unhappy so stop." She winked, prompting Ashley to tickle her torso. What erupted was a delirious belly laugh that brought her pure joy.

"What time is it?" Megan queried.

Ashley reached for her phone. "Ten."

Megan jumped up. "Crap."

"What is it? Do you have to be somewhere?"

"I'm expecting a call from my agent at eleven and my phone's dead."

Megan grabbed her clothes and ran to the bathroom to freshen up. She returned five minutes later.

"I'm sorry that I have to leave so soon."

"That's okay, I understand."

"I had a great time."

"Me too."

Megan reached her arms around Ashley's back and leaned in for a kiss. "Those lips…" she murmured.

"What was that?"

"I like kissing you."

"Yeah?"

"I wouldn't mind doing it again, sometime."

She held Megan's face in her hands, softly cradling the angelic features of a person she barely knew but wanted to. As she parted her lips and made contact with Megan's again and again, her want became a need. The smell of her perfume still lingered on her body from the day before, an intense fruity scent with coconut created a summer smell she would never forget. The feel of Megan's hand running through her hair made her knees go weak and her stomach flutter, all the tell-tale signs of a real connection forming.

"I would really like to see you again." Ashley pressed her lips against Megan's between each word she spoke. "Soon."

Megan smiled before stepping back and placing her hand on Ashley's chest, "I will call you later and we can arrange something?"

"Okay."

"I really need to go now."

"Go then."

Megan turned to open the door, her eyes never wavering from Ashley's. "Just one more kiss."

Ashley obliged willingly. One soon turned into five. They made their way slowly to the apartment door and then, all of a sudden, she was gone. Ashley ran her fingers through her hair as she pressed her back against the door, left with overwhelming memories of the best date of her life.

***

"So, what was it like?" Emily said.

"What?"

"You know, the sex?"

"We didn't have sex."

"Yeah, and I'm the Virgin Mary."

"Seriously, it didn't get to that."

"What? You were all over each other when Mads walked in."

"Yeah, thanks for that by the way." Ashley glared at Madison, who sat sheepishly across the booth at their local diner.

"I don't know why it didn't happen. If I was to say it just didn't need to happen, would that make sense?"

Emily raised her eyebrow, perplexed. "Absolutely not, no."

Madison rolled her eyes as she often did in Emily's presence, "Ignore Mrs. I-sleep-with-everyone-on-a-first-date. Tell us what you mean."

"Everyone? I'm not a whore."

"You could have fooled me."

Emily launched one of her french fries in Madison's direction, subsequently, it landed in her iced tea.

"Brilliant, now you can get me another."

"That's karma."

Ashley coughed purposefully, the bickering between her two best friends often reached a boiling point, "Guys, back to the original conversation."

"She started it," Emily sulked.

"How old are you?" Ashley taunted.

They both fell silent.

"I'm assuming you wanted it to happen? Like, you find her attractive?" Madison asked.

"100%, how could anyone not be attracted to her? It was just different, there was no pressure to have sex. We were just so comfortable with each other. Like, she literally fell asleep in my arms and we stayed that way the whole night. Who does that on a first date?"

"Yeah, that's not normal." Emily agreed.

"See?"

Madison toyed with her grilled cheese sandwich. "It's not normal to you because you just see it as an opportunity to get laid. I wouldn't say it's not normal. I'd just say it's a little uncommon."

"That's basically the same thing," Emily sniped.

"Don't laugh because I'm not trying to sound cliché here, but I just felt like I already knew her. Sometimes dates can be a bit formal and uncomfortable, but she was familiar to me. The connection was clear from the second we started talking."

"Okay, so what you're saying is you're in love after one date?" Emily baited.

Ashley rolled her eyes. "I literally hate you both."

"On a serious note, how did the date go? I have to get back to work in twenty minutes so make it sharp."

Emily noticeably turned her wrist to look at the time.

"In short, it was amazing. Do you know the bar Nancy's? On the east side?"

"The place on Lexington that's run by the old guy?" Madison replied.

"Yeah, well, turns out that's her grandparents. Well, Nancy is her grandmother. They have an amazing love story and Megan took me to Central Park, told me all about it and said I should write it. I even met Nancy and she gave her blessing."

"Seriously? That's certainly a creative first date."

"I was confused at first, but honestly it's a beautiful story and I'd love to write about it."

"What will you do? Approach some magazines with it?" Emily questioned.

"I haven't thought that far ahead, but maybe this could be my breakthrough. They always say a personal story is more likely to get published."

Madison smiled authentically. "I'm proud of you. It's time to put yourself out there. I won't allow you to be a bartender forever. You've got too much talent."

"Thanks, Mads."

Ashley's skin tingled; a broad grin appeared. A love story like Nancy and Christopher's filled her with joy. There was so much more to uncover, and she promised herself she would do the article justice. It would be *Romeo and Juliet*, but with a happily ever after.

"Oh god, I almost forgot."

Emily slid from the booth, ready to leave. Almost knocking over the waitress and the tray of drinks she so delicately balanced, "What is it?"

"Last night, when I text you saying we were on our way to the apartment, I had a text message from Georgina."

"Georgina, as in your ex, Georgina?"

"Yep."

"What did it say?"

Ashley removed her phone from her pocket and read out the message in question. "*I know you've been with a girl today. My sister saw you together at Dos Caminos. Why didn't you tell me you were dating someone else? Did I mean that little to you?*"

Madison scoffed, "She's got some nerve."

"She's kidding, right? After the crap she put you through?"

Emily sat back down, visibly annoyed.

"Don't you need to get to work?"

"Work can wait five minutes. So, what did you reply?"

Ashley shrugged, "I didn't. I don't know how to respond. I was occupied last night, but now Megan's gone all I can think about is Georgina."

"Please tell me you wouldn't consider getting back together with her?"

"No, it took me long enough to get over her. You know she has a boyfriend now, anyway."

Emily scoffed, "That didn't stop her sleeping with you though, did it?"

"That's old news."

"Ash, it was literally three weeks ago."

Ashley held her hands up, surrendering to the onslaught from which she would never emerge victorious. When it came to Georgina, there was always an excuse.

"That was a mistake."

"A mistake you will no doubt make again if you don't cut her from your life."

"I wish it was that easy. We have a lot of history." Ashley waved her phone at her friends. "What am I supposed to say to that?"

"Tell her it's none of her business."

"I agree," Madison held up her hand, signalling the bill, "she needs to know she doesn't have that hold over you anymore."

"That's nasty though, right? She said she wanted to be friends. I don't want to be mean."

"Ash, she literally ripped out your heart and stomped on it time and time again. If she really wanted to be friends, she wouldn't have slept with you three weeks ago. She is literally the devil."

Emily removed the black square-framed sunglasses from her head. "I second that."

"Okay, I'll ignore it. I don't need the drama."

"Good."

Ashley knew unequivocally that she would not ignore the message. She would try, but the reality was, Georgina still had a hold over her. The thought pained her and made her feel utterly weak and powerless, but it was the truth. Georgina Clark was Ashley's kryptonite.

They met through a mutual friend at the bar Ashley and Madison worked. They dated for almost a year, but throughout that year, Ashley found herself second best to everyone else. She fell hard, a slave to Georgina's charismatic nature. There were times when she thought it would work. When they were alone, she was made to feel like the most important person in the room, but in reality, she was a distraction, just another tick in an imaginary box, a list entitled 'The Tales in the Life of Georgina Clark'. That's what she came to realise when the fog faded and the clarity from her friends rang true. She was simply an experiment. When she found out that Georgina had also been sleeping with Travis—the guy she claimed was her *'best friend'*—that was the icing on the cake.

The brave face she portrayed in front of her friends in recent months was just that, a brave face. A lie that would keep things ticking along until one day she could truthfully say *'I don't love her',* and mean it. These things were easier said than done. Ashley still woke up most mornings to a text from Georgina. She became exclusive with Travis two weeks after they'd ended for good. That was two months ago. Since then, they had slept together a total of eight times—she had become her dirty little secret, a title she wasn't proud of. Emily and Madison were not aware of the eight times. She had tried to hide the majority of them, embarrassed and ashamed that she was still holding on to someone that hurt her so deeply. She settled for telling them part of the truth in the hope that they wouldn't uncover the reality. In the back of her mind, she knew there would come a day when the name Georgina Clark wouldn't feel like a kick to the stomach. The challenge being, she wasn't sure when.

***

Ashley pointed towards the group of ten middle-aged men gathered around the petite 4-seater table. Upon entering, Ashley purposefully sat them furthest away from the bar. The jerseys they wore solidified the fact that they had come from the Knicks vs Nets game, a fixture on the calendar that meant most bars in Manhattan were in for an eventful night.

"They are keeping me busy tonight."

"How are the tips?" Madison asked.

Ashley opened the zip on her black money belt revealing a bundle of bills stuffed inside. "Worth the hassle." Ashley grinned.

"Nicely done. Looks like food is on you tonight." She slapped Ashley's butt, "I'll do the glass collection."

They would often work the same shift, which included almost every Friday and Saturday. The end of the night ritual had never changed, whoever earned the most in tips bought food on the way home. Delving into a large pizza at two o'clock on a Saturday morning was the highlight of their weekend.

Ashley worked her way down the dark wooden bar top; all twenty stools were taken. A sight that would panic some bartenders, but Ashley was one of the best. It had taken her less than six months to master the role—mixing beverages was now her speciality. Often, the patrons' orders were aimed directly at her for personal recommendations.

"What can I get for you?"

"Three of your best house cocktails," slurred the woman in the skin-tight red dress.

"Do you have a preference in spirit?"

"No, you choose."

"Okay." Ashley went to work; the tequila was poured first, followed by Ancho Reyes, a hint of lime and lastly, grapefruit juice. It was an acquired taste, one of her favourites, but the bitterness wasn't for everyone. One by one she filled the requests of the customers, often doubling back to the most generous tippers. That was what paid her bills, so she favoured the lavish customers.

Madison appeared at her side in a hurry, "Don't look now, but you will not believe who's just walked in."

Ashley glanced towards the door.

"I said don't look."

"Is that who I think it is?"

"Yes," Madison clarified.

"Why is she here? She doesn't come here anymore."

"Would it have anything to do with the fact you ignored her?" Madison raised her eyebrows suggestively. "The ball's in your court now, Ash."

Georgina Clark stood at the end of the bar, closest to the door. The silver pendant light fitting that ran along the bar stopped at the very edge, the intensity of the light revealing Georgina's features in the darkly lit room. Ashley tried to concentrate on the $350 bottle of Dom Pérignon a gentleman had just ordered to celebrate his engagement, but it proved difficult. Dropping the most expensive bottle of champagne they served would have been a disaster. Once it was safely in the hands of the man, she could breathe again.

"Is she with him?"

"No, she's with a group of girls."

Ashley scanned the room, settling her gaze on Georgina. There was no denying she looked good; that was the difficult part. The long, flowing black hair partly covered her face, so Ashley could only make out her side profile. She remembered so vividly the way that hair smelled, what it was like to be kissed by those lips, and how it felt to be the one that Georgina wanted.

Madison nudged her back to reality. "Are you going to finish making that cocktail or what?"

They spoke in between serving customers, "Do you think I should go and talk to her?"

"Pass me that glass." Madison pointed. "Not at all, she's come here to try and make you feel uncomfortable and that's not fair."

"Has she though? Or is she just wondering why I'm ignoring her?"

"You can believe what you want Ash, but deep down you know she just wants to have her cake and eat it too."

Ashley did know that—all too well. "You're right."

Madison reached for the cocktail strainer. "Look, she's clearly jealous. That should make you feel good, there's no harm in playing on that a little bit, just don't get attached again."

Again being the crucial word. There had to be a point when she'd feel unattached for that to work. The tension between them was obvious. Every time Georgina looked over, Ashley looked away.

"Are you okay if I take a break?"

"Sure."

She headed for the back area. Through the brown double doors stood a row of lockers, a brown leather sofa and a stand-alone coffee machine. She'd been on her feet for six hours solid, with only four to go. When she removed her phone, she was met with a missed call and a message from Megan. In that moment, she felt guilty that she hadn't crossed her mind sooner. The minute she'd left the apartment that morning, Ashley's attentions had turned to Georgina—out of habit, not desire.

The message read:

Hey, I tried calling. I forgot you'd be at work. Call me when you've finished? I have some news. Don't worry if it's late, I'll wait up.

Ashley placed the phone back in her locker. Whatever the potential news could be was swiftly put to the back of her mind when she turned to find Georgina standing in the doorway.

"What are you doing back here?"

"Hello, to you too."

The garish yellow dress she wore was figure-hugging enough to make anyone look twice. If the intent had been to cause Ashley discomfort, then Georgina had already succeeded.

"What do you want, Georgina?"

"I want to know why you're ignoring me?"

"So, you came all the way over here tonight to ask why I'm ignoring you?"

"Yes."

"That's not normal."

"Why is it not 'normal'?" Georgina made air quotes, emphasising the sarcasm.

"Why does it matter to you?"

"You matter to me."

Ashley scoffed. "Yeah, okay."

"Why is that so hard to believe?"

"Oh, I don't know, maybe because you ripped out my heart on numerous occasions." Ashley slammed the locker shut.

"I thought we'd been over this? I said I was sorry."

"Just because you say you're sorry and then we sleep together, it doesn't make everything okay."

Georgina walked towards Ashley, closing the gap between them—there was nowhere for her to retreat. "You're right, but I am sorry for the way I treated you."

"You have a funny way of showing it."

"I still care about you and, for what it's worth, I really would like to be friends."

"Friends don't have sex, Georgina," Ashley hissed.

"Oh, I must have missed that memo."

Ashley composed herself. She would not allow the slip in self-control again—it wasn't healthy. "Too soon."

Georgina held up her hands, apologetically. "Can we at least try to be friends?"

"Why?"

"What do you mean?"

"Why do you want to be my friend?"

"Because I want you in my life."

"I don't know if I can be in your life the way you want me to be."

There was a brief pause. "Can't we at least try?"

"It's still too raw for me." Ashley looked deep into the hazel eyes of the woman she used to love. The dimly lit ambience made for an intimate scene. The pain was still present whenever she thought about what they used to be.

"Will you think about it at least?"

"Being friends?"

"Yes, like real friends. No sex, no flirty messages, just genuine friends."

"And you could do that?"

"If it means I get to have you in my life, yes."

"See, that's the difference between me and you because when I see you, I have to fight the urge to kiss you every damn time. I don't know if that will go away anytime soon."

"Then kiss me."

Ashley shook her head in disbelief. "No! That's the whole point, Georgina. That's what we cannot be doing. I hate that I want to kiss you, I actually hate it."

"Did you hate kissing that girl last night?"

"That's none of your business." Secretly, Ashley enjoyed watching Georgina squirm. The jealousy was evident and she would bask in the glory of that for days to come.

"So, you did kiss her?"

She considered taking the high road, but the opportunity presented itself perfectly. "We spent the night together, Georgina. So yeah, we kissed." As soon as the words left her mouth, she felt petty—childish—for implying something more had happened in order to hurt her.

"Oh. Well, I really hope you enjoyed her company."

Georgina pulled a photo from her bag and forcefully pressed it against Ashley's torso.

"I guess it's time for me to stop carrying this around." She spun dramatically and headed for the door.

"You're kidding, right? You're mad at me?"

"I'm not mad. I just realised it's time to stop holding on."

The look on Ashley's face said a thousand words. "Since when were you ever holding on?"

She wished that was the truth, but something inside told her to stay strong. There was a visible tear in

Georgina's eye as she left, theatrics that came naturally to her—she was an aspiring actress after all. The mixed signals over the past two months had sent Ashley running back and forth, late-night phone calls, 'good morning' texts and secret meetings in the park. She could have been completely over her by now, but the loneliness crept in every time she considered saying no.

The night before, with Megan, was the first time in a long time she'd felt content, like the universe had come together to plant a small seed of happiness, and now the responsibility lay with her to help it grow. She looked down at the photo of her and Georgina—it was of a happier time. In the beginning, when they'd fallen blissfully in love, before the betrayal, before the lies, a time when Ashley thought she might be the one. They were sitting on the sofa in Ashley's apartment, Georgina on her lap, cradling her face as Ashley looked up in awe, completely in love. The picture would have brought her to tears a month previous, but now the sorrow was manageable, small progress she was extremely proud of.

The photo was of a time she had to forget; it took an unimaginable amount of mental strength to tear the photo in two. It signified all she hoped she would one day feel towards her—absolutely nothing.

7

Megan

Megan sat upright in the window of her aunt's condo; the tactically placed accent armchair engulfed her body. Accompanied only by a cream throw, she thought about her earlier conversation with her agent Cheryl. She reached for her laptop. The screen came to life immediately and the email she had read through four times already sat open in the web browser. Cheryl had revealed her future and a whirlwind of emotions now surrounded her. She read the email once again for clarity.

Meg,
Congratulations once again!!
Below is a brief overview of what I have attached and what I need from you so we can officially accept and get the ball rolling.
I have attached the contract agreement and highlighted a few things I think we can negotiate on. Have a look through and let me know if there's anything else, but the majority looks good to me.
The salary was a stat better than Lyon, the performance-based bonuses are achievable and your general quality of life will be better in terms of accommodation, career development, travel, etc.
I know your dad will want an input, so I have sent the email to him as well. This is what we wanted though! This is the perfect stepping stone to one day get into the

WNBA. You will have a starting role with the Mystics, a league that is just starting to make a name for itself. The English league is getting a lot of press lately and the momentum is building, so we will be sure to take full advantage of that.

I am already working on some advertisements we can get you involved with and start to build your brand.

Talk to your dad about getting back to England as soon as possible. Your contract won't officially start until August, but you want to be in close proximity. Stay ready, keep working hard and I'll be in touch.

Cheryl

Megan found it all so surreal; she would soon be a member of the Manchester Met Mystics, which meant a return to England for the first time in four years. The prospect filled her with excitement. It meant a new beginning and the chance to spend some quality time with her parents. There was a momentary wave of disappointment when Cheryl revealed her new team. The natural choice would have been Lyon, but it wasn't meant to be. She would make the most of the opportunity given, that much she knew.

Megan took note of the time before closing the laptop—it was 12:30 a.m. The view over Central Park at night was utterly mesmerising. The New York skyline was always a photo to be captured, but the park being so vast had a more mysterious effect. Many New Yorkers would deem it unsafe at night, which was the main reason she would not walk through it after dark, only admire it from afar.

The evening had been a wholesome one, eating and drinking with Julie. When the time came to leave, she would miss their routine. The adrenaline still burned in her veins; it was nights like this when Stanford proved its worth. If ever she couldn't sleep, she would head to the gym and play until she was so physically drained that the only option was to sleep—basketball had always been her release. The two hours that afternoon on the local court had done nothing to ease her excitement or the anxiety she felt about leaving—it was a mix of emotions. Her phone was conveniently balanced on the arm of the chair. She glanced towards it impatiently, as she had done for the past hour. There was one last person to share the news with before she could retreat to bed. The lack of experience in such a situation left her feeling nervous.

How do you go from having a game-changing first date to potentially never seeing that person again? All in the space of twenty-four hours? Life has a funny way of throwing curveballs like that, and Megan felt the full force of this one. There was absolutely no way she could put any emphasis on being more than friends—they would be 4000 miles apart. It was impossible, that realisation had already hit. The hard part would be trying to let go of the *what ifs* that clouded her mind. Just as she pondered her life choices for the tenth time that day, the phone screen lit up. Her stomach dropped immediately— it was Ashley.

"Hey." Ashley's voice made Megan smile instantly.

"Hey, you're done early?"

"Well, I didn't want to keep you waiting all night, did I?"

"Don't flatter yourself, I was wide awake."

Ashley gasped, "I'm so hurt." Followed by a laugh that warmed Megan's heart. "There was me thinking you'd waited up especially for me."

"Maybe a little part of me did."

"I'll take that."

There was a loud crash of bottles on the other end of the phone that startled Megan.

"What the hell was that?"

"Just one of the bars filling their dumpster. I'm just walking home. You get some strange noises in Chelsea at this time of night."

"Is Madison with you?"

"No, she drew the short straw. It was quieter than expected so we flipped for who would stay until the end."

"And of course, you won."

"Technically no, but she knew I was ready to leave tonight."

"How come?"

"It's been eventful, but I can tell you about it another time." Megan sensed the reluctance on Ashley's part, so she didn't pry.

"What news did you want to tell me, anyway?"

Megan stalled with the words on the tip of her tongue.

"You remember I told you I had a call with my agent this morning?"

"Yeah?"

"Well, I finally have an offer."

"That's amazing, Megan. Congratulations. Will you be playing on the east coast?"

The plan had never been to stay in America, as much as Megan would have loved that to be the case.

"Not quite."

"Oh really? Don't keep me in suspense."

"I'll be going back to England."

Ashley inhaled. "Wow."

"I know, it was a surprise to me too."

"That's amazing, though. It's what you've worked so hard for, isn't it? You must be super happy."

"Yeah, it is, and I am. With change always comes fear though. I hope I can make an impression on the English league."

"I have every faith that you will."

"You've never seen me play," Megan declared.

"I have seen some videos."

"Since when?"

"Since I stalked your social media the day after we met."

That was like music to her ears, but the enjoyment that came with the reveal wouldn't be made public knowledge. "Oh, so you're that girl? You're giving off complete stalker vibes."

"Are you telling me you didn't look at mine?"

Megan responded sheepishly, "No."

"I'm calling bullshit."

"Okay, maybe I looked once or twice." Megan cringed inside. *How lame*, she thought, thankfully, Ashley changed the subject.

"So, when do you leave?"

"A week tomorrow."

"That soon?"

"Yeah, it's actually my mom's birthday in two weeks, so my parents like the idea of having me home for that."

Megan struggled to contemplate the idea of missing someone she didn't even know. She felt like it was the end of something that had never even started, not really, but the thought of never seeing Ashley again felt unjust.

"Would you like to meet up before you leave?"

"Is that weird?" Megan scrunched her cheeks; she was airing on the side of caution whilst only hoping for one answer.

"I suppose it's a strange one with you leaving, but there is no harm in us being friends, right?"

Friends, it felt like a form of rejection. Megan knew that a romantic relationship was off the cards. Couples with solid foundations didn't last 4000 miles, never mind two people that barely knew each other. She wasn't naive to that fact. Ashley was offering a friendship, which was exactly what was expected, but all she could seem to focus on was the potential to be more that was now being withheld.

"Of course, I'd like us to be friends too."

The words she spoke sounded confident, believable, almost.

"Good. I don't know if it's weird for me to say this, but I'm proud of you, for following your dreams."

"Thank you, that's really sweet. I'm sure I will say the same to you one day."

"Well, I'm offended that you're not proud of me for working in a bar?"

"Hey, I have nothing against you working in a bar, but it's not your dream. So when you become a big fancy writer or editor-in-chief of a New York magazine, then I promise I'll be proud of you."

"Well, at least one person will be," Ashley joked.

"You have to make a joke out of everything." Megan rolled her eyes, unseeable to Ashley on the other end of the phone, but she felt it was appropriate.

"Do I make you laugh, though?"

"I'm laughing at you, not with you."

"That hurts."

Megan grinned. Her eyelids felt weighted now. The last person had been informed of her future plans so she could finally relax. Ashley was the last person she told, but oddly, the first person on her mind when she found out.

"Are you almost home?"

"Sure am. Two minutes away."

"Good, I'm ready for bed. You must be exhausted?"

"You get used to the late nights after a while. I'll wait up for Madison and we'll probably eat pizza and watch a movie before we finally crash."

"Seriously? Oh god, I don't know how you do it."

"Habit, I guess."

"Will you text me tomorrow and we can arrange something next week?"

"You bet."

"Great. Goodnight, Ashley."

"Sweet dreams, Megan."

The only thing to do now was rest her head, recharge and let the unpredictability of her dreams sweep her to a place where everything made sense. That was the thing about dreams—they help to process emotion, subconsciously prioritising thoughts and feelings, allowing humans to make sense of the challenges they face.

***

The next day passed with no contact from Ashley. When the clock struck 10:00 p.m. she assumed there would be a reasonable excuse—an early start at work, a family emergency, some unforeseen circumstance that would stop her from checking in. Then, as the night turned into early morning, she was left disappointed. She couldn't help but think that Ashley's desire to see each other again didn't match her own.

Megan had no right to expect anything from her—she knew that. People go on dates all the time and never see each other again. That was life. She told herself she would text her the next day if she'd heard nothing. That wasn't needy at all, because she'd waited a full twenty-four hours. That alone highlighted everything that was wrong with her generation, too worried about pride.

Megan poured herself a glass of freshly squeezed orange juice. The perks of living with Julie. She was a health enthusiast; nothing entered her body that didn't add nutritional value. The fridge was always filled with fresh fruit and vegetables of every kind, and the bonus was a freshly squeezed glass of juice every day. The day before it had been celery, this morning it was orange—she couldn't complain.

"How's your juice?" Julie emerged from the bathroom.

"Perfect, thank you. I thought you'd have left for work by now."

"I have a quiet day today. I don't need to head in until lunchtime."

"But you've still been up since five this morning?"

"Of course."

"Don't you ever just want a morning in bed?"

Julie side-eyed Megan. "Do you ever have a day where you don't want to play basketball?"

"Nope."

"Exactly, because it's a habit. If you build strong habits, you have a happy and healthy life."

Megan thought about that. "I see."

"What do you have planned today?" Julie reached for a bowl and began her usual morning breakfast routine, another habit Megan observed.

"I'm meeting Sofia for breakfast."

"Sofia Diaz?"

"Yes, do you remember her?"

"Yes, of course. It's been a few years since I saw Sofia, but her father works for the police department. I see him regularly around town."

Megan used to have a huge crush on Sofia's father— she and Sofia had known each other since being three years old. Despite the distance, they managed to stay close friends throughout Megan's time in England. Whenever she returned to New York, Sofia would be up there with her family on the list of people to see.

"Good old Mr. Diaz. He's like a fine wine," Megan joked.

"Do you remember when you came to visit? You must have been fourteen, and Sofia was having a birthday party. You said to me, 'when I'm older I'll marry a man like Mr. Diaz, he's perfect'. You had such a crush, it was adorable."

"I think my taste in men has changed significantly, Aunt Julie."

"You mean you added *wo* in front of men." They both laughed hysterically.

"Well, yes, there is that. Mr. Diaz doesn't quite do it for me anymore."

"What about young Sofia? Is she more your type?"

"God no, she's like a sister." Megan ferociously shook her head.

"Have you spoken to your parents yet? About preferring a Miss over a Mr?"

Megan looked awkwardly at her hands. "Not quite."

"You know they'll be okay, right?"

"Yeah, I know that."

"Then what's stopping you?"

Megan often asked herself that very question. She had told her aunt about her attraction to women when she was nineteen; she'd never gone as far as to say *'I'm gay'* as the idea of being placed into a box and labelled made her uncomfortable. As the years went by, her sexual preference switched mainly towards women—the intimacy, the passion, the relatability and comfort of being with a woman felt like nothing she'd ever experienced.

"I guess I'm waiting for the person worthy of telling them about."

"Do they not ask? About your love life?"

Megan sneered. "Can you imagine my dad asking me about my love life? I don't know who that would be more uncomfortable for. I think he assumes I'm still a virgin and will not be told otherwise."

A small blueberry fell from Julie's mouth as she grinned. "What about your mom?"

Megan leant over the marble kitchen surface, her aunt's food making her stomach groan.

"It's just not something we discuss. She used to ask me if I was dating any boys, then I think as the years went by, she stopped asking. I was always reluctant to talk about it—she must have sensed that." She glanced at her watch; it was almost time to leave.

"You should tell them soon. I know your grandma knows and your friends. Nothing will change."

"I know that and I'm not keeping it from them because I fear their reaction. It just doesn't define me, yanno? I'm still Megan Davis whether I'm gay, straight, bisexual or transsexual. I just don't want to make a big deal out of it."

"Okay, you do it whenever you're ready, sweetheart. I'll support you no matter what."

"Thanks, Aunt Julie." Megan kissed her aunt on the cheek. "I've got to go. I said I'd meet Sofia in twenty minutes."

"Do you want dinner tonight?"

"Yes, please."

"It'll be ready for seven then. See you later."

***

Megan approached West 35th Street. She could see Best Bagel & Coffee, their favourite breakfast stop. Standing outside was Sofia, casually leaning against the wall, headphones in, her shoulder-length black hair poker straight.

"Hey, girl."

"Meg!" Sofia embraced her.

"It's a nice day, isn't it? Shall we grab a bagel to go and head for a walk around Central?"

"Sounds perfect."

They emerged five minutes later with a bagel in one hand and a coffee in the other. Megan's choice was a bacon and cheese bagel, hardly the breakfast of an athlete, but not everything had to revolve around protein shakes and juice cleanses.

"Have you seriously just got a butter bagel?"

"Yeah?"

"When did you get so boring?"

Sofia grasped her chest, offended. "I'll have you know my bagel choice does not reflect my lifestyle."

"Oh really? The Sofia I knew would've had a garlic and salt bagel with peanut butter and jalapeño."

Sofia grimaced at the thought. "That sounds absolutely disgusting."

The conversation stalled in between mouthfuls of bagel, but by the time they reached the Strawberry Fields entrance, their bagels and coffee had been disposed of.

"So, are we going out again this weekend? One last hurrah before you leave me?"

"I fly Saturday afternoon, so we can go out Friday, but it would have to be low key."

"Okay, I can speak to the guys, see what they're doing." The guys were some old elementary school friends. Sofia still kept in touch with them often, but Megan only predominantly saw and spoke to them when she returned to NYC. All the gossip in between would come from Sofia's weekly Thursday night phone calls.

"That would be nice. I don't know when I'll be back again, so I'd like to see everyone."

"I'll miss you. I thought I'd have you back for longer than a few weeks." Sofia pouted for dramatic effect.

"I'll miss you too." Megan reached out to put her arm around her. The little 5'2" frame of Sofia made her feel like a giant.

"The girl you met last weekend, Ashley, wasn't it? How's that going?"

Megan tucked both her hands into the short black running shorts she sported and shrugged. "I don't know."

"What do you mean you don't know?"

"We had an amazing date, but then I told her the other night I was leaving and we agreed to meet up one more time, but she didn't speak to me all day yesterday."

Sofia pulled her by the arm away from the oncoming cyclist, who was speeding through like a maniac. "Cuidado idiota." She bellowed.

"Why does anything you say in Spanish sound sexy? Even when you're quite clearly angry?"

Sofia winked. "It's a sexy language."

"I need to get myself a Spanish girl."

"You had one right here and you rejected her," Sofia teased.

"I did not reject you!"

On the contrary, it did fall under the umbrella of rejection. Megan visited New York as often as she could—two years prior, she had stayed for most of the summer. She and Sofia grew closer than ever, and Sofia got her wires crossed. The awkwardness of the situation smoothed over quickly and they now chose to joke about it.

"It's okay, we were better off as friends, we both know that! Besides, I will find myself the perfect girl one day."

"Are you trying to say I'm not perfect?"

"Perfect for someone else, yes."

"Nice answer."

"Stop changing the subject anyway!" Sofia side-eyed Megan, waiting patiently for her to divulge some more information.

"She hasn't texted me. I don't know what more there is to say."

"Have you texted her?"

"No...but—"

Sofia raised her eyebrows.

"Don't give me that look."

"What look is that?"

"The look you give me when I'm normally in the wrong."

"I didn't realise I had a look for that, but I'm glad it works."

"You think I should text her first, don't you?"

"Yep."

Megan dropped her bottom lip like a child throwing a tantrum. "But why? I told her to text me?"

"Have you ever thought that maybe she's thinking the same thing? Waiting around for you to reach out to her?"

Megan rubbed at her forehead; she knew Sofia had a point. "I just assumed...."

"Never assume, Meg. That gets you absolutely nowhere."

"You sound like my aunt."

"You know I'm right."

"Yes, and it pains me to admit it."

"Just text her now." Sofia reached for Megan's pocket. "Give me your phone I'll do it."

She smacked her hand away. "There is absolutely no way I am letting you text anyone."

They passed The Lake and made their way towards Shakespeare Garden. The picturesque body of water appeared so calm; the light summer breeze didn't affect the flow of the water and two large swans made their presence known to passers-by.

"Stop admiring the view and just text her."

"What do I say?"

"Just say 'Hello', and ask her when you're going to see her again."

Megan knew it was time to swallow her pride. She stopped to compose a message; Sofia's beady eyes watched as she typed away.

Hi Ashley,

Hope you're okay? When are we going on that second date then?

"Is that too forward? Should I make small talk first?" Megan queried.

"No, that's fine. It just shows you're interested, there's nothing wrong with that."

She felt uncomfortable—needy somehow—just by asking Ashley about plans that had already been agreed in theory. After hitting send, the gulp was audible.

"What if she just doesn't want to meet me again?" Megan felt foolish. "Or even worse, what if she recites some lame excuse like, I have to pick up my dry cleaning or I had to take this tiger to the vets because it got hit by a car. I will literally crawl under a rock."

"A tiger? Really?"

Megan shrugged. "The first one is probably a little more realistic."

"Remember, I was there that night. She couldn't take her eyes off you. There will be no such excuse, trust me."

The confidence Sofia had in Ashley's reply far outweighed her own. "We'll see."

Sofia linked her arm. "Shall we take a gondola ride and wait for her reply?"

Central Park was suggested by all New Yorkers as the perfect place to spend a summer's day. The sightseeing gondola rides around The Lake were one of many ways to do just that.

"Sure, why not."

"That's the spirit. Come on." Sofia took off towards the boathouse, dragging Megan along with her.

8

Ashley stared at the same four walls of her bedroom, admiring the intricacy of her favourite painting and then turning her attention to the laptop that was gathering dust on the new wooden desk. She'd had it specially made to fit the corner it currently housed, hoping that would give her some inspiration. Two months later, and the desk was rarely used, considering she aspired to be a writer, the time she spent staring at the laptop was greater than the time she spent typing on it. There was an element of self-belief needed, a quality Ashley struggled to manifest.

The idea of writing Nancy's story excited her. It was a love that stood the test of time, true love at its finest and in Ashley's opinion, it was one for the storybooks—a love that deserved to be written. The nervousness she felt was due to the self-doubt in her ability to do it justice. The ability to condense a lifetime of emotions and feelings into a two-page magazine article. It was possible; she'd seen it before. The way in which writers would tell a story so vividly, pulling on your heartstrings whilst keeping the wit that it takes to be a magazine writer.

Do you believe in soul mates? She would ask the reader. *Is there such a thing as one person for each individual on the planet?* The idea was something Ashley often laughed off, putting it purely down to an unrealistic storyline in the movies. This incredible, all-encompassing kind of love that defines us as people and makes everything else seem dreary in comparison. That was unattainable, at least for most. But what if Ashley could convince the good people of New York that it wasn't? That every now and again a story makes you believe in fairy tales. The story of Nancy and Christopher might do just that. Maybe it was even enough to convince Ashley that true love was real—anything was possible.

Firstly, she had to tell the story. That required a number of things; silence, motivation and more background, the latter she needed Nancy for. After deciding she couldn't proceed without some more information, the hour of procrastinating came to an end.

It was a Wednesday in June; the month was almost over. July would soon come around and Ashley despised the humidity that came with a New York summer. The locals would often go away on vacation and the tourists would flock.

The conversations with Megan had been brief, Ashley would be the first to admit that she was holding back. The fear of getting attached to someone who would leave in three days' time made her do just that. She had avoided the idea of a second meeting for that reason, though the urge to message Megan had been uncontrollable, she found herself thinking about her often. It wasn't until Megan messaged her that she realised whatever plan she was trying to hatch wouldn't work, all it did was fill her mind with unknown possibilities. *They could just be friends after all, right?* Ashley hoped.

They both agreed to do something fun, Coney Island the choice. Neither had been since childhood, so it was the perfect last hurrah. They agreed to meet outside Ashley's apartment, a cab was ready and waiting. In just under an hour, they were transported from the glitz and glam of Manhattan to the old-style amusement of Brooklyn's Coney Island. On arrival, they admired the white and red wooden frame of the famous Cyclone rollercoaster stretching high above the sandy beaches below.

"Can you believe that was made in 1927?" Ashley informed.

"Seriously?"

"Yep! Apparently, it's the second steepest wooden rollercoaster in the world."

Megan looked in awe at the rickety old fixture. "How is it even still standing?"

"I have no idea. I suppose that's part of the fun, isn't it."

"What is? Wondering if I might die today?"

"Exactly!" Ashley chuckled.

The wonder wheel could be seen spinning in the distance. A unique take on the Ferris wheel, the passenger cabins were not fixed directly to the rim of the wheel leaving room for movement—that excited Ashley. Children ran by in every direction enjoying ice cream cones and cotton candy, parents chased aimlessly, trying to keep up. The sound of rollercoasters, carousels and numerous fairground rides brought back a flash of memories from her childhood. There was once a time her parents had been happily married. She adored her sister—minus the normal sibling rivalry, of course, they were the perfect all-American family. That changed quickly as she got older, a time she tried to block out.

"Are you hungry?" Megan asked.

"A little. What do you fancy?"

"Where do you recommend?"

Ashley pointed towards the large building painted in shades of green and yellow—it said 'Nathan's Famous'.

"Hot dogs?"

"Sure, it's the original. If you come to Coney Island you have to get a Nathan's Hotdog, it's the law."

"Okay, lead the way."

The queue was surprisingly short for such an iconic franchise. Megan found a place to sit, the red and yellow parasols highlighting the wooden benches reserved for Nathan's Famous customers. Ashley appeared five minutes later with two hot dogs smothered in chilli and cheese.

"I got you the same as me. I hope that's alright?"

"Of course, thank you."

The hotdogs weren't about to win an award for presentation, but the taste never disappointed. She watched Megan take one large bite, the remnants of cheese covering her lips, an insatiable release of noise left her mouth indicating her enjoyment of said hot dog.

"Good?" Ashley enquired.

"So good. I don't remember them being this nice." They savoured every last delightful bite. "I didn't even offer you any money. How much was it?"

"Don't be silly. It's on me."

"Do you buy all your friends' hotdogs?"

"Just the pretty ones." Ashley winked.

Megan blushed, hiding behind the paper napkin she dabbed at her face. She quickly changed the subject.

"Are you doing anything for the Fourth of July?"

"I normally go home and visit my mom for the weekend, but I think we might have a party at our house this year. Macy's sponsors a huge firework display in the city—the view is great from our rooftop. What about you? England doesn't celebrate the Fourth of July, right?"

Megan shook her head. "Nope. I wish I could stay for that."

"Can't you?"

"It would be too late to change my flight now."

"That sucks." Ashley watched intently as Megan fidgeted with the long strands of hair that whipped with the wind, adjusting it to avoid knotting.

"Do you think we can stay friends?" Megan gazed intently.

"If that's what you want?" It wouldn't have been her first choice. She favoured the chance to explore what they could have been, but Ashley had been left with no alternative.

"I would really like to." Megan smiled. "I will come back to New York at least once a year—it would be nice to catch up when I do."

Ashley agreed half-heartedly, "Me too." There was no real intent to have a once-a-year friendship with anyone, but she felt obliged.

"Is it weird that..." Megan stopped dead in her tracks.

"What?"

"Nothing."

"Don't do that." Ashley leaned on the bench in front, hands clasped together, staring deep into Megan's eyes. She couldn't help but smile in response.

"It's embarrassing."

"Come on. It can't be that bad." Ashley reassured her.

Coyly, Megan looked down at her hands. "Is it weird that I will miss you?" Immediately after she'd said it, she covered her face with her hands. Ashley found it amusing, quickly reaching over to pull her hands down so she could look into the piercing emerald green eyes when she spoke.

"Not at all. In fact, I'll miss you too."

Megan's eyes widened. "Really?"

"Weirdly, yes."

"Why do you think that is?" Megan asked.

Ashley considered the question posed. "I don't know." She looked out towards the beach, focusing purely on the ebb and flow of the sea. Then she said the first thing that came to mind, "I think we have a connection. It doesn't necessarily have to be on a romantic level. That is everyone's first instinct, but sometimes life throws a curveball or two and here we are. You leave in two days and I don't know when I'll see you again." Ashley shrugged.

"So, we don't make it anything more than what it is, right? I'm leaving, but there's no harm in staying friends."

It seemed simple enough. "Exactly."

"So, I have a proposition."

Ashley raised her eyebrows, intrigued. "Okay."

"How about we forget that I'm leaving and for today we just enjoy each other's company?"

Ashley nodded. "I can do that."

"Okay then, so where to next?"

The boardwalk filled up suddenly. The entrance to Luna Park became crowded as people gathered below the giant archway guarded by the grinning clown.

"Follow me."

The park was filled with rides, each one offering its own unique thrill. Thunderbolt was the newest addition; Ashley had heard about it in the newspapers. The large steel rollercoaster had been built a year prior. The feeling of adrenaline took over, they were quickly strapped into the nine-seater cart and the restraint system came forcefully down around them. The cart set off and the ascent towards the 90-degree drop began.

"Oh, God." Megan reached for Ashley's hand, she could feel her nails grasping tightly. "Shit. This is high."

"Are you ready?" Ashley yelled.

"No."

They looked directly at each other as the cart dropped. The G-force was enough to make their eyes widen like they'd seen a ghost. The cart catapulted into one turn after another. The twisted layout erupted into the sky, each plunge causing another loud roar from the people on board. The ride eventually came to a stop and Ashley prized Megan's hand off her own, the grip tight enough to cause a brief loss of circulation.

"You have one hell of a grip," she said, shaking her hand dramatically as they climbed down from the platform.

"I was clinging on for my life."

"No round two for that one, then?"

"Never."

"You didn't strike me as a chicken."

"Yeah well, I am. Surely, there's a children's ride around here somewhere?"

Ashley laughed, doubled over. "I got you. I know the perfect ride."

Swinging like the pendulum of a clock in the distance was Luna 360. Ashley pulled Megan towards the ride; the short length of the queue didn't ease her nerves.

"See, nobody wants to go on this one. I wonder why?"

Ashley rolled her eyes and pulled Megan by the hand. "You'll love it."

They were strapped into the large red contraption in seconds. The music started, followed by the gliding back and forth, capturing the G-force it required to send the ride dual swinging into the atmosphere. The fluid spinning motion filled the air with screams of joy. She heard Megan's above all, causing the outburst of laughter that erupted from her core.

"I hate you."

"Why?" Ashley laughed.

"That was horrific."

"Oh, come on. Didn't you enjoy it just a little bit?" Megan linked her arm through Ashley's—seemingly for convenience, but she welcomed the touch.

"No. My legs feel like jelly. I don't remember rides being this traumatic."

"When was the last time you came to a theme park?"

"I honestly can't remember. Maybe eight years ago."

"Seriously?"

"They scare me."

"Why?"

"They're just unpredictable, aren't they?"

Ashley couldn't comprehend the fear of theme parks, she'd always been an adrenaline junky when the opportunity presented itself. The chance to jump out of a plane had been taken three years ago, since then a theme park seemed nothing in comparison.

"You've got more chance of Donald Trump becoming president than you having an accident on one of these rides."

"I don't like those odds." Ashley looked down to watch Megan's left hand link with hers, the other cradling her upper arm. The touch sent a shiver down Ashley's spine.

"You ready for the next one?"

"Sure, it can't be any worse than that."

They rode the Brooklyn Flyer, followed by Steeplechase—much to Megan's dismay—and finally, The Cyclone, before stopping for some sorbet at Coney's Cones. The weather permitted an hour on the beach. Neither had prepared for the sun beating down; no sunblock meant no longer than an hour, neither wanted to resemble a ripe tomato. They found a comfortable spot on the sand, watching the world go by.

Ashley felt sadness knowing that it would not be a regular occurrence, there would be no coffee dates or walks through Central Park with Megan. They spoke about her plans once she returned to England, the excitement she felt at playing competitive basketball again, the chance to spend time with her friends and her parents. The positives far outweighed the negatives, but she would miss New York and California—both had been extremely good to her over the years. The intention was to always return. The WNBA was the league she desired to play in, the work ethic she would need to adapt in order to achieve such a goal was immense, but she expressed the desire to do whatever it took.

Ashley asked about Megan's parents, Michael and Amanda—she spoke so fondly of them, their admirable careers and role model marriage. Ashley couldn't say the same about her parents. Whenever the subject arose, she quickly moved on. She knew she'd have to visit her mom at some point over the Fourth of July weekend—that was not the problem. The inability to quit talking about her father and all his wrongdoings was what bothered her, even after four years of separation she hadn't found it in herself to move forward and that frustrated Ashley.

The sun began to set on the horizon, and there was just one last thing Ashley wanted to experience. "It shuts soon, so we need to hurry."

"What does? Please don't say it's another rollercoaster."

Ashley grinned. "No, it's not quite as thrill-seeking, but it's fun."

The large multi-coloured wheel could be seen from anywhere on Coney Island, lit up in red fluorescent lights spelling out the iconic title 'Wonder Wheel'. As they got closer, Megan's panic-stricken face relaxed.

"The Wonder Wheel? I can cope with that."

The blue and yellow striped cart awaited them as they jumped in. The sign stated the ride would take around ten minutes to complete the full rotation, so she paid the operator double—it was quiet, so he accepted without hesitation.

"This wheel is a little different to the normal ones."

"What do you mean?" The cart shot forward and back at speed, causing Megan to grab hold of Ashley with one hand and the side of the cart with the other. "What the hell! Is it broken?"

"No, of course not. Just wait until you get to the top and it does it."

Megan's face dropped. "And you've paid for two turns? Are you crazy?"

Ashley shrugged. "I like the view at the top."

"Of course, you do." Megan crossed her arms.

The cart movement happened every minute or so, but Megan became more comfortable once she knew what to expect.

"So, I thought about Nancy's story the other day."

"Did you start it?"

"Not quite. I thought about starting it. I think I need to talk to Nancy though. Do you think she'd mind?"

Megan smiled the most heart-warming smile. "Not at all. Shall I give you her number? Then you can arrange to speak with her?"

"Do you mind? I didn't want to just turn up at the bar and start bombarding her with questions."

Megan pulled her phone from her pocket and sent the contact information over.

"Thank you."

"That's okay. I can't wait to read the article when it's done."

Ashley frowned. "Hmmm."

"What?" Megan braced herself for the next drop before turning towards Ashley. "Why do you look like that?"

"Like what?"

"Like you have absolutely no confidence in your own ability to write the story?"

"That's deep. You got all that from a look?"

"Am I right?"

The silence confirmed her assumption.

"Can I ask you something?"

Ashley nodded reluctantly.

"What happened to make you lose confidence in your writing? You told me when we first met that you moved into the city with the hopes of being a writer. That was three years ago. I have known you for almost two weeks and I haven't once heard you speak about something you're working on—until now with Nancy's story—and I'm pretty sure you're just trying to appease me before I leave by saying you'll do it."

Ashley looked out towards the beach. The wheel had reached the pinnacle and was beginning to descend again; the view looking out to the sea was what she loved the most about the Wonder Wheel. Everyone down on the beach seemed so small. It was a different world atop the wheel and that made Ashley feel superior somehow, as opposed to her normal inferior mindset. The two weeks she had known Megan, they'd spoken most days, but she had tried to avoid referencing her parents for fear Megan would want to know more. The thing she found the most confusing was the urge she possessed to talk about it with Megan, an urge lost even with her best friends.

"Ashley?" Megan brought her back to reality.

"Sorry. I guess it's to do with my dad." When she didn't say anymore, Megan tried to lead the conversation.

"Was he a writer too?"

"Yes."

"What did he write?"

"Politics and War, he was in the Army growing up so it interested him the most."

"Is that why you wanted to write?"

"Initially, maybe."

"What changed?"

"I realised he was a complete asshole and our whole bond in my late teens had been based on a lie." Ashley clenched her jaw.

"A lie? How so?"

The inner corner of her eyebrows slanted upwards as she inhaled deeply. "He was cheating on my mom for five years. He literally had another family. The woman he was seeing had two kids. He used to go and stay there 2–3 nights a week. He'd tell us he was working on a story. I was so gullible, believing all his lies about these amazing trips he'd been on." Ashley looked down at her hands, pushing her lips firmly together, obviously uncomfortable discussing the deep-rooted pain she carried. "He'd tell us he was *'following the story'* and how that was the most exciting thing about being a freelance writer. The whole time he was staying with his other family."

"Wow." Megan chose her next words carefully. "So, you had these dreams of being a writer and following in your dad's footsteps. Then all that was shattered when you found out the truth?"

"Pretty much." Talking about her father always conveyed the same rigid expression. "The dream had always been to move into the city and pursue a writing career because that's what my dad did. When I finished college I planned my move and literally, a few weeks later, I found out exactly what he'd done."

"That must have been tough."

"They'd already been separated for almost a year by that point, but my mom never told us why. She said they'd grown apart, she said she wanted to protect us, but I think she was more bothered about saving face with the neighbours."

"How did you find out?"

"I saw him at a diner in Long Island. He was with the other woman and her kids. I went home and told my mom. She's always been a terrible liar, so I could tell straight away it wasn't a surprise to her."

Megan listened intently, waiting patiently for her signals to prompt the conversation further. "So, then your mom told you everything?"

"To an extent. She tried to forgive him, she'd known for six months before they separated properly and he left our home. I'm just thankful I wasn't young enough to go through custody battles because what followed was horrendous."

"Where is your dad now?"

"He moved to the west coast with his new family. My sister, Samantha, took his side and moved with him."

"Seriously? Why?"

"She's always been a daddy's girl. She's a few years younger than me, and she saw the opportunity to be the centre of attention in a new state. She knew Dad would give her anything she wished for if she went with him. I suppose both parents got to keep a daughter. They truly got half of everything in the divorce settlement." Ashley was cynical.

"And that's why you don't speak to your sister anymore?"

"Exactly. My mom didn't deserve to be treated that way. How her own daughter can abandon her like that, it didn't sit well with me." The cart was on its second trip around the wheel. The movement not causing so much as a flinch now.

"Have you spoken to your father since?"

"Only on holidays. He sends a present or a text every now and again, but that's it."

"Do you think you'll ever be able to forgive him?" A loaded question.

"I have forgiven him for what he did, he wasn't happy, but he stayed with my mom for years because he didn't have the guts to break our family apart, I suppose there is something admirable in that, weirdly, in some way." Ashley smiled shyly, conscious of her ramblings.

"But?"

Opening up to Megan was easier than she anticipated. "I haven't forgiven him for making me a part of his lies. That still hurts."

"You feel like your whole career choice has been built on a lie?"

"I guess so. My years spent at college, my move into the city—it was all to follow in his footsteps. Since I found out the truth, I lost the inspiration. All I think about now when I open my laptop is all the times he sold me a pipe dream, made out as though writing was this amazing career and that we would one day write stories together. It was amazing for him because he got to be with them, that's the only reason."

"What if he believed it was amazing? What if the writing was never a lie, but instead the only genuine thing he could discuss with you?"

Ashley considered that theory. "I never looked at it like that." It was a new take on an old situation.

"I'm not defending him, but if he was keeping all those secrets and lying to you and your mom, maybe the bond he had with you over writing was his saving grace. It probably made him feel less guilty, knowing that he was having a positive impact on your life despite his wrongdoings."

"Is that the only reason, though? The guilt?"

"Have you ever asked him?"

"No."

Megan reached to hold Ashley's hand, playing with the tips of her fingers intricately, as if she would hold them for the last time. "Well, maybe you should. It might help."

"Maybe."

"I think regardless of what happened, if writing is a passion of yours, then pursue it. You'll only regret it in ten years' time when you look back at what could've been."

"I know."

"So, promise me then."

"What?"

"That you'll write the best version possible of Nancy's story and publish it for the world to see."

"I can't make that promise. It's not that easy."

"I believe you can."

Ashley smiled—just hearing the words made her emotional. The belief she had lost was in the heart of a girl she barely knew, only two physical meetings, yet spiritually, it felt like many more. Ashley felt even closer to Megan now, knowing they would soon be physically apart. They connected on a level that was beyond anything she had experienced before. Through their body language, their eyes, their voice, the slightest touch. The opportunity presented itself, Ashley leaned in, her lips brushing softly, delicately against Megan's. The warmth of her skin and the scent of her perfume lingered as the cart came to a stop, neither wanting to pull away too soon.

"I'm sorry."

Megan inhaled, catching her breath. "Don't be." She whispered.

"Not a great start to our friendship."

"We can always start tomorrow." Megan smiled.

They hopped off the ride and headed towards the fairground exit. Ashley had a habit of biting her lip when she felt nervous, her gaze fell to the floor.

"What's wrong? You've gone quiet." Megan observed.

"Can I come and visit you? In England? Only if you wanted me to of course, no pressure."

"Of course. I would love to show you around." Megan seemed genuinely excited.

"I'd love to see it one day."

Ashley reached her arm around Megan. She had to tip-toe slightly to make it work in her favour. "Thank you for the best second date I've ever had."

"I should be thanking you. It was all your idea."

"That's true, actually. I take it back." They laughed uncontrollably, a common theme in their short time together. The sun had fully set on a day that Ashley hoped they would one day repeat. The timeline was unknown, but one thing was for sure, she would never forget their time spent together.

9

September 2014
Ashley

August gave way to September, and the days quickly passed by. The summer was drawing to a close, which meant the bar became busier during the week as the regular locals returned from their vacations and began to wind down, ready for the winter. When Ashley wasn't working, she found herself writing. The inspiration she'd lacked for so long had found its way back—she had Megan to thank for that.

On Wednesday morning, she stopped by Nancy's bar. A place she now often frequented alone. She found solace within the four walls. She took her usual spot to the right of the bar; the plush velvet green chairs were the comfiest, accompanied by a charging port for her laptop and the proximity to the bar—it was the perfect spot. A grey, short-haired man with a slim build and rough stubble appeared moments after she sat down with a glass of soda.

"Hi, sweetheart." He placed the glass down and smiled broadly, happy to see her as always.

"Thanks, Christopher. I hope you're adding these to my tab."

"Sure, sure." He waved her off. Ashley knew he wouldn't. She had tried for two months to pay for her drinks, but he refused.

"Why don't I believe you?"

He shrugged and walked away, laughing to himself, wiping the tables as he went. Ashley had grown close to Nancy and Christopher since their first sit-down conversation two months prior, and in return, they had grown rather fond of her. The conversations about their story often turned into deep meaningful exchanges about life, love and oddly, forgiveness. The latter being the one Ashley struggled with the most. The days turned into nights so easily, and she found herself learning and growing with each interaction. It started off as an assignment, a way to build her confidence again in the hope her love for writing would return. If she happened to write an article that got published, then that was a bonus. After a few weeks, it became so much more, it took on a deeper meaning and the guidance she received from Nancy whilst she followed the journey to the final finished article was invaluable.

Ashley's mom was adopted and her dad's parents died when she was young, she felt a void from not having grandparents, especially growing up, when other kids would talk about staying at their '*Grams*' for the weekend. The bond she had created with Nancy and Christopher brought her a sense of belonging. *Is this what it feels like to have grandparents?* she often asked herself. The advice and the wisdom they offered with every conversation brought her great satisfaction.

Nancy appeared by her side. Her shoulder-length grey hair looked lighter than usual; it was pulled back off her face with a large old-fashioned barrette and a matching set of small, diamond hoop earrings. The lines around her eyes seemed less prominent—she'd applied make-up today.

"You look amazing."

She took a seat beside Ashley. "Thank you, darling."

"Are you going somewhere?"

"Just out for breakfast with my daughter." Ashley had heard all about Julie from Megan, and more recently from Nancy, but they'd never met.

"Lovely. Anywhere nice?"

"I'm not sure actually, I told her to surprise me."

"That sounds exciting." Ashley reached into the folder to the left of her laptop. "I actually have something for you, if you've got a minute?"

"I always have a minute for you, dear." Nancy's eyes widened when she saw the newspaper. "Is that the article?"

Ashley's dimpled grin emitted pure delight. "It might be."

"You got published?" Nancy squealed.

"Yes! Can you believe it?"

"Yes, because I knew you would." Nancy embraced Ashley, squeezing tightly with enthusiasm. "When did you find out?"

"I only found out yesterday that it had been brought forward and it would be printed in today's paper." Ashley held the paper in her hands, careful not to crease it.

"You didn't even tell me you'd sent it."

"I wanted it to be a surprise."

Nancy held out her hands. "Can I read it?"

"Of course. I thought you should be the first."

"Haven't you looked at it?"

"No, I'm too scared."

Nancy turned and signalled for Christopher to join them. "I'll get Christopher to read it to us."

He appeared by her side seconds later. "What is it, dear?" He glanced down at the newspaper in her hands. "Is that what I think it is?"

They both nodded in agreement.

"I am so proud of you, Ashley. That's incredible." He glanced again at the paper. "And with *The New York Times*? I am so thrilled for you. I knew you could do it."

There had only been one newspaper in mind when she wrote the article. The amount of research she did into previous articles, current writers and their styles, what the editors were looking for and the gaps within the newspaper. There had been a long list of requirements she had to meet, from the word count to the unique readability. The whole article had been written with *The New York Times'* readers at the forefront. It was the holy grail of newspapers; it was a case of *go big or go home*.

"Thank you. You'll make me cry." The words she longed to hear made her instantly emotional. He reached out to stop Nancy from opening the paper.

"This calls for a celebration."

"Sweetheart, it's 10:00 a.m."

"It's never too early for champagne."

Christopher darted towards the bar, reasonably agile for his age—seventy-six looked good on him. He returned moments later with three champagne flutes and a bottle of Louis Roederer Cristal.

"Will you read it for us?" Nancy handed the paper to Christopher, who took a seat opposite. Luckily, the bar was nearly empty. A couple finished their breakfast and a young man sipped his coffee silently whilst he typed away. Christopher flicked through the paper, stopping immediately at page number ten. In bold writing, the heading read, *'Do you believe in soul mates?'* followed by a small sub-heading that read, *'True love is a myth, right?'*.

"Here it is."

Ashley knew what to expect, but that didn't calm the butterflies. She had shown snippets to Nancy and Christopher, but the pressure of the big reveal made her stomach knot.

"We are all sceptical, it's human nature to question and doubt. That is how great debates begin. If you're reading this article, I can guarantee you are sceptical about one of the following: God, UFOs, the afterlife, or whether Kim Kardashian's butt is real. I got you, didn't I? It was the last one? Anyway, the reason I started this way is because I am sceptical, or I was. How many times have you heard, *'there is someone out there that's perfect for you, you just need to find them'*? The idea of meeting your soulmate is the glorious stuff of rom-coms, a picture created to give us hope that one day we will meet someone and it will simply *click*. The sudden overwhelming clarity will identify that you have always been meant for each other, despite every instinct to the contrary. The concept excites us, builds our expectations up so they can never truly be met, but sometimes, once every so often, a couple prevails." Christopher paused, took a sip of champagne, and continued.

"This was never an article I thought I would write, but inspiration comes when you least expect it. A good friend of mine once told me about a young couple. Nancy and Christopher met in 1958. It was a year of breakthroughs, America sent their first satellite into space, NASA was formed and the Microchip was created—thank you, Jack Kilby; without you, I would not be able to type this article. The year was as impressive as any, but these are not the things you will remember once I share the story. Why? Because love is the most powerful emotion we experience as humans and everything else falls to the wayside. Let me start at the beginning. When Nancy met Christopher…"

The middle of the article was purely their story, just as Megan had told it. That part had been the easiest to write, because she wasn't trying to fool anyone. There was no ulterior motive, she simply wanted to share the story in its simplest form, knowing positively there would be no bells and whistles needed to engage the reader.

"Yes, Christopher did create a plaque. I apologise to the men reading this article for including that part because the bar has been set. As far as romantic gestures go, that is right up there with Richard Gere climbing the fire escape to capture the heart of Julia Roberts in Pretty Woman—*swoon*." Christopher smirked at the nod towards his romantic side. "You can see it for yourself to the left of the lake. I haven't created an unrealistic picture here; I have merely shown you a blissful vision of a couple destined to be together. I didn't dramatise the story in any way, nor did I add emotion that wasn't present. I bet, if you were a complete sceptic at the start of this article, it made you believe just a little, didn't it? I know it did because it did me. Going back to my original point: do you believe in soulmates? We all have a different version of what a soul mate should be, so here's mine." Nancy grabbed Ashley's hand and squeezed it tight for the second time; she took that as a good sign.

"My belief is that we will all cross paths with people that have a significant, earth-shattering effect on our lives, even if we don't realise it at the time, but a soul mate? I think that is up for debate. In the movies, the discernibly incompatible couple find out they are really soulmates when they realise their favourite band is the same. All of a sudden, their problems melt away and they are blissfully in love for eternity. No wonder everyone wants one, right? Love, regardless of beliefs, takes hard work and sacrifice. I don't believe a soulmate is totally devoid of all realism, certainly not after learning about Nancy and Christopher, but I am still curious. What do I need to do to find mine? If you know the answer, please inform me via email or even better, if you are my soulmate, that would really move things along nicely." Nancy laughed out loud at the final line. Christopher placed the paper down on the table and walked around to hug Ashley.

"It was amazing."

"Really?"

"Absolutely."

"I was so worried, especially talking about the two of you. It took me a while to find the perfect words because, despite my feelings about soulmates, I didn't want to downplay the realness of your love story."

Nancy reached for the paper so she could see it for herself.

"It was perfectly balanced. It was relatable and witty in all the right places. You did a fantastic job."

"Thank you, Nancy."

"I need to go across the street to get a copy."

"Already got you one." Ashley pulled two more newspapers from her bag.

"This is going on the wall." Christopher beamed. "I must see to the customers, but amazing work, kiddo, I really mean it." He wandered off with the newspaper in hand.

"You must be so proud of yourself."

Ashley had dreamt of the day she would see her first piece of writing published; throughout her teenage years, it consumed her. The reality, however, was far from what she imagined.

"Yeah, I am."

Nancy cocked her head to the left. "You could've fooled me. You have just been published in *The New York Times*, now, I don't know much about the writing profession, but I would imagine that's a pretty big deal."

The facade drained, followed by a pronounced sigh. "You're right."

"Is it about your dad?"

"I guess, deep down. I think I imagined today differently. I created this picture that down the line became unattainable and I never accepted that until today. It was never going to meet my expectations. It's my own fault." Ashley lowered her head, disappointed. "Anyway, let's not talk about that. Today is just as much your day as it is mine."

"I didn't write the article."

"No, but you inspired it, and that is critical. Without you, there would be no article."

"Our story was merely the spark. You turned it into a fire, my dear, and now you have to keep it burning. Don't you ever let the flames burn out, that is too much talent to waste."

Ashley placed her head on Nancy's shoulder. She watched as the delicate, wrinkled hand reached to brush the side of her cheek.

"I like that metaphor."

"Good, you can keep it."

Ashley took a sip of champagne, conscious that Christopher had opened a bottle just for them. The woman taking a seat two tables away glanced in their direction. She would, without doubt, pass judgment on their early morning drinking habit—Ashley couldn't help but giggle at the notion.

"Have you told Megan yet?" Nancy enquired.

"No. I thought you would like to do that."

The truth, Ashley hadn't heard from Megan in almost two weeks, but Nancy didn't need to know that. The assumption that the two of them were the best of friends remained firm in Nancy's mind since Megan's departure two months prior. There was absolutely no reason for the lack of contact. There was no bad blood from either side, the relationship had just become what was expected—a long-distance friendship. At first, they spoke every day, all day, much to Ashley's delight. The delay in conversation was one minute or six hours—time difference depending. It took a week or so to get used to. They called each other every day, a nicety that transported her to a place where time and distance didn't exist.

They spoke freely about work, basketball, friends, family—the details Ashley knew about Megan's life became more than she knew about her best friends' lives. The faded scar under her chin came from falling down on the ice when she was a kid. Her mother, Amanda, was the youngest of six siblings, the oldest being an alcoholic and a racist that the rest of the family tried to avoid. The first car she ever drove was her dad's vintage Camaro. At Stanford, she got so drunk in her freshman year that she woke up in the middle of the basketball gym the next morning dressed as a Disney princess with the men's team staring at her. The details Ashley had absorbed in such a short period of time deepened the bond between them, but it didn't change the reality. They were on different paths—completely separate, painfully contrasted paths.

Unsurprisingly, their contact had diminished; it was easier that way, Ashley told herself. Megan crossed her mind from time to time, but the urge to speak to her lessened soon enough. Ashley recalled the last goodbye before Megan left for the airport. They had kissed again, despite the joint agreement that they would remain friends. The kiss, however, lacked passion. It wasn't the type of kiss that would bring someone to their knees, but rightly so, Ashley had already detached herself from the situation knowing the outcome all along. The kiss however felt comfortable and instinctive, which actually made it harder to say goodbye—that's what initially gave Ashley a few sleepless nights. She could only assume that Megan was living the life she had dreamed of—the pictures on social media highlighted just that. The more she settled back into her life in England, the less time she spent talking to Ashley. The realisation that friends don't talk all day every day allowed Ashley to take a step back and lessen the confusion clouding her mind. The yearning to be her friend had not weakened, but she did wonder whether you could truly be friends with someone you once had a romantic connection with. Maybe she would write about that—her next article needed a subject.

Ashley overheard two young girls on the table adjacent to her whisper, *"This is the place. I wonder if that's Christopher?"*.

They looked towards him as he greeted an older couple at the door and then a well-dressed gentleman after that.

"Shall we ask him?" the young black girl said.

"There is even a drink on the menu called 'Nancy's favourite', honestly this is the cutest thing ever."

They continued like that, much to Ashley's amusement, for five minutes before they eventually caught Christopher's attention and plucked up the courage to ask him if he was the man referred to in *The New York Times* article.

He smiled politely and nodded, to which the young red-head squealed, *"OMG they should so do a movie about you."*

Christopher indulged them before taking their order and returning to the bar. On his return, he placed another soda on the table and removed the empty glass.

"It's getting busy in here this morning," Ashley nodded to the full tables surrounding the bar.

"Thanks to you."

"What do you mean?"

"The guy over there, the young couple, the two girls—they're all here because of your article."

"You're kidding?"

"No, they told me so."

Ashley scanned the bar, noticing that all the people he had just described were looking in her direction.

"Why are they staring?"

"Probably because I told them you were the one who wrote the amazing article."

Christopher placed a hand on Ashley's shoulder. "Thanks, kiddo, you might just have given us a new lease of life."

Nancy or Christopher had never mentioned that the bar wasn't profitable, but the lack of custom over the past two months felt light compared to the bars she was used to. If the article had done anything to help bring new customers to the bar, then that was an unexpected bonus.

She received a text message from Georgina, which meant it was time to go. The day was planned in favour of trying to rekindle any form of relationship between Georgina, Emily and Madison. The thought made her instantly question her life choices.

10

Megan

Megan brought the ball into the frontcourt; she glanced at the shot clock. They trailed by two with 14 seconds left. The opposing team set their zone defence perfectly. Megan half expected the quick foul, but when it didn't come, she knew there was time to run the coach's first play of choice. Megan passed the ball to Miller, the team's point guard, who set the offense at the top of the key.

Megan made a deep cut on the left behind the defence whilst Miller dribbled left, then right, to create a better passing angle. The double screen was set whilst Megan cut to the right side and found herself open. She pulled up from beyond the arc with 3 seconds left on the shot clock. With a snap of the wrist, the ball soared through the air. The catch and shoot technique she had practised for years was put to the test. The shot fell through the net with perfect precision; she imagined the crowd going wild, her teammates storming the court and propelling her up on their shoulders.

In reality, it was only the second pre-season game, and it had absolutely no relevance whatsoever other than to build team chemistry and enhance fitness levels. The shot, however, was one she hoped to re-enact when it mattered the most. Since joining the Mystics one month prior for training camp, she was made aware of their lack of three-point shooters. That's where she came in, the coach had told her on the first day—no pressure.

Megan shook hands with each of the opposing team. One after another, she received appraisal: *'nice shot'* or *'great game'*. Afterwards, the coach sat the team down in the dressing room, his 6'7" frame bent slightly to avoid hitting the roof. An air of composure surrounded him; he was inspiring, constructive and knowledgeable, a huge contrast from *'Nasty Natalia',* the nickname her former coach earned within the first week of playing at Stanford.

"Great job, ladies. A solid performance against a very good team." He turned towards the TV behind him. "Liam, do you have the stats?"

The tech guy in the corner frantically tapped away on his laptop. Within seconds a document containing every player and their performance highlights appeared on the screen. One by one, he reeled off what went well and what part of their game they needed to improve—Megan was third on the list in alphabetical order.

"Davis, you were firing deadly from the field tonight, 80% from beyond the arc is incredible. 5 assists and 6 rebounds to accompany your 24 points." The coach observed the stat sheet, looking for some form of improvement. Her game had been strong all around, but there always had to be at least one learning opportunity. "And of course, the game-winner. Pre-season or not, that was a hell of a shot. Work on your perimeter defence for the next game. It needs to be tighter without fouling, but great job."

"Yes, coach." Megan had played three pre-season games with the Mystics, and in each of them she put on a decent performance whilst others tried to regain their form. The early morning runs and late-night pick-up games with her father over the past two months put her in fantastic shape.

"Megan." She was in the process of swapping clothes for her post-game workout when a familiar voice called to her.

"Hey."

"Are you shooting?"

"Of course."

"If I join, do you think you could give me some tips?"

It was an unexpected request, but a flattering one. Candice Williams played point guard; she was fairly new to the league after moving from Philadelphia a year earlier. Megan had observed her overall game, and it was impressive, but the reigning PG had ten years of experience and captained the team, so she would never be the first choice unless she significantly improved her game—starting with her three-point shot, something Megan noticed the starting PG lacked.

"Sure."

Candice grabbed her things and followed Megan to the gym. The lights were out; it was a Wednesday night and nobody else thought it necessary to get up some post-game shots. That would have been unacceptable at Stanford. It had been engrained into her mentality from her college days, so much so, that it became routine, despite any plans she had, they would always come second.

"Do you want to start under the basket and we can do twenty each from five spots around the arc?"

"Sounds good." Candice ran towards the basket and hurled the ball in Megan's direction. The first twenty from the left corner hit the net seventeen times. An 80%

shooting percentage was her target in practice, 90% if she was being extra hard on herself.

"I'll be lucky if I hit five." They swapped places and Candice pulled up for her first shot which hit the front of the rim. The second hit the back and bounced out.

"Can I give you a few tips on your form?"

"Yes, please."

"Keep your feet shoulder-width apart and bend your knees more in the build-up to prepare yourself to jump. Most of the power for a three-point shot comes from extending your legs."

Candice readied herself once again, focusing on the placement of her feet. The third shot rolled in and out.

"That was better. Now, when you come up, keep your arm locked at that 90-degree angle. It's too flimsy right now. You need a strong arm to follow through with the shot."

"Like this?" Candice took another shot, this time it rolled around and went in.

"Exactly, now keep doing that."

She managed 8 of 20, and they moved to the next spot. Megan fired 18 for 20.

"How did you get so good? You shoot the ball so freely."

"Practice, I guess. I knew growing up that I didn't have the height to be automatically considered, women who are six feet tall have a better chance of making it in the basketball world. I had to stand out in other ways, three-point shooting was one of them. My dad was a great three-point shooter, so he taught me a lot."

Candice took Megan's place once again. "I wish my dad had played basketball. I bet that was so much fun growing up."

"Like anything, it had its challenges, but it was nice to have someone who understood and could guide me. Although it was like your coach sitting around the dinner table, or coming on vacation with you. The sacrifice could be hard when your friends were out playing during the holidays and you're running drill after drill."

"But it paid off though, right?"

"When I play in the WNBA, then it will have paid off."

"So, that's the dream?"

"Sure, isn't it yours?"

Candice took her final shot. "It was, but after I got injured, I knew I would never return to that type of form again. I am just happy now to play the sport that I love professionally. I don't care where I play." Her next shot was nothing but net.

"Nice shot." Megan grinned. "When did the injury happen?"

"My third year at college. I fractured my kneecap."

Megan grimaced. "Surgery?"

"Yep, two of them. The recovery was rough, I thought I might not play again."

"How did you come back from that?"

"A lot of rehab. It was hard. I wanted to give up, but I thought about my life and what I wanted to achieve. Basketball was the only thing that made sense."

"Well, I admire you for coming back from an injury like that. Do you think you'd ever go back to Philadelphia?"

"Maybe, my family lives there, so it gets a little lonely over here sometimes, but I have some good friends around me."

"No girlfriend?" Megan asked, her focused gaze still firmly on the basket.

"You're assuming I'm gay?"

Megan jumped, launching the perfect three-pointer. The sound of the net swish brought her great pleasure.

"You're not?"

"Yes, I am."

"Well, then." Megan laughed.

"Is it that obvious?"

"It wasn't until I overheard you describe word-for-word what you liked about the opposing team's shooting guard the other night."

"That's kind of a giveaway, huh?"

"You did say, and I quote, *'How does she get such a nice ass, it just sits perfectly in her shorts'*. That was a slight giveaway."

Megan used her dramatic, high-pitched American socialite voice.

"I do not sound like that." Candice crossed her arms underneath the basket. The wrong move as the ball soared through the air, fell through the hoop and onto the head of the distracted point guard.

"Ouch." She rubbed aggressively; Megan found the whole ordeal amusing.

"You're up next."

"How many did you hit?"

"Nineteen."

"Seriously? I hate you."

They traded places; Megan smelled the perfume as she passed Candice. That was not the scent of a girl who had just played a full game of basketball; the rose and jasmine aroma appealed to Megan.

Without thinking, she said, "You smell good."

Candice in the arc of shooting fumbled the ball. It missed the net completely. "Thank you."

"So, back to the girlfriend, was that a no?" Megan enquired.

"No girlfriend. I have been single since I came to the UK. I suppose it's easier that way if I ever end up going back to Philly. What about you?"

Megan walked towards Candice, ball in hand. "When you go up for the shot, you need to snap your wrist more. Like this." Megan locked in her position, arm at 90 degrees, knees bent and poised. When she jumped, her arm extended and her wrist jolted forward, giving the ball the arch it needed to sink comfortably into the net. "Did you see the way my wrist flicked forward? You need that to be able to propel the ball further, it'll give it more of an arch. Your arm also needs to extend fully." Megan demonstrated once again, another perfect shot— a broad smile appeared.

"Our very own Steph Curry. I can't wait to see how you get on during the season." Candice followed Megan's instructions to the letter. The shot fell short. "You make it look so easy."

"You have to give it time, you're altering your shot completely so you need to adjust to it. Keep trying."

"You didn't answer my question."

Megan launched the ball back towards Candice. The sequence was repetitive, but it was a necessity. "No, I have no girlfriend."

"Huh." Candice smirked.

"What?"

"I find that hard to believe."

The muscles around Megan's mouth tensed and her lips closed. She tried to remain composed despite the obvious flirting.

"I only came back to England two months ago. I don't move that quickly."

"There was nobody at Stanford?"

Megan answered honestly. "There was for a while, but we split in Senior year."

"How come?"

"We wanted different things."

Megan's phone interrupted the conversation. She ran to the bench to see Nancy calling. That was unusual for a Wednesday evening or early afternoon in NYC, so she picked up immediately. "Hey Gram, everything okay?"

"Hi, sweetheart. Don't sound so panicked, everything's fine."

Megan breathed a sigh of relief. "You never call at this time."

"Well, I have some exciting news."

"What's that?" Megan signalled one finger towards Candice, indicating she wouldn't be long.

"Ashley's article got published!" Nancy screeched.

"Seriously? Wow, that's incredible. When?"

"Today! It's in *The New York Times* on page ten. She bought us a copy and it's amazing."

At once, Megan was met with contentment that brought great joy to her soul. She was undeniably proud of Ashley and what she had accomplished, a feat she believed her capable of all along.

"I knew she'd do it."

"And guess what?" Nancy could barely conceal her delight. "It's actually bringing people into the bar."

"Like, new customers?"

"Yes! Can you believe it? I went to breakfast this morning with your aunt Julie. When I returned, Christopher told me he'd had four or five different people ask him about the article."

The tone of Nancy's voice fluctuated throughout, so shrill towards the end that she had to remove the phone slightly from her ear. This made Megan laugh quietly to herself.

"I am honestly so happy for you, and Ashley, of course."

"She refrained from telling you so that I could. So don't be mad at her."

Megan stared at the floor, watching her feet shift slowly from side to side. If only she had a right to be mad at her, their relationship had become non-existent and at times that made her sad, but the ability to switch off those emotions was a skill she attained from the years of travelling alone.

"I won't." Megan glanced at Candice, who was shooting patiently. "Gram, I need to go, I'm in the gym training, but I'll call you tomorrow."

"Okay, Meg. Love you, sweetheart."

"I love you too."

The call ended and suddenly Megan's motivation drained. The thought of Ashley fully consumed her mind, to the point where she missed 10 of her 20 shots from the right corner—which was almost unheard of. Pinpointing the reason behind her sudden loss of concentration was elusive.

"Did you just get some bad news?"

"What do you mean?"

"The phone call? You just missed half of your shots."

"My mind's just elsewhere I guess."

"Do you want to talk about it?"

"Not really."

Candice sat on the bench and proceeded to take her shoes off, trading for a more comfortable slider.

"Okay, suit yourself."

Megan had spoken to Candice on several occasions, but never about anything other than basketball. Her willingness to share with someone she barely knew was absent.

"Sorry, I just don't really have anything to say."

"Not that I was eavesdropping, but I'm assuming your gram isn't the reason you missed 10 shots. That would leave someone called Ashley?"

Megan raised a curved eyebrow. Candice was observant. *Almost too much*, Megan thought.

"Ashley's a friend from New York."

"Oh, so she's the reason you're not openly looking to date anyone?" Candice teased.

"Not at all. As I said, she's a friend." Megan tried to be convincing, but the avoidance of eye contact said otherwise.

Candice rolled her eyes and gathered her things. With the gym bag over one arm and the basketball under her other she walked towards Megan and kissed her softly on the cheek.

"If she's just a friend, then maybe we could go out sometime. Let me know."

Megan's head was slightly down-turned, but she held eye contact the whole time as she watched Candice saunter towards the exit. The way she walked reminded her of Ashley; their body type and facial features were similar, the slim athletic build and even down to the blonde hair, although Candice's had a natural curl which gave it more volume.

Megan shook her head. The thoughts of Ashley were unnecessary. The extent of their romantic relationship had been minimal, not enough to warrant the sporadic comparison of her features.

***

Megan arrived home two hours later. The drive from Manchester to York was roughly seventy miles—a journey she made two or three times a week. The organisation offered to put her up in a local apartment with another girl from the team, which she happily accepted, but whenever she had a day off, she would go back home. There was nothing like home comforts. Her career left her often wondering when the next move would be, so she made a conscious effort to enjoy her parent's company as often as her schedule would allow.

The journey had been a blessing in disguise. She took the time to assess her emotions. The playlist she chose seemed to match her every mood. The lyrics from the songs helped determine what it was she felt. She cranked up the volume to Beyoncé's 'I Miss You'—she connected with the words like she never had before. In her college days, the song was simply another song that she liked to sing along to. Now, as she drove with nothing but her thoughts for the first time, she really listened to the lyrics and what they were trying to convey.

The driveway leading up to the house was the part she enjoyed the most. The house was spectacular and her parents had done renovation after renovation over the years to make it into a beautiful family home. They refused to downsize, despite the fact it was just the two of them taking up a five-bedroom house. The drive, however, brought the fondest memories. Megan was immersed in a feeling of belonging whenever her tyres hit the gravel. The house had been subject to her coming and going over the years and although she had changed and grown up, it still maintained the same character and charm, reminiscent of that when she was younger.

It was late, too late to go to the stable and see Fred, she noted. The temptation was there, but he was getting older and the thought of disturbing his sleep didn't feel right. The house was quiet, as expected—her father would be sound asleep. Michael Davis preferred to go to sleep early and wake up early. The routine became a habit throughout his basketball career, regardless of his retirement six years ago. Before the rest of the world was awake, he would have two hours' worth of training under his belt, an abundance of email responses and the rest of his day planned accordingly.

As Megan entered the kitchen/dining area, she noticed her mother perched in the corner on the burgundy-red chesterfield armchair. It had no business being in a room that was purely decorated in light, grey colours, but that's what Amanda loved about it.

"Hey, baby girl."

"Hey, Mom." Megan walked over and placed a kiss on her cheek.

"I'm so glad you decided to come back tonight. It means we get the whole day tomorrow."

"I know, me too. I'm so thirsty, do you have any juice?"

"In the fridge." Amanda pointed.

Megan glanced at the tablet in her mom's lap. "What are you reading?"

"It's the article about your gram and Christopher, have you read it yet?"

"No, she only told me a few hours ago. I'll take a look tonight."

"It's really good. Your friend's incredibly talented."

"I know she is," Megan said matter-of-factly.

There was no doubt in her mind that she would read the article and fall in love with Ashley's words. She had seen snippets early on, and when she was asked about her opinion, there was always very little critique. Megan didn't know a lot about writing, but the emotional rollercoaster she experienced spoke volumes.

Amanda laughed out loud unexpectedly. "This part here where she says, *'if you are my soulmate that would really move things along nicely'*. You can tell her from me, I laughed at several points and teared up in the middle. It was really something."

They didn't even know her and they found her hilarious. *How was she supposed to pretend like she had no romantic feelings at all?*

"I haven't spoken to her much lately, but when I do, I'll let her know."

"Have you fallen out?"

"No."

"Why aren't you speaking then?"

Megan shrugged. "I don't know Mom; friends don't talk all day every day, you know. Do you talk to Janine all the time?"

"Not all the time, but she can be annoying."

"Yes, I agree with that." Megan refilled her glass and wandered to her mom's side. "I'm going to bed. It's been a long day."

"You sure everything's okay?"

"Yes, Mom, everything is absolutely fine. Stop being weird."

"Stop with the lip." Amanda playfully smacked her across the butt. "I just worry about you."

"You worry about me when there's nothing to worry about. God help me when I actually have a real-life problem."

"That's what parents do. Now, go to bed before I ground you forever."

"You're hilarious. Night, Mom."

"Goodnight."

Her bedroom wrapped around the right side of the house, giving it an L-shape. Everything was as she left it a few days earlier. The solid white desk sat up against the wall as she walked in, piled high with basketball magazines and letters she would never open. The bank didn't need to inform her on a monthly basis just how little money she actually had; the letters often made their way down to the shredder in her dad's office, unopened. She threw her holdall in front of the chest of drawers, then rounded the corner to see her freshly made bed. The scatter cushions had grown significantly in recent years and it felt like a full-time job removing them to put them back on the next morning.

The day had drained every ounce of energy. Her knees felt weak; she stood at the foot of the bed, spread her arms wide and crashed onto the arrangement of pillows, and within minutes, she fell asleep.

***

Megan roused; the moonlight could be seen casting a shadow through the exposed window. She was still in the same position that she'd collapsed into. The alarm clock on the bedside table confirmed the time as 03:26 a.m. Megan gathered herself, swapped her sports gear for a pair of pyjamas, and rinsed her face. She climbed back into bed before placing her phone on charge. The sudden urge to check her socials removed her from the sleep haze. Despite the time, *one quick look wouldn't hurt,* she told herself. She scrolled aimlessly, without direction, just getting lost within the rabbit hole that was social media, until she came across a photo of Ashley.

The photo had been uploaded by Madison, the caption read, *'Congratulations to this legend, a New York Times writer? That's got to be worth celebrating'*.

Megan stared at the photo for longer than necessary; Ashley sat on a black leather sofa, her legs crossed, with a bottle of champagne in hand. The sweet smile extended to her eyes and deep into her soul—it was genuine. The happiness deep inside spread throughout her body, creating a picture that Megan couldn't take her eyes off.

Megan only wished she knew what it was about Ashley that brought a sudden halt to everything. Was it the unknown? The classic fear that the *friend* could have been so much more? Megan had tried since her return to England to tuck away any romantic thoughts—the notion was easier said than done. She would tell herself over and over again that there had been no connection, there had been no spark to light a thousand fires, no frighteningly apparent familiarity that she couldn't explain. Two girls met, they had a great time and then they moved on with their lives, or so she told herself, but that didn't explain the burning in her chest, it didn't explain the impulse that submerged her into a pattern of denial.

The denial that what they had experienced was nothing short of remarkable, she refused to believe that their experience was different in spite of every conflicting instinct. Irrespective of this, Megan did something next that was uncharacteristic, but the truth. The message composed was out of the blue, she battled with herself for thirty seconds before she hit send.

I miss your face.

Instantaneously she buried her head face down in the pillow. The mocking from the alter-ego within began. The part that would laugh when you felt embarrassed, tell you that you're terrible when you had a bad game, or bring up traumatic childhood memories to warn you off ever stepping outside of your comfort zone again. We all have that alter-ego—Megan felt hers as present as ever at that moment. The gesture showed a dependency that surprised Megan. *Was it socially abnormal to tell someone you'd met twice that you missed their face?* Megan considered the response she might get from Ashley, it wasn't until she received the reply that she realised she might be right—perhaps she was a bit socially abnormal.

Was that meant for me?

Now she felt foolish.

Yes, of course it was.

Megan sat upright in bed. Suddenly, she was wide awake.

I miss your face too.

The response she had hoped for left her feeling underwhelmed. The realisation that they were thousands of miles apart and unable to act on a whim came flooding back. Had she been in New York, she would have gone to Ashley at that moment, declared the want and the need to be close to her and maybe even so much more. Instead, Megan lay in bed alone, fully aware of Ashley's whereabouts and the torturing inability to be near her.

Are you sure about that?

Megan questioned.

Positive. New York isn't the same without you here.

Did she really mean that? Megan wondered. *Maybe she was drunk?* That made more sense.

Well, that's nice to hear. I miss it.

"And I miss you. Did I tell you that already?" Megan muttered while rolling her eyes at herself.

I hope you come back soon. I'd love to see you.

The gesture was well received. If only she could go back tomorrow.

Me too.

There was no further response from Ashley. The embarrassment subsided and Megan realised she had nothing to be ashamed of. The reciprocal confession, whether genuine or not, meant something. The weight was lifted, the ability to say how she truly felt in that moment left her feeling triumphant. She would unapologetically, without hesitation, do it again.

11

Ashley reached around Emily, searching blindly for the large, fresh cup of coffee. A conversation she'd already had with Madison seemed to be the only topic of interest; the three attempts at changing the subject were unsuccessful.

"Why do you do it to yourself?"

Ashley shrugged. "I don't know."

"You know she's never going to commit to you, right?" The harsh reality that Emily was never too afraid to point out.

"Maybe she—"

"Ash, seriously? I just wish I had a crystal ball so I could fast forward six months and show you what your life looks like. I guarantee you, she won't be in it."

The words were hurtful, yet true. Ashley knew Georgina was merely filling a gap in her schedule until the next all-American guy came along to sweep her off her feet, in reality, all he required was large muscles and a six-foot frame—two things Ashley could never offer. *Was Georgina worth the trouble/heartbreak?* A question she often asked herself. Her friends indisputably thought not.

"I know, but can't I just enjoy the company for now?"

"Do you enjoy it, though? Does it bring you happiness or are you just waiting for the day you wake up and she's found someone else?"

Emily watched intently, leant on the kitchen surface with her clenched fist pressed against her cheek.

"I enjoy her company."

"But?"

"You're right, there will probably always be that nagging feeling in the back of my mind."

"I know you're not stupid, so I don't understand why you do it to yourself."

Ashley considered her reasoning. "It's easier."

"What is?"

"Being with Georgina. I know she's going to leave, so it won't come as a shock. I've already grown numb to the idea, so I suppose it's easier because I know what to expect with her."

Georgina had separated from her boyfriend, Travis, a month ago. Their short-lived relationship had been full of lies and deceit, behaviours not uncommon to her. The next day, they'd met for a coffee. That same night, they slept together again—they had seen each other every day since.

"Okay, fair enough, if that's how you feel. I just don't want you to miss out on something real because you're wasting time chasing someone that will never give you what you want."

Ashley's darting glance and fidgeting hands revealed the cause of their tension.

"So, about tonight…"

"No," Emily raised her eyebrows, "not happening."

"You haven't even let me finish." Ashley's nervous laughter filled the room. The reaction was as expected.

"You don't need to. I know exactly what you're going to say."

Ashley had been gathering the courage all day to make her best friends aware that she planned on inviting Georgina on their night out.

"Emily, come on, we are going out to celebrate. Can it just be civil for one night?"

"I don't mind if you want to damage your own mental wellbeing, that's up to you, but forcing it upon me isn't fair."

"She isn't that bad, the cheating aside."

Emily rolled her eyes. "She is undoubtedly the most self-absorbed, infuriatingly annoying person I have ever met."

"Say how you really feel."

"Well, she is. What she's done to you in the past is bad enough, but if I have to sit and listen to her tell stories about her holidays on an island with Richard Branson, I will flip."

"You know she's never been on holiday with Richard Branson, right?"

"It's hypothetical. I can't actually remember who she said because I stopped listening."

Ashley traced the edge of the large blue coffee mug. "Okay."

"Don't do that."

"What?"

"You know what."

Ashley's pleading expression looked like that of a puppy wanting to be loved.

"Nope."

"That look. You always give me that look when you want me to co-operate. It's infuriating."

Said look continued for a few more seconds. "It works though, doesn't it?" Ashley pouted for effect.

"Annoyingly, yes." Emily placed her mug in the sink. "I need to shower."

"Will you behave? Please?"

She paused, walked around the island and ruffled Ashley's hair from behind. "Only for you."

"You're the best."

"I know. Now, get ready, we don't have long."

Emily's idea of being on her best behaviour involved enough tequila that she couldn't remember the night, which allowed for an occasional slur of abuse that would then be taken lightly due to her intoxication. Ashley preferred that over the alternative.

It was a Friday night, the first one Ashley hadn't worked since Megan was in town. The thought of Megan often brought a wave of emotion that was difficult to process. She created the idea in her mind that Megan would be there to celebrate the article even though she knew that couldn't happen—just the fantasy alone made her smile. Regardless of the distance, there was still a prominent desire to build a relationship—a desire that was unrelenting at times. She remembered vividly her mom telling her, *'You always want what you can't have, but in the end, it leaves you heartbroken, it ruins your life'*. She had been referring to her father. His take on the situation, however, was completely different.

Did the mounting desire for Megan only exist because she was unattainable? The thought accompanied her in the shower, whilst she got changed and it followed her into the evening.

It was 8:00 p.m. when she entered Nancy's with Georgina on her arm, followed closely by a reluctant Emily and Madison. They'd been talkative in the cab ride over, involving her in conversation. Emily only rolled her eyes on one occasion when Georgina started to reel off all the designer handbags she owned. The self-centred part of her personality made Ashley wish she could detach herself from the situation, but Georgina was a welcome distraction and walking away was easier said than done.

Jason waved from the bar as they entered. Wearing a cream suit jacket buttoned up with no t-shirt, a single gold earring and some flashy sequined loafers—he oozed style. Ashley was eager to meet his new boyfriend. They'd been together for five weeks and she was yet to have the pleasure.

"Baby girl, look at you." Jason jumped from his seat and wrapped his arms tightly around Ashley's waist, almost knocking Georgina over the foot of the stool—Emily sniggered.

"Hey, handsome. Who do we have here?" The figure hidden behind Jason perched on the edge of his seat, glancing from his hands, to Ashley, and back, differing from the flamboyant persona Jason had.

"Ash, this is Derek, Derek, this is Ash." He introduced each member of the group the same way until he got to Georgina, "That's Georgina," he swung his arm out unenthusiastically towards her. Emily sniggered again, the dislike for Georgina was felt equally across the group.

"It's lovely to meet you, Derek."

"You too, I've heard a lot about you."

"All good I hope?"

"Oh, of course, he loves you." Derek eyed Jason, who was beaming with pride.

"So, it seems becoming a New York Times writer has increased your fashion sense," Jason joked.

"Excuse me? I'll have you know I have always had a fashion sense, it just gets lost from time to time." Ashley glanced down at her modern attire, pleased with herself for such a bold choice.

"The pantsuit is so now. And the colour!" Jason lifted the corner of the jacket into the light. "Blue looks good on you. I want one!"

"Georgina picked it out."

The mention of her name made her take notice straightaway. "Yes I did, I knew it would accent all the best parts of her." She winked in Ashley's direction. Jason pretended to be sick, then swiftly changed the subject.

"What do you want to drink?"

"I'll have a Cosmo please."

Ashley turned towards her best friends. The conversation was light-hearted. They made a conscious effort to include Georgina, as painful as that was for them. Nancy's felt like the perfect place to start the evening. Without it, there would be no article and no start to what she hoped would be a long career in the publishing industry.

Nancy and Christopher came over in between serving customers to congratulate Ashley once again. They took great enjoyment in revealing the large black frame that hung to the right of the bar. It sat proudly underneath a light that illuminated the article inside.

"What do you think?"

"I think it looks amazing." She almost welled up. "Thank you for supporting me. It means so much."

Nancy placed her arm around Ashley. "Have you told your father yet?"

"No. I told my mom, she was happy for me, but I can sense the disinterest whenever I speak about writing. It just reminds her of him." Nancy nodded, allowing her to continue. "I thought about sending a picture to him, I just haven't gotten around to it yet."

"Don't put it off forever, sweetheart. This might be the thing you need to try and fix your relationship."

"What if I don't want to fix it?"

"Nobody's forcing you, but I think you'll regret it if you don't try. Trust me, I know all about regret." Nancy smiled softly; she understood better than anyone. Ashley had confided in her on numerous occasions over the past two months and was incredibly grateful for all that she had to say. "Go and enjoy your night anyway, you can't spend it talking to an old girl like me."

"I'll let you in on a secret. I actually like talking to you the best." Ashley professed.

Nancy touched the base of Ashley's chin with her finger, "I know," before she sauntered back behind the bar.

Ashley wasn't about to let thoughts of her father and their indifferences ruin her evening—that was a conversation for another day.

Jason pulled Ashley to one side. She looked around the room to check for Georgina, aware that she'd left her alone. She spotted Derek engaging in what seemed to be a deep conversation and assumed she would be fine.

"Don't worry about her, Derek's good at holding a conversation." He handed her the Cosmo.

"Thank you." They raised their glasses.

"To you. You did it, Ash, you finally started to chase your dreams."

"I know, it's surreal, isn't it?"

"I suppose you have Megan to thank for that."

"I wouldn't be here without her, that's for sure."

Jason pressed his lips to the edge of his glass, eyeing Ashley the whole time. "And yet, you don't talk to her?"

"Why is everyone so fixated on whether I speak to Megan or not? Madison mentioned it yesterday."

Ashley couldn't understand the sudden obsession. *How did a girl she had known for two weeks play such a big part in her life? Did the others know something she didn't?*

"I'll say no more." Jason made a zipping gesture across his mouth and threw away the key.

"Do you know something I don't?"

"Nope."

"Then why is everyone mentioning someone I went on two dates with?"

Jason rolled his eyes blatantly. "I think we both know it was a little more than just two dates."

"That's the reality of it though."

"Yes, it is, but I remember the week after she left you told me you couldn't stop thinking about her. You told me there was a certain pull towards her that you couldn't shake. I knew you were in trouble as soon as you said it."

"That was two months ago."

"Yes, but I'll bet my life that it hasn't changed."

Ashley felt instantly uncomfortable. Jason stared so intently that she was conscious of her facial expressions and what they would imply.

"So what if it hasn't? It's not like I can do anything about it." Ashley shrugged. "That's life."

"Maybe not right now."

Ashley felt her phone vibrate in her pocket. The caller ID showing a name she wasn't expecting.

"What have you done?" Ashley flashed the phone in Jason's direction.

"I didn't do that." He smiled. "The world works in mysterious ways." Jason removed the now empty Cosmo from Ashley's hand. "Answer it then, I'll get you another one of these."

She took a deep breath and hit accept.

"Hey."

"Hi." She made her way down the corridor and into the outdoor area. "One second, I can't hear you very well."

"Where are you?"

"At Nancy's actually."

"I wish I could be there. I miss that place." There was a long pause.

"Did you need something?"

"Sorry, no, I don't know why I called to be honest."

"Oh, what time is it there?"

Megan replied sheepishly, "2:00 a.m."

"So, you randomly call me at 2:00 a.m. but you're not sure why?"

Megan laughed. "It's not 2:00 a.m. where you are."

"That's true."

"I just felt like saying hi."

"Well, hi."

"And congratulations, of course. I read the article yesterday, three times over, actually. It's really great, Ash."

Ashley couldn't help but think the abbreviation of her name sounded so much better coming from Megan's lips.

"Thank you. I hope I did it justice."

"You did, I knew you would."

Ashley sat on the black metal chair closest to the door. She felt arms suddenly wrap around her shoulders—it was Georgina.

"What are you doing out here?"

"I'll be back inside in a minute, I'm just on the phone."

"Who to?" Georgina asked suspiciously.

"Just an old friend."

"Okay, well hurry, I miss you."

"I will." Ashley watched Georgina walk away and then placed the phone back to her ear. "Sorry about that."

"Who was that?"

Ashley was hesitant, but saw no reason to lie. "Georgina."

"The Georgina?"

"Yes."

"Oh, are you two a thing now?"

"Not really a thing as such. I don't know, it's hard to explain."

"I'll take that as a yes." Megan chuckled.

"Well, I couldn't wait around for you forever, could I?" Ashley joked.

"I guess not. Anyway, I will let you go back to your friends, you're out celebrating. I shouldn't have called."

Ashley didn't want the conversation to end. "You can call anytime you like."

"That's good to know, old friends really should keep in touch." The emphasis put on *'old friends'* was intentional—a jibe.

"Are you mocking me?"

"Not at all." Ashley could sense Megan smiling through the phone. It eased the tension.

"I guess I will speak to you soon then?"

"I'll speak to you soon then."

The phone line went dead. Ashley sat for a moment, contemplating. The conversation, although brief, clarified a number of things. Megan's voice filled her with an overwhelming surge of happiness and oddly, she had called her for absolutely no reason. *Did friends do that?* Ashley wasn't so sure. As she sat alone at the back of Nancy's bar, she couldn't help but wonder how she would feel if she were celebrating the night with Megan and not Georgina.

Whatever they had experienced in their short time together, one thing was abundantly clear—Megan had left a mark on Ashley's life that was hard to erase. However, dwelling on the *what ifs* would not change her current situation. Megan had never been an option. Ashley had known the outcome from the beginning, but not knowing what could have happened made it increasingly difficult to forget.

One day, she hoped they could be something to each other. If that was as friends, then she would accept that, but for now, she would thank Megan for every feeling, every touch and every word of encouragement in the hope that their paths would one day cross again.

12

August 2015
Ashley

"Can you believe your sister is having a baby?"

Ashley loaded the bags into the trunk of the yellow cab. There was no help from the disgruntled driver, who had already been waiting impatiently for five minutes.

"No, it's surreal, isn't it?"

Madison hopped in. "Sure is. She might only be three years younger than us, but I still see her as that little girl who used to annoy us at any given opportunity."

Ashley slammed the trunk shut forcefully. The driver took off before she had the chance to fasten her seatbelt.

"Someone's in a bad mood," she whispered to Madison.

"I know. He said traffic is quite bad on the 678 interstate so it'll be about one hour and twenty minutes to JFK."

Ashley pulled the tickets from her backpack; they had enough time.

"How are you feeling? Nervous?"

"Very."

"About your dad or Samantha?"

"Both."

"You spoke to your dad though, so everything's still okay with you two?"

"Yeah, but I haven't seen him face-to-face in over a year."

The conversation with her father had consisted of an hour-long phone call in October 2014. There had been tears, brutal honesty, and by the end, a mutual understanding between the two. Ashley felt like a weight had been lifted just hearing the words, *'I am so proud of you',* and it helped her realise that relationships are complex. No one person is the same and everyone handles things differently. He loved her; that was enough.

"That might be a little awkward." Madison fidgeted. "What about Samantha? Have you spoken to her yet?"

"Nope, well, she was in the background when my dad invited me, which I told you about, but not since then."

"How long has it been?"

Ashley considered the length of time since she'd last seen her sister. "Maybe three years?"

"Has it been that long already? Wow. Why are we going again?" Madison joked.

"I honestly have no idea. I apologise in advance for what will be the most awkward weekend of your life."

"Oh, God." Madison hit her hand against her forehead. "I forgot your mom's coming too, isn't she?"

Ashley laughed, "Yep."

"Why have you done this to me?"

"At least you can sit back with some popcorn and enjoy the show. I have to be in the middle of it."

"That's true. I can't believe Emily got out of this."

"Conveniently, she has to work all weekend. We both know it's because she can't be away from her new obsession."

Emily had recently been promoted to Executive Assistant to the CEO. As far as personal assistants go, she was now at the top of the food chain, working closely with a powerful, strong-minded, multi-millionaire—a job she relished. The hours had naturally extended—with more money comes more responsibility. Throw in the mix a new girlfriend and Emily was unavailable.

"Do you think this one will last?" Madison asked.

"It's only been three months, so I won't hold my breath, but who knows? She seems pretty hooked."

"I like her though, she seems nice."

"It's the Spanish for you, isn't it?"

"Maybe." Madison bit her lip. "How can you not find the accent attractive?"

"You need to start finding your own girls." Ashley teased.

"We all know I am about as useless as a wooden frying pan when it comes to finding the right girl."

Laughter erupted from Ashley. The driver looked in disgust through the rear-view mirror.

"A wooden frying pan?"

"I am!"

"Well, I'm not much better. I mean, you're accompanying me to my sister's baby shower instead of a smoking hot date—that says it all."

"That's rude. Shall we pick up Georgina along the way?" Madison smirked.

"We agreed not to mention that name ever again."

"That was until you insinuated I wasn't smoking hot."

Ashley glanced at her phone. "Speak of the devil."

"Is she still trying to get you back?"

"Pretty much."

"Well, look how the tables have turned. I bet it feels good, doesn't it?" Madison adjusted her posture to sit angled towards Ashley.

"Do you want my honest answer?" Madison nodded. "It feels fucking great."

"What is she saying? It's literally been two months."

Ashley unlocked her phone and read out snippets of the last few text messages that had gone unanswered.

"Can we try and work things out? I miss you. Why are you ignoring me? Stop ignoring me. I heard a song on the radio, it reminds me of you. I'm sorry. Blah blah blah."

"Nothing new then?"

"Nope. She just doesn't get it. Although, Jason told me he'd seen her out with some guy last week. She's definitely dating other people. She just doesn't like the fact that I was the one who dumped her."

"Can I just say, and I speak for me and Emily collectively, we are so glad you did."

"You've never told me that before." Ashley rolled her eyes. "Oh no, wait, you have. At least every other day."

"I just want to make sure you don't go back."

"I already told you, I am so over that. It took ten months for me to realise, but here I am, newly single and ready to mingle."

Madison covered her mouth with her hand so the words came out muffled. "You didn't just say that."

"Too much?"

"Absolutely."

Ashley removed her laptop from her bag. "Do you mind if I write while we travel?"

"No problem. What are you working on?"

She turned the laptop towards Madison. The heading read, 'LGBT+ love in NYC'.

"Cool, do you want to write about my experiences?"

"That would make a very boring article."

"That's nasty. True though." They laughed. "What is it about? Other than the obvious."

"I start by making reference to the Stonewall riots. Then I go on to talk about the culture in NYC. New York has such a thriving LGBT+ community, I wanted to shine some light on that. I've spoken to quite a few members of the community with strong stories about overcoming adversity; it's all underpinned with diversity in mind, the idea that love finds us all despite what hardships we may have to face. Love always wins."

"I love the concept. I think it's great that they want you to write about LGBT+ love, it's so underrepresented."

"They told me to pitch something I am passionate about, so I hope they like it."

"They will. Your writing is so poetic, you always do an amazing job." Madison pointed to a bit at the bottom of the page. "You should have that as your title. Love always wins. It's catchy."

"Good idea."

The cab fell silent as Ashley's fingers moved skilfully over the keys. With each new piece she wrote, came a new mound of pressure. After the success of Nancy and Christopher's story, she had been asked to go and find something similar, so she did. Shortly after that, she was asked to do a piece on dating apps and the controversy. She'd found some entertaining experiences and some scary ones. All in all, it made for a good article. The editor at *The New York Times* asked to see an article of choice, whether it would be published remained unseen, but given the opportunity, Ashley chose to write about the LGBT+ community.

One month prior, she'd cut her hours at the bar by one day to focus on writing. It was a dicey move, but the series of events that followed proved it was the right move to make. The next day, she had the phone call to write her current article. The next week, a position became available for a bar manager and Madison was promoted. She took that as a sign that the universe was letting her know she was on the right path.

***

The plane touched down at San Jose International Airport, California. The time: 2:00 p.m. and the sun was beating down. The decision to wear shorts benefited her greatly now. Alternatively, the beads of sweat could be seen rolling down Madison's cheeks, her normally pristine hairstyle now curled at the ends slightly.

"I told you to wear shorts." Ashley eyed the choice of skinny jeans and a hoodie. "At least take your hoodie off."

"I can handle thirty-degree New York heat, so I can handle this."

"Oh, really? You should tell your face that and FYI, you can't handle New York heat. Just last week you were lying on the apartment floor in nothing but your underwear rubbing yourself with ice cubes."

"That was a very hot day."

"So is today, you can't say I didn't warn you."

Madison began to peel the hoodie over her head. There was still no sign of Ashley's dad.

"What time did he say he would pick us up?"

"About ten minutes ago. Typical really, he's always late to everything."

"The baby shower is tomorrow, right?" Madison enquired.

"Yes, all day, unfortunately."

"How many people are going?"

"My dad said roughly fifty people."

"Do you think Grace will be going?"

"I really hope not, but it's possible. I didn't really think about that."

"So, I will add her to the list of people to avoid. There's going to be alcohol, isn't there?" The statement was less of a question and more of a plea.

"Plenty. We'll make sure we are intoxicated for the full event. Don't you worry."

A 1969 white Chevrolet Camaro rounded the corner at speed, beeping at two different cars before pulling up wildly in the arrival bays. Ashley rolled her eyes, expecting some teenager to climb out and a blonde socialite to run into his arms.

"Is that your dad?" Madison nudged her sunglasses to the end of her nose to double-take. Ashley spun back around to find a bearded but balding middle-aged man with a pair of sneakers and a beige matching summer co-ord. That was Benjamin Stewart.

"Oh, God. Is he having a mid-life crisis?" Ashley muttered under her breath. She waved back whilst recoiling internally. "Is he wearing Jordans?" Ashley said through gritted teeth.

"Yes, yes he is."

"Oh, God, I can't cope."

Ashley gathered her case. "Here we go."

Strolling over, she noticed the colour of her dad's beard was darker, disguising almost all the grey, his grin displayed a set of whitened teeth that would stop traffic and his usual figure—what Ashley would categorise as a 'dad bod'—looked slimmer.

"My little girl, come here." The embrace was slightly dramatised, as if he was in the running for some secret award unbeknownst to her. Since her parents split, Ashley had only seen her father a handful of times. Each time it felt uncomfortable; she couldn't shake the blame she placed on him. She vowed to make sure this time was different. They had cleared the air. Even her mom had learnt the art of forgiveness over the past year since she'd found a new love interest, so it seemed there was no reason to be mad at Benjamin anymore.

"Hi, Dad."

Benjamin turned his attention towards Madison. "Maddie, it's great to see you, kid. Come here."

Ashley smirked in the background, happy that Madison was also subject to the same weird, over-energetic treatment. The cringe when he called her *'Maddie'* was even more amusing—her nickname as a child that she'd hoped had lost its value.

"Hi, Mr. Stewart. How are you?"

"You can call me Dad. Even better now the two of you are here." Ashley looked at Madison confused. Benjamin placed the bags in the trunk of the car. "Get in, girls."

"Does he think we are together?" Madison whispered.

"I have no idea." They clambered into the small 2-door Camaro.

"When did you get this, Dad?"

"About six months ago. I got a great deal. I've always wanted one, but your mother disapproved, said it wasn't a family car." Benjamin smiled. "She had a point at the time, but now my girls are all grown up so it's time to treat myself."

Ashley observed the interior. It was in great condition considering it was forty-six years old.

"What about Julia's kids?"

Julia Raynard, aka, the mistress. The thirty-five-year-old desperate housewife wannabe, as Ashley liked to refer to her. She was fifteen years Benjamin's junior with two young children and a schedule that included soccer, tennis, ballet, piano lessons and weekly PTA meetings. Ashley wasn't 100% sure of her career. The desire to know much about her had never been present; the part she played in ruining their family unit stood the test of time.

"They're old enough now. They love hopping in the white stallion. They feel cool when they arrive at school," Benjamin said proudly, clearly overjoyed with his purchase.

"Did you just refer to your car as the white stallion?" Ashley raised her eyebrow.

"Not cool?"

"Totally not cool, Dad."

"Okay, I will take that on board." At the traffic lights, he lifted his sneaker slightly to give Ashley a better look. "What about these Michaels, they're cool though, right?"

Ashley placed her head against the window. "Dad, they're not called Michaels, they're called Jordans and I think the fact you've just called them that shows they're too cool for you."

Madison burst out laughing. "That's a classic, Mr. Stewart."

"Dad, are you re-inventing yourself?"

"Ethan said I need to be hipper." Ethan was Julia's fifteen-year-old son.

"Oh, I see, that's what this is then." Ashley waved her hand at the car and her father.

"Do you not like it? I look stupid, don't I?" Benjamin was being sincere, and she didn't have the guts to tell him otherwise.

"No, Dad, you look fine. I'm only joking with you. Just don't start wearing snapbacks please."

"Why would I wear a snack bag?" Benjamin questioned.

"SNAPBACK, Dad, not snack bag."

The fits of laughter from the back seat were uncontrollable. Benjamin laughed along, unphased by the amusement at his expense. Ashley felt warm and happy thinking about the fond memories of her past. She longed to be thirteen again. It was a simpler time when her father would drive her and Madison anywhere they chose every Saturday morning; it was their time, and it made her feel so grown up.

They passed through different neighbourhoods, each with the same suburban feel—sweeping driveways, large front yards with picket fences and beautiful green lawns. Ashley was in awe of the open space, such a contrast from New York City.

"This is us." Benjamin nodded towards the sign that read, *'Welcome to Silver Creek'*.

Silver Creek was known for its country club lifestyle. The views of the valley below were what attracted the rich and famous to the area. Ashley wondered how much money Julia had. The divorce settlement had left her dad with a large chunk of savings whilst her mother kept the house, but it wasn't enough to live in an area as affluent as Silver Creek.

"It's beautiful." Ashley immediately saw what appealed to Samantha.

"I have a feeling you'll love it here, darling," Benjamin beamed.

As they pulled onto the driveway, Ashley observed her surroundings. She'd seen pictures on social media—posted by her sister, of course. The bragging rights were truly on Julia's side. At first glance, the house had to be five bedrooms. A double garage sat to the right, whilst a large open lawn surrounded by shrubs filled the left side. There wasn't even a flower out of place, nor a scratch on the exterior of the house—it looked immaculate, much like the rest of the street. Ashley exited the car and watched as the residents leisurely strolled along; some walking dogs, some jogging, others chatting whilst gardening. It was enviable, such a lifestyle. She wondered, *how many of them actually work?* Much like Julia, their occupations were unknown.

Madison tugged at Ashley's arm. "The houses here don't come cheap. I searched for properties in the area and that one over there," she pointed towards a house very similar to the one they stood outside of, " is listed at 2.5 million!"

"Seriously?"

"Yep. What on earth does she do for a living? I hope she's like, an assassin or something cool."

"Couldn't just be a businesswoman, no?"

"That's boring."

"What are you two talking about?" Benjamin shut the trunk of the car, slinging both bags over opposite shoulders.

"Nothing."

"Okay, shall we go in?"

"Sure, lead the way."

Ashley and Madison followed, half expecting an overzealous greeting, but the house was quiet.

"Where is everyone?" Ashley questioned.

"Julia's carpooling the kids today. They'll be back in an hour or two. Ethan has football practice tonight and Ava has a piano lesson."

Madison raised her eyebrows up and down repeatedly.

"Busy schedule. What about Samantha?"

"She pretty much lives with Lucas now. She probably stays with us once or twice a week. Follow me, I'll show you guys straight to your bedroom."

Benjamin set off and climbed the stairs towards the second floor. Ashley's eyes flitted from left to right. The open-plan living area had large white pillars and an indoor balcony that overlooked the whole of the downstairs.

"This place is really nice. How long has Julia lived here?"

"Maybe four years now. It was her family home. Her dad gave it to her when he became ill."

Madison mouthed the words, *Daddy's girl*—as expected, the assassin theory was a little far-fetched.

"Will you two be okay in here?"

Benjamin pushed the door open to a rather basic bedroom. Ashley half-expected the house to be like MTV Cribs, but instead, a solitary wooden bed sat against the far wall, an en-suite could be seen through a slight corridor to the left that was flanked by a small walk-in closet on either side. A flat-screen TV sat on the one full wall that wasn't covered in windows and that was the extent of the room. It was pristine, as was the rest of the house, but it lacked inspiration.

"Of course."

"It's not much, but we are slowly renovating room by room. This guest room hasn't been done yet." Benjamin placed their bags on the bed. "I will leave you to freshen up. I know you've been travelling all day."

"Thanks, Dad." Ashley smiled. "What time does the baby shower start tomorrow?"

"It starts at two."

"It's at a local golf club, right?"

"Just up the road from here, it's within walking distance."

"Okay, great."

"There's a pool out back if you want to go for a swim."

Benjamin closed the door behind him. Once he was a clear distance away, Madison broached the elephant in the room.

"So, he told me to call him Dad and now we are staying together in the same bed? Why would he think we are a couple?"

Ashley shrugged. "The bed thing could purely be that there isn't another spare room."

"True."

"I'll say something if there's another comment."

Madison perched on the edge of the bed. "I mean, I'm not offended, it's just you and me, isn't it? It's weird."

"Is it? Weird?" Ashley folded her clothes neatly onto the shelves of the wardrobe.

"A little, don't you think?"

"I think we'd make a pretty good couple." Ashley popped her head back around the closet door and raised her eyebrows playfully.

"Are you flirting with me?" Madison laughed.

"You and I haven't had the best of luck with women. Who knows, maybe my dad's on to something." Ashley winked.

"Okay, this is weird."

They both laughed, equally high-pitched and awkward. Ashley wasn't entirely joking. They had been best friends for a long time, jeopardising that was unthinkable, but recently, amidst the break-up from Georgina, her thoughts and feelings had taken a different turn. What she had to figure out was whether the feelings were purely based on loneliness or a genuine want for something more. They say a successful relationship is built on friendship and communication—they had both—but a failed attempt would result in the loss of her best friend. For now, she vowed to pursue nothing, but that was always easier said than done.

***

The golf club's Italian architecture and stunning Californian views combined to create a setting perfect for a baby shower. It was extravagant and wedding-like, as expected—only the best for Samantha. The event reminded Ashley of Samantha's thirteenth birthday; she had been insistent on having a pink floral theme with ponies and puppies. Her entire class had been in attendance, and Benjamin, in the nick of time, managed to scout out a litter of puppies.

The golf club consisted of a clubhouse, a swimming pool, an outdoor dining area with a large wooden floral pagoda overlooking the valley and three miles of beautiful grounds that made up the majority of the golf course.

The night before had been relatively painless. Ashley bonded with Julia's children over their mutual love of chess—a game Ashley hadn't played for a number of years, but after the first practice round, it all came flooding back. They made pizzas and watched TV together. She hadn't expected to feel so welcome. The sense of betrayal towards her mother never left her mind, but she made the utmost effort to fit into the family unit her father had created. However, there had been no contact with her sister—she feared an awkward encounter.

The day's events had been thoroughly planned out on the digital invitation attendees had received. Welcome drinks would be available on arrival, followed by speeches, then food and finishing off with some games—with prizes. The day was predicted to last anywhere between 3–4 hours, but the clubhouse was booked until late into the evening for those who wanted to stay and continue mingling.

The dress code had been described as floral or pastels. Ashley had opted for a crisp white shirt tucked into a pair of beige cropped trousers. The Californian heat was at its worst in August, so a jacket was absolutely not necessary. Madison had opted for a long, flowing pastel pink dress with a low-cut neck—it left little to the imagination. Ashley was impressed, rarely did she see her so dressed up.

The double doors at the clubhouse opened up to a large entertainment hall. One solitary banquet table ran from one end to the other, decorated tastefully with a cream table runner, candles and a large centrepiece filled with white and pink roses. A wooden handmade bar held the pink arrival cocktail consisting of gin, lime and orange—an approved choice.

Further inside, three cream Chesterfield sofas sat in a U-shape. A large draping curtain fell behind with ten white and pink balloons, but they weren't just normal balloons—Ashley noticed the sheer size immediately. A camera was set up in that space, ready for photos. Ashley observed the room, looking for the enormous table of gifts where she could deposit her own.

The un-organisation on her part had resulted in a last-minute trip to the mall that morning. A candle and a sleepsuit that read, *'I love my auntie',* seemed appropriate. Although the amount of time she would spend in the baby's life was yet to be determined.

"She's over there." Madison pointed towards the gifting table.

Ashley rolled her eyes. "Of course, she's guarding the gifts."

The person she was talking to had her back turned. Her sister looked stunning in a white no-sleeved gown that accentuated her bump and still showed just how in shape she was, despite being seven months pregnant. Her long brown hair had been curled and pinned up on the left side so that the bulk of her hair flowed onto her chest over her right shoulder. She held her bump with one hand and accepted gifts with her other—she was glowing. Ashley teared up, blinking ferociously to try and stop the floodgates from opening.

Samantha grinned as wide as the Cheshire Cat when she spotted Ashley—an unexpected reaction. Three years was a long time, people change. There was so much Ashley didn't know, so much she wanted to know.

The space between them closed rapidly as Samantha threw her arms around her.

"I am so glad you came."

"Me too." Ashley pushed her waist back, conscious not to apply too much pressure to the bump, whilst her sister squeezed tighter.

"Samantha," Ashley croaked, "a little less squeezing."

"I missed you. I'm so sorry. Like, really sorry. I should have called. I should have explained. If I could go back I would."

Ashley raised her finger to Samantha's lips.

"I see nothing's changed in three years," Samantha creased her forehead, confused, "you still don't know when to shut up." Ashley smiled.

"I mean it though, I really am sorry."

"I know, so am I." Ashley reached for the bump proudly. "I can't believe my baby sister is having her own baby."

"Crazy, isn't it?"

"I haven't even met Lucas."

"You will. He's outside at the minute, but he's really great, Ash."

"Was it planned?"

"Oh, God, no. One minute, I had dreams of being a physio for the highest-paid athletes in the world, next I find out I'm eight weeks pregnant. Life changed pretty quickly."

"And how does Lucas feel about it?"

"He was shocked at first. Now, I think he's more excited than I am."

"I doubt that. You're beaming, it's amazing to see."

"I'm putting on a brave face. Deep down I'm terrified. How is this," Samantha grabbed her stomach with both hands, "supposed to come out of me?"

"Many other women have done it before you, so there must be a way," Ashley teased.

"Is this my gift?" Samantha pulled the gold gift bag from Ashley's hands. "I wonder what it is?"

"You can open it later. You have a lot of guests to tend to."

"I don't want to. I want to spend time with you."

"We have all day and tomorrow too. I don't fly home until Monday morning so we can catch up properly."

"Do you swear?"

Ashley crossed her heart. "I promise."

"Let me just put this on the table."

Samantha briefly sparked a conversation again with the same woman she'd spoken to when Ashley walked over. "Have you met my sister?"

The figure had beautifully curled golden-brown hair and a floor-length pastel grey dress—she turned around to acknowledge Ashley. The jolt that surged through Ashley's body left her completely rooted in position. Her eyes widened, but her facial muscles barely moved. The hand that gripped her cocktail tightly felt weak, like she would drop it at any moment. Their eyes locked and the world stood still.

13

Ashley

There are certain people that come into your life on a merry-go-round—they get on and off as they please. When they appear, it is as though the time you were apart was no time at all. The distance created was merely a mirage that no longer exists the second they step back into your life.

"Megan?" Ashley blinked rapidly.

"Ashley?"

"You know my sister? How?"

Megan glanced in Samantha's direction, who was understandably confused by the whole exchange.

"You two know each other?" Samantha probed.

"We met in New York about a year ago. You never told me you knew my sister?"

"I didn't know Samantha was your sister."

"The second name didn't give it away?" Ashley jested.

"Believe it or not, there are a lot of people with the surname Stewart." Megan folded her arms.

"Okay, fair enough. How did you two meet?"

Ashley glanced back and forth between her sister and Megan.

"We went to Stanford together. We met through a mutual friend on the basketball team and we've been great friends ever since."

"And you came all the way from England to congratulate my sister at her baby shower?" Ashley looked sceptical.

"I was actually travelling around America for a few weeks. It's the off-season, so Samantha gave me enough notice and I made this one of my stop-offs," Megan challenged back.

They watched each other intently. Ashley often dreamt about Megan—a month ago had been the last time. The dreams were unusual. She would see her in the distance and not be able to reach her or be racing against time to stop her from leaving. Ashley tried not to dwell on them. Dreams, after all, didn't actually mean anything—or so she told herself. They were merely electrical brain pulses that pulled random imagery from our brains. Now Ashley stood before Megan in person, the imagery that surrounded her dreams didn't compare in the slightest. It didn't show the delicate way her dimples appeared at the slightest smile, or the creases in the corner of her eyes when she laughed uncontrollably. Her green eyes were more prominent than Ashley remembered, but above all else, she looked happy.

"I sense weird energy here. Wait…" Samantha looked around for prying ears, "…did you two get together?"

"No," they both replied in unison.

"It didn't get that far," Ashley finished.

"Well, I'll be damned. What are the odds? My sister and one of my best friends, I feel a sense of déjà vu."

"She's not here, is she? Grace?"

"Nope, luckily for you she's on vacation."

Ashley breathed a sigh of relief.

A woman appeared by Megan's side. Confidently, she placed her hand on the base of her back as though it belonged there. The tension had built to an unavoidable climax, there was no way to divert the attention away from Megan and Ashley.

"Ash, this is Megan's girlfriend, Candice."

Candice outstretched her hand. "Nice to meet you."

Ashley obliged. "You too." Her down-turned mouth barely cracked a smile, her gaze never once dropping from Megan's.

"Anyway, I need to go and mingle, so Ash, why don't you go and check on Madison? She's over there waiting for you." Samantha pointed to the Chesterfield sofa, where Madison sat alone.

"No Georgina?" Megan asked.

Ashley turned to walk away, looking back over her shoulder with a wry smile. "Ancient history. Life moves on."

When Ashley reached Madison, the broad grin and flashing eyes indicated she had already spotted the scene unfold.

"Is that who I think it is?"

"Yep."

"Who's the chick?"

"Candice, her girlfriend."

"Why is she here?"

"She knows my sister from her Stanford days."

Madison's eyes widened. "Seriously? I never would've predicted that. Was it awkward?"

"A little. I haven't spoken to her in probably six months."

Madison peeked around Ashley to observe the women, who were huddled together in deep conversation.

"They look to be having a detailed discussion."

"Really? What do you think they're talking about?"

"I don't know, I'm not a mind-reader."

"Today's going to be fun, isn't it?" Ashley said sarcastically.

"Extremely entertaining, for me, anyway. And your mom hasn't even bumped into your dad yet. I have been keeping tabs on that one."

"Don't remind me. If that is anything less than a car crash, I'll be pleased."

Ashley took a seat next to Madison. Her eyes scanned the room—it was filling up. She noticed her uncle in the corner with his wife and kids. A couple of Samantha's old friends from school were there; one of their cousins sat uncomfortably at the end of the table, she'd always been socially awkward. Ashley was surprised at how many people had willingly taken the five-hour plane journey from New York. It was a testament to Samantha, either that or she'd threatened them all with social media slurs and the fear of spilling secrets—the latter was possible.

"She's attractive, isn't she?" Ashley said.

"Megan?"

"Well, that's obvious, but I meant her girlfriend."

"Do I sense a hint of jealousy?"

"No."

"Liar."

"Maybe a little."

"She's attractive, yes, but she's not as attractive as you." Madison placed her hand on Ashley's arm. To an outsider, it would seem more intimate than intended.

"Are you flirting with me again?"

"Shut up, she's looking. I'm doing you a favour."

Ashley turned her head toward the gifting table where Megan was last located. Madison pulled it back quickly with the hand that wasn't currently holding onto Ashley's arm.

"Don't make it obvious, you idiot. Pretend like she's not even there. That will drive her wild."

"Why though? She isn't thinking about me."

"Course she is. I guarantee you."

"What makes you so sure?"

"I saw her face when she saw you."

"Shocked?"

"No. It was more than that."

"What do you mean?"

"Do you remember when we went to watch that low-budget play? It was the most random thing, that guy approached us and asked if we wanted tickets for $10? They were just trying to fill the seats. Do you remember?"

"Yeah, of course, it actually turned out to be really good."

"And do you remember what you said to me at the end of it?"

"Nope."

"You said, *'I hope someone looks at me one day the way the two main characters looked at each other'*."

"Okay."

"That's how Megan just looked at you."

Ashley recalled the play in question, the way the male lead had gazed at the female lead so intently. The looks had captivated her, made her believe in true love, even for a brief fleeting minute. It was desire, passion and intrigue all rolled into one. Ashley had even gone to the trouble of staying behind to congratulate the unknown leads. The play had touched her, but she remembered the intensity of that gaze—no way had Megan looked at her that way.

"I don't believe that."

"You weren't watching her."

"I was literally standing right in front of her."

"Yes, but you didn't watch her, not really. When you looked at your sister, she never took her eyes off you once. When Candice appeared, she didn't even look at her. Samantha introduced her, but Megan didn't take her eyes off you the whole time."

"Seriously? What do you think that means?"

"I don't know, but that girl feels something towards you—that's undeniable, I know that much."

"Who knows." Ashley shrugged. It didn't matter how hard she tried to play it cool, the grin on her face gave away her true feelings.

Madison was still holding her arm throughout the conversation. "You just leaving your hand there?"

Madison slapped her arm and then pulled away. "My bad."

After ten minutes, Samantha assumed everyone who was due to arrive was there, so she announced the food was ready. A buffet-style serving had been prepared by the chefs. The selection was a delightful one, an array of different flavoured sliders, frittata, several large charcuterie boards, Italian pasta salad and meatballs. The latter sent Ashley's tastebuds into a frenzy.

A blush pink place card indicated where each guest should sit. When Ashley and Madison found their positions at the top right of the table, Ashley was relieved to see Megan and Candice on the opposite side, six seats down.

The afternoon went smoothly. After the food, the games began. 'Guess That Tune' was a crowd-pleaser, 'Hit Me Baby One More Time' by Britney Spears and 'Always Be My Baby' by Mariah Carey the only two songs Ashley guessed correctly. The winner was Samantha's future mother-in-law. The scowls from other family members indicated she was the least liked.

The game 'Find The Guest' involved socialising, getting to know people in order to fill in the card with who each fun fact belonged to. That was the one game that would continue throughout the evening, the prize had been donated by Lucas's dad. A three-course meal at The Valley Hill Bistro, the poshest place in town, according to his dad, but then again, he did own it.

Ashley instantly knew which fact belonged to Megan. The third box from the top read, *'I play basketball in England, but my dream is to play in the WNBA'*. Samantha could have made it more difficult. After an hour, Ashley had twenty-five of the thirty boxes filled and she was feeling pretty confident.

Other than the occasional smile across a packed table, Ashley and Megan had barely spoken two words to each other, not since their opening encounter earlier in the day. It seemed they were both just as intent on avoiding each other. Ashley watched Candice leave, assuming she'd gone to the restroom, but when she didn't return, Ashley started to wonder whether she'd called it a night. Megan remained, continuing her conversation with Samantha and a few of their Stanford friends—their names she'd forgotten.

It quickly reached the time in the evening where adults with children went home, grandparents retreated to bed and the DJ brought out the more provocative music. Ashley had tried to avoid her mom for most of the evening; the show of affection she displayed to her new boyfriend was deemed excessive in most people's eyes. Surprisingly, Benjamin didn't rise to Christine's childish behaviour. They'd stayed at separate sides of the room for most of the night, which suited both parties equally.

It was Christine that started the slow dancing, requesting 'You're Still The One' by Shania Twain. Ashley rolled her eyes. It was one of many songs played at her parents' wedding and just another dig at Benjamin. The desired effect was actually the opposite of what she wanted to achieve, but Ashley figured it was better than her sobbing in a corner for the duration of the baby shower.

The whole event could have been mistaken for a wedding at first glance. It had the atmosphere that you would expect; everyone dressed in their best attire, flowers, favours, gifts, a photographer. The DJ continued with the slow songs after another five couples joined the dancefloor—his prepared set of 90s pop and classic country would have to wait.

Madison was happily conversing with one of Lucas's cousins for over an hour. Little did she know that she was as straight as a ruler, but Ashley wasn't about to burst her bubble. The next song caught Ashley's attention; the slow piano introduction sounded familiar. She couldn't place it right away, then she glanced towards a small circular table by the DJ booth. There sat Megan, quietly swaying, watching patiently. *Thinking about what?* Ashley wondered. Then it clicked. The song was 'I Should Go' by Levi Kreis, the song played on their first date in Dos Caminos. They had discussed how odd it was to play such a slow song; it wasn't the right atmosphere, but Megan had expressed her love for said song and knew every word.

It took Ashley the whole first verse and chorus to pluck up the courage to ask Megan to dance. She strolled over, so unsure of herself that she could trip at any moment. Her heart thudded hard in her chest, yet on the outside, she looked calm and composed. Megan's eyes grew wider as she approached.

"Would you like to dance?"

Madison grinned. "What took you so long?"

The nerves eased immediately. Ashley extended her arm hoping chivalry points would work in her favour. They took their position on the dancefloor.

"Did you request this song?"

"Yes, I love it."

"I remember."

Megan raised her eyebrow, surprised or suspicious, Ashley couldn't tell.

"I was surprised to hear about you and Madison."

"What about us?"

"That you're a couple. Doesn't she mind you dancing with me?" Megan questioned.

"We're not a couple."

"Oh, your dad said—"

Ashley interrupted, "Ignore my dad, he always gets the wrong impression."

"That would imply there was an impression to give?"

Ashley laughed. "No impression. You know how close we are. Maybe it's wishful thinking."

"From your dad's point of view or Madison's?"

"You'd have to ask them that." Ashley smirked. "Anyway, how long have you and Candice been an item?"

"About six months."

"Do you love her?" The question escaped Ashley's lips before she had time to lessen the blow.

"Wow, straight to the point."

"Sorry, it's none of my business, really."

"Honestly? I'm not sure, I think I could one day."

"Interesting."

"What?"

"Nothing."

"Don't do that. You always do that."

Ashley chuckled at the familiar way they conversed, as though no time at all had passed.

"What's funny?"

"I just like to see that look." Ashley nodded.

"What look?"

"That look. You cock your head slightly and raise your eyebrow as though you're really annoyed, but there's always a hint of a smile buried in your lips. You can't hide it, even though you try. It's the look you give me whenever I purposefully try to wind you up. I remember it well."

Megan lowered her head, trying to hide the obvious blushing.

"You think you're so charming, don't you? Easily making girls grin and blush with your laid-back, fascinating approach."

"You think I'm fascinating?"

The song switched to 'Back At One' by Brian McKnight and all of a sudden Ashley became intensely aware of Megan's body as it pressed against her own.

"I never said that." Her words were now just above a whisper.

"I think you did. I love this song."

"Me too." Megan twined her arms around Ashley's neck and leaned in closer. Their gaze remained locked. The soft silk of Megan's dress moved from side to side with the rhythm of their bodies. There was lingering energy between them now. Ashley was fully aware of her heartbeat as it grew steadily with every motion. They were close enough that a kiss would've seemed inevitable. The intensity prompted such a display, but then without warning, Megan pulled away with a hint of regret in her parting smile as she left the dancefloor.

***

Outside, the moon began its slow rise. A warm summer breeze gently ruffled the trees. Ashley's reflection could be seen in the pool. The lights from the clubhouse dimmed as a figure approached. A familiar scent of perfume filled the air, the breeze revealing her identity.

Megan stood beside Ashley now, a half-empty wine glass in her hand. The day was coming to a close, as good days often did.

The glare from the outdoor lighting cast a glow over Megan's luminous skin; it shocked Ashley that she somehow got more beautiful as the hours passed by.

"What are you doing out here on your own?"

"It's an incredible view. I'm just trying to appreciate it before I head back home."

"To the Big Apple. I miss that place."

"Do you plan to stop by on your trip?"

"I already did, two weeks ago." Ashley's heart dropped. "Only for one night, just to see Julie and my gran."

The disappointment was made obvious by the deep-seated frown. "Oh, I thought you might have called."

"We hadn't spoken in six months. I thought it might be a little weird. Plus, Candice was with me and to be honest, I don't really know how I would categorise our relationship."

"I thought we were friends?"

"We are."

"Then why didn't you call?" Ashley probed.

"I suppose after I found out you and Georgina were an item, I didn't think we could be."

"What does me being with Georgina have to do with us being friends?"

"It just wouldn't have been fair to her, she knew about us. I didn't want to put you in that position." It seemed even Megan wasn't entirely convinced by her speech, but she wasn't willing to admit the truth.

"Tell me this, do friends call each other in the middle of the night just to say hi? Or get jealous when the other person is with someone else? Do they slow dance to Brian McKnight? I'm not so sure."

Ashley looked back towards the valley.

"Are you trying to say I was jealous of you and Georgina?"

"You weren't?"

"Were you jealous of Candice?"

Ashley scoffed, "As if."

"You're a terrible liar," Megan challenged.

"Touché."

Then came the silence. The sound of the crickets chirping around them brought a calming atmosphere. The faint sound of the DJ could be heard announcing his set finished in five minutes' time. The night was drawing to a close, a night full of unpredictability.

"Why did Candice leave early, anyway?"

"She didn't feel great last night. She couldn't shake it, so she went to get an early night."

"Where are you staying?"

"At a motel about twenty minutes out."

"Where are you heading tomorrow?"

"The plan is to drive through Arizona, then on to Kansas, Iowa and finish in Chicago. I have a flight home from Chicago to England in two weeks' time."

"That sounds exciting. I'm happy for you."

Megan linked her arm through Ashley's and leaned her head upon her shoulder. There was so much unsaid, so many words that could have changed the dynamic. The urge to express her deepest thoughts didn't rise to the surface. She kept at bay anything that might jeopardise whatever they had worth saving. If they were to one day truly be friends, Ashley's feelings, however disconnected and uncertain they may be, had to stay under the surface. That was the one thing she knew with certainty.

"Would it be weird if I told you I'm going to miss you?" Ashley instantly regretted the words until greeted with a response so sincere.

"I'm going to miss you too."

Ashley instinctively kissed her on the forehead. There was a part of her that wished for more, to be able to kiss her lips once again. The reality, however, was far different.

"I should go," Megan whispered.

"Don't be a stranger, okay?"

Megan nodded; she lifted Ashley's hand towards her lips. A final parting gesture.

"Take care, Ash."

"You too."

There was a recognisable ache in Ashley's chest as she watched Megan walk away. The same ache had only been present once in her life—the first time Megan had left New York. There was no denying the connection they had, but a connection was just the spark. Time was its own master; time couldn't alter the distance between them, that ultimately, kept them apart.

***

"Ash, everyone's leaving. Are you staying out here all night?" Samantha called out from the doorway of the clubhouse.

"I'll be right inside."

Samantha walked the short pathway to her sister. "You missed the 'Find The Guest' game winner."

"Who won?"

"Megan, she got twenty-seven out of thirty. Do you know what's even more interesting?"

"What?"

"She was the only one who got your clue correct, aside from our parents."

The clue read, *'At the age of 10, I got lost in a theme park. The authorities searched for hours to find me'.*

"I told her about that when we went to Coney Island. Do you remember that?"

"Briefly, I remember the number of officers that were looking for you."

"I got separated, so I ended up crawling under the space beneath one of the rides. I was so scared. I literally just sat there for hours because I had this fear someone would kidnap me."

"Did we even go back to Coney Island after that?"

"Not until we were a lot older. I think it traumatised them." Ashley laughed. "It's funny now, but at the time I was in serious trouble."

"You were always in some sort of trouble. I'm surprised Megan remembered that. I've known her for nearly four years and she didn't even get mine without me telling her." Samantha eyed Ashley suspiciously. "Why do I feel like there was more than just a brief encounter between the two of you?"

"Wild imagination, I guess." Ashley winked.

"I saw the way you two were dancing."

"She was sitting alone—I felt sorry for her, that's all."

"Okay, if you say so."

"I do."

"Fine."

"Okay, great."

"Fantastic."

Samantha turned to walk back inside as she called out, "Just come in, stupid."

Ashley reflected on the short trip to California. Monday morning, she would fly back to New York, leaving behind half of her family and a fond memory of Megan. It was a weekend she hadn't expected. The time spent with her sister made her realise just how important family was. The years of not conversing and holding a grudge that may not have been warranted felt petty now. Ashley would take away one life lesson which would prove to be vital—forgiveness. What happened with her parents was now a distant memory, they were better apart, happier it seemed, or at least they would be.

***

On the plane ride home the inspiration for her next article had come without pressure, the need to search vigorously for inspiration had not been present. Sometimes life just handed you the perfect story—that, she was grateful for. Freelancing was tough! Ashley found it to be an unpredictable task. She had been fortunate enough to strike up a relationship with one of the editors, who, after the first article, was more than willing to read any future pitches she had. Three of the further six she had submitted over the past year had been accepted and published, a rate she was proud of. Ashley had been surprised to find out that 75% of commissioned stories were from first-time *New York Times* writers—that gave her the confidence boost she needed to continue her journey.

The follow-up to her soulmate article had been on the cards since day one. The inspiration to do it justice and to really understand the readers' wants had been lacking though. *How do you get someone to care?* That was the ultimate question. The readers' investment is paramount to any successfully written piece. Ashley had been trying to figure out how to approach it.

We live in a fast-paced chaotic world, filled with many different types of people whose paths we cross on a daily basis, but not just anyone can mould perfectly to you. The real-life story element of the first article was what caught the editor's attention and captured the hearts of the reader, so Ashley searched for another story that would provoke the same emotions. What she found difficult was the ability to know if two people were destined to be together. After all, there is no soulmate detector. You can't walk around hoping the device beeps when it sees someone who meets your compatibility. *If only life was that easy*, Ashley thought.

Ashley removed her phone from her pocket and typed the first few lines, hoping it would lead her on to something momentous:

I am here again to ask you the question: do you believe in soulmates? We, as humans, are biologically designed to fall in love, but that doesn't mean we get it right the first time. We find ourselves in numerous 'temporary' relationships. These can last a lengthy period of time, but eventually, we realise the incompatibility and close out that chapter of our lives. If soulmates are real, then there is one question we have to ask whenever we find a new love interest: Is this the one person I was obligated by destiny to spend the rest of my life with?

Then you might ask: how would I even know such a thing? Is there a checklist? Some ancient tick box exercise that has been tested and proven to be unequivocally accurate—that would help, right? If you know of one, please let me know.

I have been searching for another couple with an undeniable love like Nancy and Christopher's that would eradicate any doubt in my mind about soulmates and the destined paths laid out before us. There was one couple; they lived in Texas, fell in love instantly, had children, and then got divorced. Another couple; high-school sweethearts who seemed to have the perfect love story— until they got divorced. Then there was a young couple who defied all odds—including two tours in Iraq and a fatal car crash—to find out that the wife was terminally ill. She left behind three children and a grieving widower. How is that fair? It's heartbreaking, but it got me to thinking: can we have more than one soulmate in a single lifetime?

The idea that her life was always destined to end that way seems unjust, but if we believe in fate and destiny, which in turn leads us to soulmates, then we believe that our lives are mapped out before us and every decision and choice we make is somehow predetermined. Ten years later, the widower re-married. He found someone else compatible with his lifestyle and he fell in love...again. Some might call that luck. He was lucky enough to have two people who he would class as 'the love of his life', but if you asked him, luck would not be his word of choice, far from it. You see, luck would have prevented his first wife from becoming ill.

The moral of the story is this, no one person can prove categorically that soulmates are real. I can provide stories that make you believe, but equally, I can provide stories that contradict that same statement. The truth is, we all like to think indisputably that 'everything happens for a reason'. We get divorced so that we can marry the right person the next time. We get our hearts broken so that the next person can show us how we deserve to be treated. We slow dance with the person we know we can't have, hoping one day the connection and timing will prevail…

I cannot convince you to believe in true love, soulmates, destined companions—whatever you want to call it. Only you know what it feels like. Only the 'lucky' will know what it's like to experience such a euphoria that words can no longer describe your feelings.

Ashley typed each word without pre-determination, simply allowing the words to flow through her, unsure to a degree where the words would take her. She often found that was when she produced her best writing.

14

May 2016
Megan

A solitary bead of sweat dripped from her forehead to the dry concrete below. The high humidity sent her body into cool-down mode. Megan received the inbounds at half court; one-on-one with her father was the pre-dinner ritual whenever she stayed home. Michael's extra foot in height aided him tremendously when it came to defence, which meant Megan had to be quicker on her feet to create enough space to pull up uncontested from behind the arc, or blow right by him for the easy lay-up—the first was often her weapon of choice. It was the first one to eleven baskets and the game was currently tied at 10–10.

The words of her first coach rang true in her ears, *'You only need three dribbles to make a move. Your first dribble should always be towards the basket, your second loses your defender, and your third is only necessary if they counteract and recover from the second dribble.'* Megan knew the better-conditioned player always won one-on-one—that was her strength. Michael was still athletic for his age, but he wasn't game-ready. Megan was.

The first five shots had been heavily contested on both sides, but then he eased up slightly, tiring as they got to the final shot. They had stood in the same position hundreds of times in the past, but Megan could only count on one hand the number of times she'd won. Her father never went easy on her, often reciting the same lines, *'nobody else will give you a free pass to the hoop'* or *'do you think the women in the WNBA will take it easy on you?'*

Megan gathered the ball and dribbled to the right wing—that was her favourite spot. One sharp Iverson-style crossover dribble sent her father left, but he recovered fast.

"Where you going now? Huh? You think you can beat me with that weak cross-over?" The goading continued as it had all game.

Megan performed a simple jab step, then planted her inside leg to establish her pivot foot, spinning rapidly back in the opposite direction. The change of pace took her past Michael and towards the open rim for the unopposed lay-up and the win.

Megan hunched over, exhausted and victorious.

"Great game, Meg. That move you just did there," Michael pointed towards the very spot, "that was a perfectly executed move. Any player in the WNBA would be proud of that."

"Thanks, Dad."

"You continue to pull out moves like that next season and the call will come."

"I hope so."

"Let's head inside, dinner will be ready."

Megan believed in her ability. She fought hard every single day to be the best she possibly could be. The work ethic instilled in her from a young age remained—always be the first to practice and the last to leave. If she wanted to be the best at her game that was the sacrifice required. Whilst others maintained their social lives, she trained intensely and furiously until her ankles swelled. The team had stopped inviting her out on the weekends. At first it bothered her, but that ultimately was what separated the all-stars from the role players. Megan had the ambition and drive to make it to the WNBA. The rest of the team had the ambition to make basketball a career, to play as long as they could, or to simply be a starter.

One of the girls—Brianna—already knew what it felt like to grace the league and then fall from that same grace. Megan had unsuccessfully attempted on numerous occasions to gather insight and information that might help her better ride the wave when the time came. Brianna was a woman scorned—one bad season and the dream was over. After that, she'd lost all motivation to try and avenge. Now, she walked around with a chip on her shoulder and everyone else had to take the brunt.

In three months' time, Megan would go into her third season as a Manchester Mystic. In that time, they'd won the WBBL cup once, but never made it past the quarter-finals of the play-offs—that was her Achilles heel. Ultimately, she knew that her performance in the play-offs is what would get her the opportunity she longed for. The stat lines she produced were in the top 5% in the league, but that became insignificant if the production of a title didn't follow.

Megan dragged her exhausted body into the kitchen, pulled a large bottle of water from the fridge and slumped into the dining room chair.

"You're both sweaty, do you have to sit directly on the furniture?" Amanda pleaded.

Michael looked at Megan, they both shrugged and nodded at each other in unison.

Amanda rolled her eyes. "Who won, anyway?"

"Me." Megan smiled proudly.

"A pure stroke of luck. She pulled out a mean spin move. It had to be a fluke."

Megan launched a cushion at her father. "I hate to break it to you, Dad, you're just getting old."

"We'll see in tomorrow's rematch."

Amanda pulled the casserole from the oven and plated it up for three.

"Darling, did you say you wanted to fly out to New York on Monday?"

"Yeah, it's Sofia's birthday on Tuesday, so I'd like to surprise her."

"Okay, I'll book some flights for you later. I had a quick glance, but I wanted to double-check. Will Candice be going?" Amanda queried.

"I told you we broke up, Mom."

"I know, but I wasn't sure if it was like a real break-up or just a temporary one."

"Why would it be temporary?"

"Well, you didn't seem sad about it."

"Fair point, but no, it's definitely a real break-up."

"Has that been awkward? At practice?"

"A little, but the season is over now and I think Candice is going to play in France next year."

"Oh, that's a shame. She was a nice girl."

Megan decided to take the plunge and tell her parents she was gay a year earlier. She had been ready to set off travelling around America with Candice—it had seemed the right time. As expected, and predicted by Julie and Nancy, her parents had accepted the news without so much of a flinch. Megan was fully aware not everybody was that lucky. Candice still refused to have the conversation with her parents back in Philadelphia. After seeing their reaction to her cousin, she figured it would be ten times worse when it was their own daughter.

Since that day, Megan felt closer to her parents. Being able to divulge all parts of her life with them meant she could be her true self and that brought her great happiness.

The relationship with Candice ended abruptly after almost fifteen months together. A cheating scandal that she was yet to discuss with her mother. Megan found out Candice had been speaking to her ex-girlfriend, who recently, and conveniently, moved to England. The messages proved to be rather provocative, which made Megan's decision an easy one. The ordeal brought to light something Megan had been struggling with for months—she'd been coasting, comfortably drifting along because that was the easiest thing to do. Candice had told Megan she loved her on numerous occasions, and eventually Megan told her what she wanted to hear, but deep down she knew she would never reciprocate the same feelings. The cheating simply gave her the push she needed to end things. Candice was distraught with her choices, trying to redeem Megan's trust over a number of messages, phone calls and surprise gifts. Little did she know, nothing would change the way Megan felt.

Amanda checked her digital calendar. "We have an important meeting on Tuesday, but we will fly out to meet you on Wednesday."

"Sounds good. Are we still going to Nashville?"

"Yes, the plan is to stay in NYC for a few nights at your Aunt Julie's, head to Nashville for about a week, then fly to Miami to look at some potential real estate options."

Megan had never been to Nashville. Despite travelling to many American states, she'd never had the pleasure of the great music city.

"You guys are still happy for me to tag along?"

"Sweetheart, we would love nothing more than for you to come with us. I don't know how much longer I will have with my baby girl."

"Mom, I'm twenty-four years old."

"You're still my baby girl, whether you're twenty-four or forty-four."

Amanda had been overly affectionate of late, adamant that family meals were spent together, family movie night every Friday shouldn't be missed and she was extremely insistent that Megan travel back from Manchester at any given opportunity. The four years at Stanford had been tough on her mother. Seeing her only child for a few weeks out of the year had been daunting. Amanda knew, deep down, the time would come when Megan would return to the US and the infrequency of their time together would return.

"Will you make any other plans whilst you're in New York?"

"Well, we only have a few days. I'll see Gram and Aunt Julie, meet Sofia for a few hours and then you guys will be coming."

"You won't be seeing your other friend? Ashley?"

"I'm not sure." Megan glanced at the time. It was getting late—perfect timing to try and end the conversation. "Is it that late already?"

"Why not?" Amanda completely ignored the change in subject.

"We haven't spoken much. I've seen her once in two years, Mom. We aren't exactly best friends."

"Oh, I just assumed you two were close. You seem to mention her more than Sofia."

"I don't." Megan's defensive walls shot up.

Amanda smirked. "If you say so."

"What does that mean?"

Michael remained silent. The hint of a smile could be seen as he lowered his head and focused on his food.

"Nothing, darling, nothing at all."

"Mom, seriously, enlighten me." She crossed her arms like a ridiculed child.

"I think you mention her more than you realise."

Megan scoffed, "When? Give me an example."

"Every time she puts a post on social media. Every time she randomly messages you to check-in. Whenever you speak with Nancy on the phone, she's always brought into the conversation. Then there's the photo."

"Photo?"

"Well, when you moved back to England you only put up a few photos in your room. Remember, you had them printed? There's one of you, Nancy and your Aunt Julie, one of you and Sofia and one of you and Ashley."

Megan unfolded her arms—Amanda made a valid point. *Why did she keep that photo?* And in such a prime position, right next to two photos with people she had known her whole life—she didn't have an answer that made sense.

"I like that photo. It was the view from the Ferris Wheel that made it special." That was a lie.

"Oh really? Just the view?" Amanda mocked.

"Shut up, Mom." Megan looked at her father. "And why are you so quiet? You usually have my back."

"I'm scared to say anything controversial. I'm not sure what the point of this conversation is."

"Me neither, actually." Megan laughed before turning towards Amanda. "What was the point?"

"You're in denial."

"About what?"

"About the weather. What do you think I mean?"

"Calm down, sassy Sue."

Michael chuckled. "I'm going to miss this. I think what your mother's trying to say is, you spend quite a bit of time playing down your friendship with Ashley. Either you're friends or you're not."

"So, now he speaks." Megan lifted her arms in disbelief. "Mr. Voice-of-reason."

Megan felt pressure at that moment to have all the answers, but the cold, hard truth was, she had none. The conversation with her parents revealed her inability to self-reflect. She'd had no idea how frequently she mentioned Ashley, or why for that matter. *Why did she feel the need to discuss her at any given opportunity?* Their last conversation had been in response to Ashley's fifth *New York Times* article. The news had been shared on her social media channels, so Megan had responded. The conversation had been a brief *'congratulations'* and *'I hope you're okay'*. There was always a lingering fear whenever she spoke to Ashley—the fear of saying too much. They both had their own separate lives to live. Lives that didn't require each other's presence, but the absence of it made for a sad revelation.

There was an overwhelming desire to be in Ashley's life. A wish that one day, their different worlds would spin together, not necessarily romantically. Megan would be lying if she said that hadn't crossed her mind, but she would settle for a solid friendship if that was what Ashley wanted. The trouble was, she had no idea what Ashley wanted. *Did she think about her as often? Did she wish that they could be something more? Did she too pin a photo of them on her bedroom wall, reminding her of a happier time?* These were all questions she longed to know the answers to, but the fear of rejection reigned supreme.

***

Megan lay back on the freshly made bed. After finishing up dinner and helping her mom with the dishes, she'd retreated upstairs to a nice warm bath. In two days' time, she would fly to New York. The excitement of being back in her favourite place trumped anything else. After dinner, her mom had booked the earliest available flight on Monday. Her arrival into JFK would be 13:48, leaving her plenty of time to make her way to Upper Manhattan, dump her belongings and venture into the city. The plan was to see Nancy on Monday afternoon, but due to her aunt having a late meeting with a patient, Monday evening was wide open.

Naturally, thoughts of Ashley returned. She recalled the disappointment in her face at Samantha's baby shower nine months earlier when she learnt of Megan's brief trip to New York without any contact. *There would be no harm in asking if she wanted to go for coffee,* Megan contemplated. If anything, it was an uncomplicated courtesy she owed Ashley—or so she told herself.

There was no Candice to cause any conflict of interest, therefore, Megan felt compelled to ask the question. Before she had time to re-think her decision, she sent a text message that would set the wheels in motion.

Hi stranger, I hope you're okay. I'm in New York for a few days next week, are you free Monday? It would be great to catch up. Megan

The message was light and breezy—not too forceful. All that was left to do was wait for a reply. Time moved by slowly; Megan remained motionless in the same horizontal position. The longer the wait, the more anxious she became. The channels on the TV changed countless times, even Alex Vause and *Orange Is The New Black* were not about to distract her from the reply she so desperately sought after. Two hours later, her phone buzzed and she jumped from the trance-like state to open the message.

Hey, how are you? Thanks for reaching out, I'd love to catch up. I can be free Monday. Where are you thinking?

Finally, Megan breathed a sigh of relief. The message showed no emotion, which she found strange. It was very robotic, like catching up with an old work colleague who you haven't seen for five years. *Was that how Ashley saw her now?* Megan felt uneasy.

That's great. I can text you on Monday when I land and we can arrange a place. There are enough coffee shops in New York, so I doubt we will be short of options haha.

The reply was instantaneous.

Sounds good. See you then.

Megan dropped her phone abruptly on the bedside table and clutched her flushed face in the open-palmed hands that stared back at her. There was always time to cancel on the day if she felt uncomfortable. That was the overriding thought in her mind. The option had to be available to stop the insanity creeping in. The two of them had a connection, it was undeniable. You could call it an earth-shattering connection that would tie them together in some form or another for eternity—if you wanted. Whatever it was, the uniqueness left Megan in unchartered waters, and she could only assume the same for Ashley. The meeting would determine the true nature of their relationship. They had a choice; everyone has a choice. Theirs was to decide whether they were thrown together on that summer evening in New York City almost two years ago to be friends, or more than that. Either way, Megan felt the pull towards Ashley. She'd felt it since the first moment she'd laid eyes on her and hundreds of times in between. The concept of them merely being friends appeared, to a certain extent, utterly naive. At heart, she recognised that, yet battled with the concept. The deliberations would continue until the moment she saw her again. Megan had three days and a seven-hour plane journey to self-reflect.

The upside to that being she had time to think. Time to really understand what it was she wanted and expected from their relationship. If they were truly to be friends, boundaries had to be set—no intimate slow dancing being the first.

The downside? She had time to *think*.

15

Ashley

Ashley climbed the underground stairs to the city streets. The delays that morning were excruciatingly long; she'd allowed time, an extra hour to be precise, but even that hadn't been enough. The rapid-fire movement of the crowds swept her along as she rushed towards the skyscraper in the distance. The smell of salted pretzel caused her stomach to grumble; there had been no time to grab breakfast, she'd hit snooze on her alarm clock one too many times. For someone who was about to have the biggest interview of her life, her choices that morning were far from impeccable.

The people around her were all so unconscious of anything going on. She squeezed her way through the crowds, one by one kindly asking people to step aside. Despite everyone being completely oblivious to their surroundings, they moved like clockwork. It was robotic the way they went about their daily lives with no care in the world for the *'crazy'* blonde-haired girl rushing her way through to get to a destination unknown to them.

There it was—almost in touching distance. The fifty-two-storey skyscraper on Eighth Avenue with the large metal racking that scaled the whole building, it formed together over the first four floors to create a brand-distinguishing sign—in the famous black letters it spelt out, *'The New York Times'*. Ashley took a right onto

West 41st and made a beeline for the entrance to the prestigious building.

The call had come on Friday afternoon; the interview was arranged for Monday morning, leaving her very little time to prepare. All weekend, she studied and gathered information that might help. The five freelance articles she'd already had published amongst the other ten she'd sent to other publications were first on her list. The likes of the *New York Post* and *New York Daily News* had both published articles rejected by *The New York Times,* which she was thankful for. Her experience in the writing world since graduating from Long Island University had been slim-to-none. The past twelve months' experience was all she had to show. She assumed the other candidates would have more credentials, but as Madison pointed out, the interview wouldn't have been arranged if they didn't think she was suitable—a publication that size didn't have time to waste.

Editing Resident was a new role; a two-year residency that looks to develop the next generation of editors. The extensive training in the newsroom would give Ashley the vital experience she needed. The freelancing would always be there, but her dream was to one day go down the editing route, so when the opportunity presented itself, it was a no-brainer. The role required three years of journalism experience—which Ashley didn't have, but they already knew that, so she assumed the interest from her recent articles was what got her the interview.

Ashley reached the glass doors and barged inside, hoping that somehow the previous interview had run over schedule, allowing her a minute to freshen up and catch her breath. The elevator doors closed behind her and she watched the steady ascent to the tenth floor. The man beside her clutched his briefcase with a vice-like grip. She noticed the beads of sweat beginning to form in the creases of his frown lines. He kept glancing at the time as though in a hurry and confused, much like herself.

"Do you have an interview too?"

The man glared and responded abruptly, "Yes."

Thankfully, the elevator ride only lasted a matter of seconds after the awkward interaction. They both exited on the tenth floor and walked directly toward the beaming red-haired receptionist.

"Good luck," Ashley whispered. Nothing in response, as expected. *What a rude man,* she thought.

"Hello, my name is Ashley Stewart, I have an interview at 11:30." She tapped away ferociously at the keys.

"Hello, Ashley, I can see you're being interviewed by Sonia. She is running a few minutes behind schedule due to a last-minute meeting this morning, so there might be a wait of around twenty minutes. If you want to take a seat over by the window, I will let you know when she's ready to see you. Feel free to help yourself to the refreshments on offer." The spiel was well-rehearsed and finished off with a beaming smile.

"Thank you so much."

"You're welcome."

The bubbly, tactically attractive receptionist was a nice touch. It seemed someone was looking down on her after all; God had granted her the time to eat a complimentary muffin to curb the hunger and relax—or not.

"Ashley Stewart."

The mouthful of exceptionally moist baked goods muffled her response, "That's me."

"Please, follow me."

Ashley jumped up, throwing the remains of the muffin directly in the trash. She ran her hands down the front of her skin-tight black shirt ironing out the creases as she scuttled to keep up. The red-haired distraction led her directly to a glass office at the far end of the corridor. Inside sat a large conference-style glass table; she gestured to enter and as she did, the lone woman stood.

"You must be Ashley." She extended her hand.

"Hello, yes that's me."

"I'm Sonia, nice to meet you. Please, take a seat." Sonia pulled the chair forward and returned to her cross-legged position.

"So, Ashley. I am one of the deputy managing editors here at *The New York Times*. I have been in this position for four years now, working for the paper for ten in total, and I started exactly where you are today. The aim of the residency is to find up-and-coming editors. There are six positions in total and over a hundred applicants have been narrowed down to just twenty who are interviewing with me this week. So, to be sitting here now is an achievement in itself—you should be proud of that." Sonia was mesmerising. The words escaped her lips with such passion and finesse. "What you're probably thinking is, that's not good enough, right?" Ashley nodded. "Exactly, you want to be one of the six, and this is your opportunity to shine. Other than a brief recommendation from a fellow editor, I don't know who you are or what you're capable of. So, the floor is yours. Why don't you start by telling me a little bit about yourself?"

***

Ashley exited the large silver doors of the skyscraper one hour later. The interview time slots had been forty-five minutes long, which left her with the confidence that it hadn't tanked completely. After all, having too much to say was better than nothing at all. Now, all that was left to do was wait. The outcome would be made public knowledge as of the following Monday. Only seven long excruciating days to wait to see if her dream career would start and she could leave the late nights in the bar behind her.

The moment she pulled her cellphone from her satchel, it started to ring; it was Madison.

"Hey, you."

"How did it go?"

"Good, I think. Sonia was really nice. She seemed interested in what I had to say and we had a few things in common, which made it flow a little easier."

"So, out of ten?"

"I'd say a solid eight."

"That's amazing. You're always modest, so that probably means it was more of a nine. I'm very proud of you," Madison said.

"Thank you."

"Are you coming back home now?"

"Yes, do you want something picking up for lunch?"

"No, it's okay. I said I'd go into work early, they're understaffed. They asked me to ask you, but I know you've got plans." The plans she'd tried so hard not to fixate on since Friday.

"I could do with the extra cash, actually. Will you tell them I'm available for the rest of the week if they need me?"

Madison went quiet. "Sure."

"Time will you be home tonight?"

"I finish at eleven, so twelve-ish."

"Okay, I'll wait up for you."

"You don't need to."

"I want to. I'm sure there will be things to discuss." Ashley was certain about that.

"Okay. Have a nice time on your date."

Ashley laughed. "It's not a date, it's two friends catching up. That's all."

"Hmmm, if you say so."

"Mads." Ashley attempted to make her intentions crystal clear.

"I know, I know. It's not like that."

"It's not."

"Okay."

The conversation came to a natural close. "I'll see you tonight."

"You will."

***

The mirror didn't lie; Ashley observed her outfit choice and the mirror told her it was time to take a vacation somewhere hot, where she could regain her glowing tan that had disappeared throughout the winter season. If there was ever a time to go to California and visit her baby niece, now felt like the perfect time. The winter had worn her down; late night after late night working or chasing her next story. Her day began at three in the afternoon, even on her days off because of her nocturnal lifestyle. It was a lifestyle that had suited her for several years, but it had finally started to take its toll.

The days had grown long, warm and sunny once again, and the weather that evening was perfect. Ashley had opted for a pair of white trainers, tapered denim jeans, a white t-shirt accompanied by an oversized grey blazer—that she'd forgotten all about—and her newest purchase, a grey fedora hat. A recent trip to the hairdressers had been successful with a new hairstyle that allowed the blonde wavy locks to sit just above her shoulders. There was a two-week transition period where she hated it most days, but she'd grown to love it after successfully exploring different styles.

The palms of her hands felt clammy, despite telling herself numerous times that meeting Megan wasn't a big deal. Deep down, she knew it was. Their contact had been minimal since Samantha's baby shower. Megan showed little interest in maintaining a meaningful friendship, but in her defence, Ashley had been too preoccupied, which allowed her to push Megan to the back of her mind. Weeks would go by without a thought, but then reminders would provoke a rush of emotion strong enough to make Ashley question everything.

They had gone back and forth about where to go for a drink, agreeing finally on Upstairs—the penthouse rooftop bar at The Kimberley Hotel. Ashley hadn't been since she first moved to New York. It was a costly venue for drinks if you planned to stay there all night, but the views—priceless. The generic ringtone sounding from her bedside table caught her attention.

"Hey, cancelling already?" Ashley teased.

"As if. I'm running a few minutes behind schedule."

"By that, you mean you lost track of time and you've not even started getting ready yet?"

"Yes to the first part, but actually, I have started getting ready. I just misjudged the amount of time it would take to have a shower, iron my clothes and put a small amount of makeup on."

"Oh, so just what you've been doing your whole life then? Somehow you forgot how long that took?" Ashley smirked in amusement.

Megan sighed. "You know what's hilarious?"

"What?"

"You don't change at all. Your sarcasm is about as predictable as..." Megan paused, "...as..."

"Do you want some help with finishing that off?" Ashley's nerves disappeared, and she felt oddly at ease.

"Honestly, if I didn't like you, I would never speak to you again."

"I'll stop playing around now. I better leave you to get ready, otherwise I'll be sitting on my own for a long time."

"That is true. Will you get us a table? I'll be as quick as I can?"

"Sure. When you get there, take the express elevator from the street level straight to the rooftop. The doorman should be able to guide you in the right direction."

"Okay. I'll see you soon."

"Looking forward to it."

Ashley ended the phone call, grabbed her keys, some money and headed for the door.

***

When Ashley arrived, the host was kind enough to direct her to a small circular table in the far-left corner. From the comfortable black leather bench, Ashley gazed at the perfect views of the New York skyline, including the iconic Chrysler Building. A mixture of ivy and hand-painted Venetian walls filled the rooftop. The bronze bar with a black granite surface added a vintage feel, complimented by the incandescent bulbs floating overhead. The rooftop expanse had a sophisticated vibe; the modern furnishings made it the perfect place to relax and unwind. She instantly felt like it was a place she should frequent more often.

Ashley sat back and admired the view. The bar was relatively quiet; roughly a dozen people congregated on the tables. The majority looked to be corporate bigwigs entertaining clients. A tall young man approached with an extremely tight-fitted black uniform and tortoise-shell spectacles.

"Can I get you something to drink?"

Ashley observed the menu once again, "I don't suppose you can do me two Mojitos?" The menu had speciality cocktails, but no Mojitos.

"Sure, I think I have the ingredients. Let me check." The waiter wandered off towards the bar and after thirty seconds, he gave a large thumbs up.

Ashley mouthed, *thank you*. She remembered her and Megan's joint love for Mojitos from their first meeting and figured it was the safest option.

A few minutes later, the elevator doors slid open and out walked Megan. *How did one person seem so beautiful, charming and seductive all at once?* Ashley contemplated. The sound of her heels clicking on the concrete slabs below sent Ashley's heart racing. She wondered how nobody else was disrupted by the elegant woman that walked from one side of the bar to the other. The bartender noticed as he finished their drinks, over-filling the soda slightly through distraction. Ashley couldn't blame him, she too was mesmerised.

The breeze rippled through her wavy curls, causing her to pull it back in front of her body. Her lips parted slightly to reveal the most honest smile when she locked eyes with Ashley. The walk from the elevator to the table seemed like a lifetime. Suddenly, people noticed her presence; two businessmen to the right lifted their heads from the mound of paperwork and observed the beauty before them.

Megan held her head high. Her walk was confident, but she was not vain. She commanded attention, but she was far from obnoxious. At that moment, Ashley admired her in all her glory, grinning with joy when she approached.

"Hey."

"Hi."

Ashley edged along creating more space beside her. "Sit beside me here, if you like. The view is incredible." She wasn't lying. The seat across from her would mean Megan had her back to the best part, but there was a small part of her that was happy about the bar's inconvenient seating arrangement.

"I feel overdressed."

The tight leather trousers, heels and cropped red top with a denim jacket cradling her shoulders looked dressy but classy. She didn't look over the top, but Ashley could sense she'd tried, which surprised her.

"You look great."

"Thank you, but you're super casual. I look like I'm about to hit the town."

"That's okay, for all these people know we could be."

Megan chewed on her lip, avoiding eye contact. Ashley sensed her insecurity and tried to make her feel more comfortable. "You haven't even commented on my hair."

"Give me chance," Megan laughed. She reached out and touched the tips of hair balancing on Ashley's shoulders, "It really suits you. I love the hat too. Very suave."

Ashley lowered the brim of the hat in a cowboy-like salute. "Why thank you, ma'am."

"I see your accents haven't improved then?"

"Excuse me? Have you heard my Australian accent?"

"Yes actually, it wasn't great."

"G'day mate," Ashley gestured towards the Mojitos, "how gnarly is this coldie?"

"Oh God." Megan covered her face.

"Crikey, don't be a drongo mate."

"Please stop."

Ashley threw her head back in a fit of laughter. "I'm sorry."

"Thank you for the drink, by the way. You remembered my favourite."

"Of course I did, it's my favourite too."

They lifted their glasses in salute.

"What shall we cheers to?" Megan asked.

"To old friends." Ashley smiled sincerely, but she noticed a hint of disappointment cross Megan's face.

"This place is gorgeous, isn't it?"

"It's incredible. I'm glad you suggested it. I bet my gram would love it up here, I'll have to tell her."

"How is Nancy?"

"She seems great. Did she tell you they're thinking about expanding?"

"No, she didn't. I haven't been to the bar in a few weeks so I haven't had a chance to catch up with her."

"Yeah, she mentioned that."

"What? That I hadn't been?"

"You know how she is. She likes to know how you're doing. She wishes you would go by more often and gets worried when she doesn't see you." Megan smiled softly.

"If you see her before I do tell her I promise I'll visit soon."

"I think it's sweet that she cares for you. I know you don't have any grandparents, so that must be nice."

"I care for her too, she's a remarkable woman. It must run in the family." Ashley nudged Megan playfully. The comment was intended to be a causal compliment, but the atmosphere intensified.

"Anyway, back to the expanding part. The unit next door has become available and they're thinking about putting an offer in to double the size of the bar." Megan's change of subject was tactile.

"Really? Wow? Shouldn't they be slowing down at their age?"

"That's exactly what I said! Apparently, the bar manager that works for them is amazing, so they think he will be able to run it the majority of the time and they can just reap the benefits."

"I don't blame them, they should be enjoying their life now not working behind a bar."

"You have inspired them for part of the expansion as well."

"What do you mean?" Ashley took a sip of her Mojito, which was already almost empty.

"They want to have a dedicated writers area with book shelves, sockets to plug laptops in, a large-screen TV playing the news, etc. They said, and I quote, *'Ashley will love it'*, so you must be the favourite because I don't see them having a dedicated basketball section." Megan crossed her arms and pouted theatrically.

"Let's be fair, it is classed as a sports bar and they often have the basketball on so don't act all misfortunate. I love that idea though. I have spent so many days writing at the bar over the past two years."

Ashley pointed towards the empty glasses. "Would you like another?"

Megan reached automatically for her purse. "Sure, but let me get these ones."

She caught the waiter's attention and signalled for two more of the same.

"So…how is basketball?" The question Ashley really wanted to ask, she decided to hold off on.

"It's good. We won the WBBL cup this year."

"I saw that, actually. I bet that was incredible."

"It was amazing to finally get my hands on a professional trophy. You saw it?"

"I watched a bit of it. I was actually at work, but I managed to sneak away to stream the last two quarters. You played great by the way."

"Thank you, that means a lot."

"It must have felt good being the top scorer and assist leader on your team this year."

"It does, but I would trade that for a championship."

"Do you think you have a shot next year? You got to the quarter-finals this year, right?"

Ashley thanked the waiter for his prompt delivery. At $18 a Mojito, it was going to be an expensive evening, but as soon as the fresh, cold taste of lime and mint caressed her lips the price tag was forgotten.

"I think we do, but it depends how we react in the off-season. We need a strong centre to really help us next year; we don't have the height advantage that the top teams have, that's what lets us down. Some games we just get destroyed in the paint."

"I'll keep my fingers crossed for you. Any word from your agent about the WNBA?"

"Not yet. She tells me to keep doing what I'm doing, stay motivated and the time will come. My dad seems to think a good championship run will make them come looking."

"Is that where the scouts go? To the finals?"

"The semis and the finals. They tend to have some representation there." Megan re-adjusted her position, crossing her right leg. The slightest touch of her foot could be felt against Ashley's calf, which surprised her. Such a simple touch felt so intimate.

"What will happen with you and Candice if you move back here?" The question escaped her lips before she had the chance to consider how it sounded.

Megan angled her body towards Ashley. "We broke up."

"Oh."

"Last month."

"Why? You don't have to tell me if you don't want to."

"It's okay, we just grew apart. She started speaking to her ex again, and I realised I didn't care. I think I knew from the beginning. At the baby shower, you asked me if I loved her. Most people would know at that point, but I was putting off the inevitable, hoping my feelings towards her might deepen over time but they never did."

"I'm sorry."

"Don't be, everything happens for a reason." Her glare remained fixed on Ashley. "Anyway, you haven't told me about your writing. How's it going?"

"I actually went for an interview this morning."

"You're kidding? Where?"

"At *The New York Times*." Ashley grinned.

"Shut up!" Megan instinctively squeezed her thigh. Ashley acknowledged the touch, but only momentarily, not wanting to draw too much attention to the closing gap between them.

"Crazy, isn't it?"

"What's the position?"

"It's an editing residency, so they basically show you the ropes and mould you to be the next big editor. There are only six positions available. I find out next Monday."

"That's honestly incredible. Did the interview go well?"

"I think so. The editor that interviewed me was called Sonia. She was super chatty and I think she liked me."

"Well, obviously she did. I'm sure you charmed your way to a position." Megan hid the seductive smile behind her drink.

"I don't know about that."

"Please," Megan scoffed, "you are super charming and you know you are."

"Says who?"

"Says me," Megan whispered.

Ashley felt the gap between them close as Megan edged even closer. The scene before her had been played out in her dreams over and over. The moment she saw Megan again; there would be no complications, no barriers standing in the way of them becoming whatever they wanted to be, except that was a dream and Ashley knew the reality. The very sudden and apparent reality that had manifested in the previous six months. The desire to kiss Megan again had built within her body for a long time. She wasn't entirely sure if she would ever have the opportunity again, but the desire was suppressed by her conscience and her inability to forget her recent commitments.

"I can't," Ashley whispered, causing Megan to pause just as her lips parted—she was within inches of kissing her. Ashley's heart raced. She felt guilty—the longing was so powerful that her ability to say no was being tested like never before.

"I'm seeing someone."

16

Megan

The warmth of Ashley's breath grazed her lips. For a brief moment, she said nothing at all, only held the position she'd been so eager to create. Staring into Ashley's eyes, she saw the same desire she felt inside—the prominent rise and fall of her chest made it clear that she was trying with all her willpower to resist Megan's advances.

"I'm sorry, I didn't know," Megan said, pulling away inch by inch. The feel of blood rushing to her cheeks warmed her face.

"Why would you? It's not exactly public knowledge at this point."

Reluctant to know, she asked anyway, "Who's the lucky girl?"

Ashley hesitated. "Madison."

If Megan's wide eyes didn't give away the surprise, her gaping jaw certainly did. "As in, your best friend Madison?"

"Yes."

"Oh, that I wasn't expecting."

"It came as a surprise to me too."

"How long have you guys been seeing each other?"

"Probably more seriously for the past five or six months, but things kind of changed after the baby shower last year."

"How did that happen? You guys have been friends forever?" Megan returned to her upright position. The lingering lean felt inappropriate now.

"Honestly? I'm not sure. I think I told you about Madison telling me she liked me a few years ago? Since then, I have kind of always known it, but I made it crystal clear at every opportunity that we were best friends— completely platonic best friends. The last thing I wanted was to ruin our friendship."

"What changed?"

"Things started getting a little more flirtatious between us last year. We found ourselves single at the same time, which hasn't happened at all, I don't think, since we were probably eighteen. One night we got drunk and things happened."

"Was that not weird?"

"For a few weeks after, it was certainly strange. We didn't know how to act around each other. And then there was Emily, of course, who let us know exactly how she felt about it."

"I can imagine that didn't go down too well?"

"That's an understatement."

"That bad?"

Ashley nodded. "I got the cold shoulder for a while, but then she realised if we move into the same bedroom, she gets the other room rather than the makeshift one she currently has, which isn't private enough now she has a girlfriend. Once she realised her benefit in the situation, she came around to the idea."

"Can't blame her, I suppose." Megan shrugged. "So, are you guys a couple now?"

"Not officially. We wanted to take it really slow to make sure we don't mess it up, I guess."

"How does she feel about you coming here?"

The awkwardness of an almost kiss faded as Megan tried to pretend it hadn't happened.

"I think it made her a little uncomfortable, but I assured her it wasn't like that."

Megan's heart dropped with the realisation that the night wasn't what she hoped it would be. "It wasn't like that?"

"Like, romantically. I think people just assume because we had that connection that it always has to be that way. We can just be friends, right?"

The old we could be friend statement felt obligatory now. Ashley's voice was calm and collected, but Megan sensed the uncertainty.

"We could."

"But?"

"No but," Megan said.

"Hmm, okay." Ashley's lopsided grin said otherwise.

"I feel stupid now."

"Why?"

"For trying to kiss you when that wasn't your intention."

"Don't feel stupid."

"I just thought you inviting me here, of all places…it kind of seemed like a date." *Was she losing her mind?* The setting had the makings of a perfect date.

"I can see why you would think that. I'm sorry, I should have been clearer, it's just not so easy."

"What's not?" Megan asked.

"Being around you in general, trying not to be too flirtatious. When you asked to see me, there was no doubt in my mind that I'd come, even if Madison hated the idea."

Megan's smile remained tight-lipped, she took satisfaction in knowing that Ashley felt the same pull she did, despite how hard she tried to ignore it. The next question was on the tip of her tongue. She so desperately wanted the answer, but feared it would be the opposite to what she hoped.

"Do you love her?"

Ashley offered a weak smile that faded quickly. "Yes."

Megan crossed her arms. "It's serious then?"

"Yes, I had to be certain."

"That it would work?"

"Exactly. I've always loved her as my best friend, but I wasn't sure if I could love her on a romantic level," Ashley answered.

"How do you differentiate the two?"

Ashley continued to stare at her. Megan sensed her want to tell the truth, but she was hesitant—uncomfortable. That surprised Megan. The blissful state of love's young dream often radiated from the people involved. Ashley was trying to hold back, to downplay her feelings to protect Megan, at least, that's how it seemed to her.

"Well, I have two best friends, one of them I want to kiss, the other I don't. It's that simple, really." Ashley shrugged. She could elaborate, but chose not to.

"In all fairness, if I had to choose one of the two for you, it would definitely be Madison. I can see why that would work." Megan smiled. "As long as you're happy, that's all that matters."

"I am."

Megan hesitated. "Can I ask you a question?"

She nodded. "Always."

"If I were single last year, at the baby shower, do you think we would have gotten together?"

Ashley thought long and hard about her answer. "Honestly," she sighed, "I think absolutely nothing could have stopped me, but that would have been a mistake."

"Oh." Megan dropped her gaze, breaking the spell she was under. Disappointment formed on her brow.

"Don't take that the wrong way."

"It's fine. It was a dumb question."

"Let me explain—"

"You don't need to," Megan interrupted. She reached for her glass; another one down. The bartender had already eyed their empty glasses as she signalled for another refill.

"But—" Ashley tried to respond, but Megan cut her short once again.

"Seriously, don't worry."

"Will you just be quiet for a minute and let me speak?"

Megan nodded, "Sorry."

"Thank you, now, as I was saying, at the baby shower I couldn't take my eyes off you the whole night, I don't know if you noticed," Ashley flushed, "I remember thinking to myself, out of all the billions of people in the world, how did I have the pleasure of meeting that girl. If only she were single. I was devastated, it took me at least a day to get over the fact you had a girlfriend."

Megan laughed. "Just a day, huh?"

"Yeah, like a full twenty-four hours, maybe even twenty-five. It cut me deep." Ashley's dimples appeared. Her grin created the small dints in her cheeks that Megan found so attractive. "In all seriousness, I thought the timing sucked. Then the next day, I realised it was for the best. If something had happened between us that night, it would have been irrelevant. You still had to go back to England and me to New York."

"That's true."

"The idea of that night and what could have been is better left as a fantasy. I think the reality would have been more complicated than either of us could handle. That's what I meant by it would have been a mistake."

"I think some mistakes should be made though."

"Me too." Ashley laughed. "I say this now with a clear head. On the day I would've ignored all reason and doubt."

"It was hard, saying no to you," Megan admitted.

"I can relate to that."

There was a mutual understanding between the pair. They both knew what it felt like to want something you couldn't have, to say no to desires so strong they would make most people crumble under the pressure. At that moment, their similarities and morals were found to be the same. Neither of them had to speak to confirm their feelings for each other, they already knew with a glance. They could see it in the other's eyes without saying a word. What they could have been or what they might one day be remained unspoken. Megan felt joy in knowing Ashley. Their connection proved more undeniable every time they crossed paths, but underneath the joy lay a niggling disappointment that she felt from time to time. She would push those feelings aside in order to be a good friend—she hoped she could at least fulfil that role without compromise.

They spoke until the sun had long disappeared behind the skyscrapers in the distance. They didn't once shy away from conversation, openly and freely they spoke about their childhoods, their high school dramas, coming out stories, first loves and finally their dreams and aspirations for the future. It became a whistle-stop tour of their lives. The more Ashley spoke, the more Megan wanted to reveal details about herself. She wanted her to know who she really was with no facade.

The initial flirtation was present, but the silent knowledge that they could be no more than friends remained strong. The air was calm. Being thirty floors above street level took away the noise of a busy New York night. The evening drew to a close at ten; the bar had cleared out almost completely, leaving a young couple in the corner who were not schooled on PDA etiquette, and then Ashley and Megan, who found the whole display as amusing as the bartender.

The luxurious setting and the panoramic views overwhelmed Megan's senses at every turn—it was a night she'd never forget. After a moment of soaking in the surroundings and enjoying the peaceful starry refuge, they finished their fifth cocktail and made their way towards the elevator.

"Did we really just spend $200 on cocktails?" Ashley's eyes widened.

"Yes, we did."

Megan covered her mouth partially with one hand as if to keep the next part a secret, "I think we just got robbed."

"How about next time we go to Nancy's?"

"Agreed," Megan said. Her body swayed as she entered the elevator.

"Are you drunk?"

"I think so," she gestured with her index finger and thumb, "maybe just a little bit."

"Scandalous," Ashley teased. She laughed and slipped her arm casually around her shoulder.

"How are you not? They were strong drinks."

"I work in a bar remember, you get used to it."

"Kind of like working in a gas station, you get used to the smell of fuel."

"Something like that," Ashley laughed. "How are you getting home?"

"I was going to walk. I realise now that's a bad idea. I'll call an Uber."

"Let me do that for you." Ashley reached for her phone and searched for the nearest available driver. Within seconds, the car was available. "It'll be five minutes."

"Thank you. I had a great time tonight, Ash."

"Is that the drink talking?"

"No, I mean it. It's always good to see you."

"It's always a pleasure, don't be a stranger, okay?"

Megan smiled. The last thing she wanted was to be a stranger.

"Ditto."

She pulled Ashley in for a hug, arms clasping tight around her neck. There was a brief second where neither said a word. Megan buried her head into Ashley's neck, breathing in the sweet scent of her perfume. They remained that way for longer than friends should. As she pulled away, she kissed her neck softly, intimately, the sombre goodbye ever-present in her mood. Next, she said what felt natural.

"I am so proud of you."

"You are?"

Ashley squinted; her chocolate-brown eyes were glistening in the moonlight. It was time to go and yet every atom in her body was telling her to stay. That was the law of attraction at work. She had nothing but positive thoughts and feelings about Ashley. Now, they came back to haunt her, to watch her squirm in situations that were almost impossible to navigate.

"More than you know," she said sincerely. "Let me know when they offer you the job."

"Shh, don't jinx it."

Megan waved at the white Toyota Prius across the street. She took one last look at Ashley and walked away.

"Hey," Megan had the car door ajar. As she climbed inside, her voice echoed across the street, "it's not a jinx if it was always destined to be."

"We will see," Ashley called out.

"Yes, we will. Goodbye, Ashley Stewart."

"Goodbye, Megan Davis."

She sat back on the worn-out leather seat—it had seen better days, but her level of intoxication, coupled with the high she felt from seeing Ashley again, left her unphased by the shabby car and its fusty aroma. She turned to look out of the rear window. The silhouette of the woman she adored stood under the gold entrance of The Kimberley Hotel. *If only she could have captured the image*, she thought.

How many times would they cross paths? How many times would she pretend like the pain in her chest was normal? she wondered. *It felt like hunger,* except the hunger never felt at bay. The more she saw Ashley, the more she wanted to see her, and the more she wanted to, the less she could.

The final words she spoke had rolled off the tip of her tongue with more meaning than intended. *It's not a jinx if it was always destined to be*—had she been referring to Ashley's career opportunities or much more than that? There was one thing apparent in her mind, a good night's sleep was unlikely.

17

Ashley

Ashley observed the sunrise from her position on the roof. There was a peaceful solitude in watching the world come to life. She found herself observing one of the only reliable things the planet had to offer. Pre-sunrise was the only time New York had an element of calm. In true fashion, it would always be the city that never sleeps, but there was a tranquil serenity even if only for a fleeting moment.

Stretching her legs out before her, she lifted her arms above her head, breathing in the fresh air. Approaching the summer months meant the crisp, clean air would soon become unbearably humid. The coffee of choice that morning originated from the UK. Maybe the choice had been a conscious one after her night with Megan, but she tried not to dwell on it too much. She liked to try other brands of coffee and her mind just happened to be drawn to the one at the back of the cupboard that was unused and unopened.

Beanies almond flavoured coffee—picked up from a local market that only sold rare European produce. The night before, Megan had picked at a bowl of complimentary almond nuts—coincidence?

The metal door creaked behind her; she turned to see Emily. Her long blonde hair looked unruly, but she pulled it off, even after a full night's sleep. The sun made her eyes narrow as she yawned, and she raised her coffee cup in salute.

"I thought you'd be up here."

"I wouldn't go applying for a detective job just yet."

"Very funny."

"Why are you up so early?"

"I have a meeting at 7:30, so I figured seeing as I'm already getting up in the middle of the night, I might as well get up a bit earlier and check in with you."

"Who are you and what have you done with my best friend?"

She rolled her eyes. "I'm regretting it already."

"How did you know I'd be up here so early watching the sunrise?"

Emily shrugged. "A hunch, I guess."

They sat in silence for a moment, taking in the surroundings as they so often did. Ashley was waiting for Emily to broach the subject. After a minute, she decided to put her out of her misery.

"You want to ask me about last night, don't you?"

"Oh, 100%," Emily sat upright, "I just wasn't sure how long to sit here before I did."

"The fact you waited at all surprises me."

"Me too. I have about twenty minutes so I'd like the full rundown please."

Ashley started off by explaining the atmosphere, the ease in which they conversed, the fact Megan was now single and every topic right up to the final wave goodbye—including the 'almost kiss'.

"She tried to kiss you?" Emily scowled.

"Yes, she didn't know at that point that I was seeing Madison. If she did, I don't believe she would have done that."

"How long exactly did you wait to tell her you had a girlfriend?"

"You know we haven't agreed on that label yet."

"Oh, come on, Ash! That's basically what you are. I wish you'd stop being so scared to commit to her."

"You know why I don't want to rush into things."

"Is that the only reason, though? Because I've heard the same excuse from you for six months."

The thought had crossed her mind. She wholeheartedly believed that she was doing the right thing by taking it slow. If she rushed, she could potentially lose not only a girlfriend, but her best friend. Their whole dynamic would change and the life she had become so accustomed to over the past five years would be no more, but was that the only reason? Ashley sometimes lay awake at night wondering if she would have committed to Madison sooner if she'd never met Megan.

"Yes, of course it is."

"It's nothing to do with Megan?" Emily probed.

"No."

"You're 100% sure?"

"Yes." She wasn't.

"Okay, so are you going to tell Mads about the 'almost kiss'?"

That was the dilemma Ashley had mulled over on her walk home and on into the night. Madison had returned home from work just after midnight, but Ashley pretended to be asleep. She needed more time to process the evening's events and decide what was need to know. That's what she hoped the sunrise would help her decide.

"I'm not sure."

"What do you mean?"

"Would you tell her?"

Emily reached for her coffee, contemplating her response. "That depends."

"On what?"

"What is your reason for not telling her?"

"I don't want it to be made into a big deal when nothing happened. I know she'll take it out of context."

"You can't really take an 'almost kiss' out of context, Ash."

"You know what I mean. If I tell her it wasn't like that, it was a misunderstanding, etc., she won't understand."

"So, what is the reason? You don't know if you'll ever see Megan again, right? Or if you do, it might be once every two years. Does it matter if you tell Madison and she resents her for it?"

Emily often made a good sparring partner—not in the boxing sense. Ashley would say exactly how she felt and she knew Emily would hit back. Whether she liked the response or not, it would always be truthful and harsh when it needed to be.

"I want to be Megan's friend. Like, really be her friend. If she moves back to New York one day, I'd want to spend time with her and build a relationship. That's why I don't want to tell Madison."

"For someone you've only met a handful of times, you really want this girl to be in your life."

"Is that a bad thing?"

"No, it's just unusual. I find it hard to believe you don't feel something more towards her."

That was the battle she faced on a daily basis—trying to understand her own feelings lately had become a struggle.

"I did, or maybe I still do. I don't know. Obviously, we are worlds apart. Timing is everything these days. I have Madison now, so that only leaves room for us to be friends and I want to try and make that happen."

Emily's eyes narrowed. She was sceptical. "Is that not dangerous?"

"Being friends with Megan?"

"Yes, when you're not really sure how you feel about her?"

"I'm not sure how I feel about you, but you're still my best friend," Ashley teased.

"Can you just be serious for one second?"

Ashley wracked her brain for a way to explain it so that Emily would understand. Then she remembered.

"Do you remember when you told me about that girl you dated in college? What was her name? Amy?"

"Yes, Amy."

"You told me you wished you could have been her friend from the beginning. You jumped straight into dating and the relationship only lasted six months. Then, every time you saw her after that, it was awkward. You knew you could have been great friends, but you'd already crossed the line. After that, you tried, but her new girlfriend didn't allow you to be friends because she found it strange."

"I see."

"Even to this day, you see her on social media and you wish she was in your life. You told me that less than a year ago."

"And that's how you feel about Megan?"

"Exactly. I don't want to regret not having her in my life."

"If that's truly how you feel, then I understand why you would keep it from Madison. I'd do the same. Let's just hope it doesn't come back to bite you in the ass."

Ashley drew her knees to her chest and propped her head. "Life's too short to fear the unknown, right?"

"I'm glad you said that. You should have no fear in asking Madison to be your girlfriend then." Emily sat back, smug.

"Touché."

18

Ashley

Ashley awoke, exhausted from the weekend's hectic shifts, coupled with the general lack of sleep. The nervousness she felt awaiting a response from *The New York Times* interview caused her to toss and turn throughout the night. Eventually, she fell asleep at four in the morning. The clock now read eight, and she wondered if she could sneak in a few extra hours, but the risk of missing the phone call was too daunting.

Madison stirred as she slipped silently out of bed. Grabbing her robe, she made it to the final floorboard before a creak disturbed the quiet.

Madison rolled onto her back and mumbled, "You okay?" She didn't open her eyes.

"Yes, are you?" Ashley chuckled to herself. There was no response after that; she'd dozed back off, so she slipped out of the door unheard.

Their relationship had grown stronger after the meeting with Megan. She'd opted not to tell her about the 'almost kiss'. Aside from that, she had spared no other details. Madison expressed her jealousy at hearing Megan was single, that combined with her outfit choice had sent her into a frenzy. Ashley reassured her, making it evidently clear she had nothing to worry about. After that, she saw it as a test—one they'd inevitably passed.

On some level, it deepened her feelings for Madison; overcoming a hurdle that allowed her to become in-tune with her feelings and understand the intensity of them. The wistful memory of Megan still dangled before her like hanging fruit in her mind, alluring her into the unknown, but she chose to ignore it. Any romantic thoughts were de-emphasised and pushed to the back of her mind in the hope of forming a solid friendship one day.

The kettle boiled on the stove as Ashley reached for her favourite mug. The antique store down the road sold unique coffee mugs, she'd gone with Madison a few months earlier to look for a gift for Nancy's birthday. They'd spent half an hour looking at the different mugs and trying to decide which one matched their personality the most. They went to the extent of sitting in an antique rocking chair and picturing what each mug would look like on the rooftop whilst they enjoyed a freshly brewed coffee. Who searches for a mug to match their personality? The idea amused Ashley now, but the picture of Madison remained as her screensaver, reminding her of a simple time, but one that brought great joy. If you could have that much fun with someone in an antique store talking about mugs, surely that was the person you could spend the rest of your life with— she was getting ahead of herself.

The rain hammered against the windows for the first time in two weeks, so Ashley opted for the comfort of the sofa instead of the rooftop.

The benefit of Madison sleeping with her meant that Emily got to sleep in the second bedroom. No official swap had been made and Emily's makeshift bedroom in the living room remained, but it allowed Ashley to get up early, make a coffee and watch TV without disturbing her sleep. They'd upgraded a year earlier from the cheap, wicker handmade partition to a sturdy, solid wood divider which gave more privacy, but it wasn't soundproof—that's why whenever she wanted company over she would forewarn or stay out.

Ashley's phone started buzzing, bringing her back to the present. It was 8:20 a.m. and the number was one she didn't recognise. Then it suddenly dawned on her who it could be, so she answered immediately.

"Hello, is that Ashley Stewart?"

"It is indeed."

"Hello, Ashley. It's Sonia from *The New York Times*. Is now a good time to chat?" *Not really*, Ashley thought, *who calls at 8.20 in the morning*? Luckily, she was an early riser.

"Yes, of course."

"Sorry to call quite early. I like to get an early jump on a Monday."

"That's okay."

"So, I have your interview feedback in front of me. I will just run through a few notes I made first."

Ashley pinched the bridge of her nose. "Okay."

"I thought you came across incredibly well. You answered each question with confidence and poise. You're very knowledgeable. Where other candidates struggled with the background of the paper and the overall requirements of the job, you excelled. I felt your passion throughout the interview and your desire to succeed within this business." Ashley felt the hard thud of her heart almost bursting through her chest as Sonia paused to gather her thoughts.

"With that being said, there are elements I felt you could improve upon. The main one being your self-belief. If you don't believe you can do it, why would anyone else believe you? You said all the right things with such grace, but when it came to me asking about your previous work, more importantly, your already published articles with us; you downplayed them. The first article you ever wrote was a sure-fire winner. I remember being sat around the board table with the other editors, discussing potential new writers. Bryan read your article out to the rest of us and I loved it. It was the first time in a long time I'd been truly intrigued by an article. The effects it could have on people and the relatable content excited me."

"So, you already knew who I was before you interviewed me?"

"Oh, of course I did. I have my assistant do extensive research before all of my interviews. I know more about you than you do," Sonia laughed.

"Surely interviewing me seems a little irrelevant, if that were the case?" Ashley joked.

"You may think that. Put it this way, I already know what school you went to, your hometown, your best friends, your work experience, your favourite food, your favourite holiday destination, what sports you play, where you like to socialise and whether you're married, single or just completely unsure. Your personal résumé and social media ultimately help me discover everything I need to know about a person to see whether or not they are eligible for the job. That's what gets you through the door, then comes the hard part."

Ashley stood, shifting her weight nervously from one foot to the other. "What's the hard part?"

"I'm glad you asked. You can fake a résumé, you can even fake a social media persona. What you can't fake are character, passion and intrigue. I can't read that on a résumé—I have to see it. What I saw from you was a strong, capable individual who could achieve anything they put their mind to if they only believed wholeheartedly in their ability. Don't let your internal ceilings stop you from achieving your goals—the sky is the limit."

Ashley made a mental note of the last sentence; a point that truly touched home. The perspiration on her forehead became visible, the jaw-clenched face in the large circular mirror stared back at her. She waited patiently for Sonia to continue.

"In summary, I have made my decision…" there was a long pause, the suspense almost sent her over the edge, "…and it was the easiest one I had to make. Congratulations, Ashley, you got a position."

"OH MY GOD, you're serious?" she squealed.

"There was never a doubt in my mind. You thoroughly deserve it."

"Thank you so much. Honestly, you don't know what this means to me."

"Don't thank me. You gave yourself this opportunity, nobody else. I simply said yes."

"Thank you, thank you, thank you. When do I start?"

"Two weeks on Monday. That should give you enough time to inform your other job?"

"Yes, definitely."

"I will have my assistant send all the details over in an email this afternoon. I look forward to working with you, Ashley."

"You too. Thank you again."

"You're welcome. Enjoy the rest of your day."

Immediately, her eyes sparkled, tears formed as she raced towards the bedroom where Madison lay sound asleep. The skin under her eyes wrinkled from the uncontrollable grin as she barged through the door and danced around the room, swelling with pride.

"I got the job. I got the job. I got the freaking job! I can't believe it."

Ashley skipped her way around the bedroom. Then without warning, launched herself onto Madison. Half asleep, she abruptly crunched inwards to protect herself from the puppy-like onslaught.

"Ash," she groaned, "I'm tired."

"I know, but did you not hear me? I got the job!"

"You got the job?" Madison clarified.

"Yes!"

"YOU GOT THE JOB?" Clarification turned into a high-pitched scream.

"Can you believe it?"

"Ash, that's amazing. I am so proud of you. Come here." They embraced emphatically, jubilant in a moment of spectacular joy. Ashley had finally caught the break she so desperately wanted. A chance to start a career in the industry that would bring her a sense of belonging and purpose—or at least she hoped it would. She knew in her heart that something was missing from her life. She had no job satisfaction working in bars. Instead, she longed for late nights in the newsroom, delving into the next leading story.

There was a bang on the door and it flew open to reveal Emily stood there, eyelids heavy and arms tightly crossed.

"I literally didn't get to sleep until two this morning. I have the week off, which means I don't want to see pre-lunchtime, and here you are being obnoxiously loud. What on earth is all the noise?"

"Guess what?" Ashley lunged from the bed.

Emily scowled. "This better be good."

"I...got...THE JOB!"

Emily unfolded her arms rapidly and ran towards Ashley, omitting a piercing shriek. With a hop, skip and a jump, she contorted herself into a position that wrapped her elongated limbs around Ashley's body.

"I am so, so, so proud of you! I knew you'd do it!"

"Thanks, Em. I'm sorry for waking you."

"Oh, I don't care about that now. This is worth being woken up for." Emily stood back and pulled down the oversized band t-shirt that had ridden up the full length of her back. "The question is, how are we going to celebrate?"

"That's a very good question." They both glanced towards Madison.

"What?"

"It's your time."

Madison rolled her eyes. "I'll sort something. Shall we say Friday night?"

"Sounds perfect."

19

Megan

The sun shone on downtown Nashville. Megan had been there four days, exploring all that the capital of country music had to offer. As she strolled through the iconic streets, something amazed her at every turn. Historic buildings, music attractions, boutique hotels and art galleries. The legendary honky tonk highway was her destination of choice. She was yet to experience it during the day, but the night before had been electric. Hanging with her parents wasn't too bad. When she was sixteen years old, it was the most uncool thing in the world. Now, she enjoyed their company.

They were staying at her dad's friend's holiday home for the week. The three-bedroom apartment in Cumberland Heights had the most amazing panoramic views of Nashville. The trip was very much a business trip for her parents, who had meetings with developers scheduled for most of the week. That left Megan to her own devices through the day; time to really take in Nashville, Tennessee, in all its glory.

The southern hospitality charmed her into thinking she could one day live there. The vibrant neon lights and energetic atmosphere were everything she imagined they would be. She strolled along 12th Avenue towards Broadway and for the second time that week, she came across Amelia's flower truck. The old cream Volkswagen truck looked vintage and homely, presenting an array of beautifully coloured flowers—the extremely adorable Labrador retriever popping its head curiously through the driver's seat window—tactfully, or not—helped the curb appeal.

Megan watched as a woman in a pink apron gracefully arranged a bouquet for a customer. She watched intently as each individual flower was picked and placed, finished off with brown paper and a cream bow.

"Hi there, can I get you something?"

Megan realised the woman was talking to her. "Oh sorry, I was just admiring your truck."

"Please, take a closer look. There is no pressure to purchase, we are just trying to spread the word with being a new business and all."

Megan loved the strong southern drawl with which she spoke.

"How long have you been here?"

"Only a couple of weeks."

"What's your dog called?" Megan reached towards the window to pet the excitable pooch.

"That's Dolly."

"Named after Dolly Parton?"

"You bet." The woman pointed towards the small sticker on the side of the truck that read, *'I'm working 9–5, just like Dolly.'*

"That's clever."

"Thank you. Does anything catch your eye?"

"I'm only here on vacation for another three days. Can any of them last two plane rides and a squashed suitcase back to England?" Megan joked.

"I wish, I would make a lot more money if that were the case, darlin'." The darling was drawn out to sound more like *'daaaarrrlinn'*—she grinned. "Here, wait a minute."

Megan watched as the florist gathered some Pink Waxflower, Italian Ruscus, White Stocks and Roses. She wrapped them neatly as she had done for the previous customer, adding a little white sticker on the front for extra presentation.

"These are on the house."

"What? No, I can't. Please let me pay for them."

The woman, whose name badge was now visible, was called Carrie. She held up her hand, protesting. "They'd only get thrown out later tonight, don't worry. It just gives you something pretty to look at for the next few days."

"I feel too bad. At least let me leave a tip?" Megan searched around for some cash. Carrie placed her hand on Megan's arm.

"There is no need. If it makes you feel any better, a pretty face like yours walking around town holding that bouquet is free advertising for me."

"I don't know about that, but thank you. Really, it's really kind of you. You've made my day."

"Then that's good enough for me."

"I will take a picture and tag you on social media if you'd like?"

Carrie beamed. "That would be great. You have a nice day now."

"You too. Take care."

Megan snapped a quick picture in front of the truck and waved goodbye with the flowers in hand. She posted the photo and five minutes later, she had a follow request from Carrie. It wasn't until then that it dawned on her. *Had she just been hit on?* Either way, she liked it.

The day before she'd been to Boot Barn, after trying on eight different pairs, the store assistant convinced her to purchase a pair of Idyllwind square-toe Western boots—apparently, Miranda Lambert wore them—that was enough to convince her. Despite the hefty price tag and the guaranteed fact that she would probably never wear them again, it didn't matter, because she felt like she belonged, even if it was just for a few days—that was worth the expense. She'd also found some vintage cut-off shorts and a plaid shirt in a local thrift store, when pieced together she was pleased with the outfit.

Passing the Music City Walk of Fame Park, Megan continued the route towards the riverfront. A local she'd met the day before recommended a rooftop breakfast bar that she forgot to write down, but she figured she'd stumble across a suitable place, eventually. Flowers in hand, she continued to explore.

***

The waitress at Biscuit Love took her order and sped off towards the counter, collecting plates as she went. Megan observed the grace with which she moved, clearly gained through years of experience. She had been warned of the wait outside due to the popularity of the Nashville bistro, and she was surprised to be seated fifteen minutes later. The concrete floors and high ceilings with heavy wood metal-framed tables and chairs gave the place an industrial feel. It was lunchtime and Megan had skipped breakfast, so the burning sensation in her stomach accompanied the rumbling sound like thunder in the distance.

The waitress had been kind enough to explain the menu, which was broadly divided into two categories:

"on a biscuit" or not. The concept of biscuit and breakfast together felt unusual, but the reviews had reassured her of a breakfast like no other. Opting for the Southern Benny, which consisted of a biscuit covered in shaved country ham, egg and country-style sausage gravy. Megan saw it as the south's version of Eggs Benedict—a dish she enjoyed regularly in England.

Whilst she waited for her food to arrive, she called Nancy back.

"Hi, sweetheart."

"Hi, Gram, are you okay?"

"Yes, darling, I'm fine. I just wanted to make sure you were enjoying your time in Nashville."

"I'm loving it, Gram. It's everything I hoped it would be."

"I'm happy to hear that. Did you go to The Country Music Hall of Fame?"

"Is the sky blue?" Megan joked. "Of course, I did. It was the first place I went."

"What about Music Row?"

"I went yesterday."

"And?"

"It was exactly how you described it."

"Did you see the studio where Elvis recorded?"

"Yes, Mom and I took one of the tours so we could learn all about it. The whole thing was fascinating."

"I'm so glad you're enjoying it, and what are you doing today?"

"I'm currently waiting for my lunch to arrive. Then I'll head out into the neighbourhood and take a look around, maybe treat myself a little."

"I don't blame you, sweetheart."

"How are things at the bar, anyway? Dad mentioned you'd been having some staffing issues."

"We had someone leave and Alec has been ill, but it's nothing we can't handle. Ashley helped out the last couple of days and she said Madison will too if we get desperate, so we have it covered."

Megan's posture stiffened, rooted in place. The growl of her stomach became more vocal. "Ashley? That's nice of her."

"She'll always help if we are desperate. She's a good girl."

"I find it so bizarre."

"What?"

"That I met a girl, got her to write your love story, and now you see her more than me. I feel like you gained another grandchild."

"Darling, I will only ever have one grandchild and nobody can compare to you, but I am grateful for you bringing Ashley into our lives. She's one of the good ones."

Didn't she know it.

"I know she is. I'm glad she's there to help you. You know I would if I could."

"As much as I appreciate the gesture, sweetheart, I remember the last time you helped me behind the bar."

Megan laughed, "Gram, I was like ten years old." She recalled the faded memory from her childhood, a flash of broken glasses and a lively ER waiting room.

"Your mom practically banned me from looking after you after that incident. I was the irresponsible Grandma. Your dad saw the funny side after you were stitched up and back shooting a basketball."

"I always had the best time with you, Gram, even in the emergency room." Megan pulled her elbow towards her eye line to see the five-inch jagged scar along her forearm. It had faded over time and was now simply a story to tell. The time she dropped a tray of glasses, attempted to pick them up and slipped onto the broken glass, wedging a large piece in her forearm—it wasn't exactly a party trick.

"Me too, darling, even if you did give me a heart attack 99% of the time."

The memories of her younger years were clouded by the thought of one person. Since her name had been mentioned, Megan was desperate to ask.

"How is Ashley, anyway?"

She'd seen Ashley less than two weeks ago, but other than a courtesy text to let her know she'd gotten home safe, their conversation had once again become disconnected.

"She seems great. She got the job at *The New York Times*. I believe they're out celebrating tonight because she said it was the only day she couldn't help behind the bar."

"That's amazing. I knew she would. Will you tell her congratulations from me?"

"Of course, but I'm sure you could text her yourself?"

The thought crossed her mind more than she cared to admit, but she refrained. Megan's gram assumed they were friends, that they spoke regularly and that no long-serving tension existed—she was wrong.

"I could, that's true."

"Did she tell you she's planning to ask Madison to be her girlfriend tonight?"

The gulp of fresh orange juice went down the wrong way. She spluttered and choked trying to catch her breath.

"Sorry." Her eyes filled with water, overflowing as she tried to compose herself. The tears were a result of the choking fit she'd just endured, but even after she'd steadied her breathing, the tears didn't stop. She dabbed at the corners of her eyes with her shirt sleeve, conscious of attracting any more attention. "To be honest, Gram, I thought they already were together."

That was an outright lie, she knew they weren't, Ashley had told her directly that they were quote, *'seeing each other'*, but she figured there was no need to make Nancy feel uncomfortable.

"No, according to Ashley, she didn't want to rush into anything, but she feels now is the right time."

"Oh, really? I wonder what changed her mind."

"She said something about finally understanding the reality of what was holding her back. She must have had an overnight epiphany. Either way, they seem good together so it's the right decision for her."

"I agree." She didn't want to make a habit of lying to Nancy, but she saw no other way.

"Oh, I didn't tell you, we got the permit through yesterday for the re-model."

"Gram, that's amazing."

"I'm not so sure. I think I'm a little too old to be doing this sort of thing, but the contractor we hired seems to have everything under control."

"Just take it easy. I don't want you tearing through walls and ripping out fittings." Megan chuckled at the thought.

"Maybe in my younger years, but I think I'll leave that to the professionals now."

Megan eyed the waitress, who was heading towards her table balancing three orders in her arms.

"Sorry, Gram, my food's just arrived. I'll call you in a few days, okay?"

"Okay, sweetheart. Enjoy the rest of your day."

"Thanks, Gram, love you."

"Love you too."

The food looked incredible, but the burn in her stomach had subsided and was replaced by a lump in her throat as she slumped back in the chair. She stared at her phone, contemplating the numerous avenues she could take. There was no doubt in her mind she wanted to speak to Ashley—she always did—but the internal struggle told her it wasn't any of her business. Surely she could congratulate her on the new job? That would be a nice thing to do, something a good friend would do. Deep down she knew that was simply a passageway in to ask the questions that really occupied her mind. *Why have you asked her now to be your girlfriend? What changed your mind? What was the revelation? Do you ever think about me? Us?* The questions flooded her subconscious. She picked at the food, her appetite diminished, but she didn't want to come across as rude.

Above all else, she wanted to know why every time they saw each other, the chemistry was so electric and the conversation so easy—it was a familiar warmth she didn't experience with anyone else. Why, after each encounter, did they lose contact? Was it just the distance that posed too many problems? Or did she not feel the same? Did she not ache at the thought of her with someone else? The kind of ache that starts at the pit of your stomach and slowly works its way up, day by day. At first, it's unnoticeable, but over time it grows stronger and before you know it you're spiralling into the unknown, waiting for someone, anyone, to break you free from the maze inside your head.

20

Ashley

"When are you going to ask her?" Emily questioned.

Ashley put her finger to her lips, gesturing for Emily to be quiet.

"Don't make it a big deal."

"It is a big deal."

"No, it's not. Nothing will change. It's a label, that's all."

"It is a huge deal. You're exclusively committing yourself to one person."

"You're talking like I'm about to propose."

"One day you might."

"If you carry on, I won't ask."

"Oh yeah, because that's such a punishment for me." Emily rolled her eyes.

"You're annoying."

"Thank you, that's so kind."

Jason entered Emily's bedroom and perched elegantly on the edge of the bed. Ashley noted the outfit of choice for the evening was a garish one—no surprise.

"What are my little MVPs talking about in here?"

Ashley grinned at the newest nickname to make the cut.

"Not talking as such, more like Emily annoying me beyond belief and me wondering when she became so irritating."

"So, a normal Friday night, then?"

"Exactly." Ashley pointed triumphantly towards Jason.

"In your honest opinion, is this outfit too much?" Jason stood twirling and posing like something out of *America's Next Top Model.*

"The blue leather suit is iconic," Ashley confirmed.

"Agreed. Only you could pull that off with a mesh top."

"Girls, you flatter me," Jason moved his hands over his outfit and stood hand on hip, "but would Tyra Banks approve?"

"I think she'd say every hallway is a runway, honey, so work it." Ashley figured quoting back his favourite Tyra quote would do the trick.

"Yes! I couldn't agree more!" There was a brief pause. "Tyra might also ask how you're feeling about tonight?"

"Not you as well." Ashley glanced towards the bathroom door. The shower was still running so Madison wouldn't be able to hear.

"Have you thought about it?"

"What is there to think about? I'm just going to ask her a simple question."

"True, but you're not going to ask her at the end of the night absolutely wasted in the backseat of a cab," he raised his eyebrow, "right? I mean, unless that's your plan."

"No, of course not."

"So?"

"I was just going to ask her when the moment felt right. Maybe before we leave, on our own. I don't think she'll be surprised. We are practically a couple anyway."

"I disagree," Jason challenged.

Emily agreed, "Me too."

"What do you mean?"

"Madison has been waiting for you to make it official for six months, Ash! That's a long time."

"She agreed we should take it slow though. It's not just her that's been waiting for me."

"Is it not? Why isn't she asking you then?" Jason made a valid point.

"Okay, that's fair. Has she said something to you?" The question was directed at both of them.

"Nothing you won't already know," Jason said.

"Like what?"

"She loves you and she would have asked you within weeks to be her girlfriend. I think she thought you were still hung up on the other girl."

Ashley knew immediately who Jason was referring to, but playing dumb seemed the safer option.

"The other girl?"

The corner of Jason's lip curled into a mischievous grin. "Megan. The one you almost kissed the other week?"

"Shhhhh," Ashley frantically waved her hands at Jason, "don't let Mads hear you say that."

He held his hands up apologetically. "Sorry."

"Anyway, why would she think that? She's never said that to me. Megan was someone I went on one date with two years ago! I barely even speak to her now. We are friends and Madison has nothing to worry about."

"Do you think that's friendship? I think Megan disagrees." Jason made a kissing face at Ashley. Emily played along.

"It's probably not a traditional friendship, no."

"You're in denial if you think it's a friendship. If it was, you'd talk often about random things with no flirtatious intent. Like we do, or you and Emily."

"You guys are my best friends. Megan is just a friend. One that happens to live thousands of miles away. There's a difference."

"If you say so."

"Now you're both annoying me."

"That tends to happen when you're in denial," Jason prodded.

"I know you like to wind me up, but genuinely, is that what you think? That I am somehow disingenuous towards Madison because I want somebody else?"

They looked at each other, debating who should answer first. "Okay, I'll take this one." Emily propped herself up on her elbows. "I think subconsciously it's maybe holding you back. Just from things you've said to me in the past and the way you talk about Megan."

"I barely speak to Megan or see her. I don't understand how that can translate to 'she's holding me back'." Ashley tilted her head quizzically.

"That's just my observation. Do you not talk to her because you don't want to? Or because you feel that's the best way to keep things platonic?" Emily's point resonated with Ashley. *Was that the reason why they didn't talk?*

"I don't know. I don't really think about it."

"You don't think about talking to her?" Jason questioned.

"No, I don't think about why I don't talk to her. Life just moves on."

"It does, but if you don't allow yourself to move on with it, you'll always be thinking about the past."

Ashley stood and strolled towards the window. The streets had darkened as the sun set behind the skyscrapers.

"I think we are going off on a tangent here. Tonight is supposed to be about me asking Madison to be exclusive."

"Okay, can I ask one more question?" Jason said.

"Yes, be quick though." Ashley eyed the bathroom door. The continuous wash of the shower had stopped.

"Do you love her?" Jason quietly mouthed the words, pointing towards the bathroom so there would be no confusion as to who the question referred to.

Ashley didn't hesitate, "Yes, I do."

"Then that's all that matters." Jason stood followed by Emily as they circled their best friend for a three-way hug.

"I'm so excited for you two," Emily chirped.

Ashley felt the warmth of her friends. The life she had created for herself was one she should be extremely proud of, but the niggling feeling that had been present on and off for months appeared once again. There was something within her body that remained cautious whenever she felt a surge of happiness. Whenever she felt as though her life was on the right path, it pulled her back like a fierce fire burning in the pit of her stomach, reminding her that not all was as it seemed. There was something missing, some emotional investment that she held back. Yet, here she was, about to ask Madison to be her girlfriend because it was the right thing to do, it was the honourable thing to do, and when she really searched herself, she knew deep down that the love she had for her would last a lifetime, through hell and high water if that's what was required. However, like a large stop sign in her mind, there was always a 'but'. Ashley pushed any doubt away, reciting to herself over and over in her mind, *the grass isn't always greener, the grass isn't always greener.*

Madison entered the room with a black towel wrapped around her body, tied just above her breasts. The water glistened as drops ran slowly down her skin. The New York summer had already given her a sun-kissed glow. Her hair always changed in the summer and Ashley noted the ends turning a lighter shade of brown.

"Why are you hugging?"

"No reason," Ashley said.

"Just love my friends that's all," Emily responded.

"And I just love hugs." Jason skipped over to Madison and wrapped his arms around her waist, lifting her slightly off the ground.

"All three of you are being weird, but I don't have time to figure out why."

"Why are you so late getting ready anyway?" Jason questioned, placing her back on two feet.

"I had to work a shift today. We were understaffed."

"Joys of being the manager, honey."

"Tell me about it. If only I could pay myself triple-time for the inconvenience."

"I hear you!" Jason preached.

Madison walked towards Ashley and allowed her lips to brush against hers delicately.

"Hey, you." She squeezed her hand and wandered towards the wardrobe in the corner. It was a sweet, brief moment that sent a shiver through Ashley's whole body.

"Em, where are those jeans I let you borrow the other week?" Madison searched the wardrobe to no avail.

"They're at the dry cleaners," Emily responded sheepishly.

"Why would they be at the dry cleaners?"

"I spilled a teeny tiny bit of red wine on them."

Madison flapped her arms up and down like a bird. "Why am I not surprised?"

"Luckily for you, we are the same size and I have a drawer full of jeans you can borrow."

Madison opened said drawer and pulled out the first pair.

"Except those ones," Emily removed them from her grasp, "or those. Actually, they are really expensive so maybe not those either."

Jason wrapped his arm around Ashley and led her towards the door. "I think we can leave them to it. Drink?"

"I thought you'd never ask."

***

Jason poured himself another glass of bourbon as Ashley observed. It was only her second compared to Jason's fourth and she already felt tipsy. They sat comfortably, listening to some R&B classics whilst Emily and Madison finished applying their makeup.

Like almost everyone, Ashley experienced moments of déjà vu; she remembered the last time she'd experienced the uncanny sensation. The year before, she'd been paddle-boarding with Emily and Madison. Whilst her arms motioned underneath her body, gliding across the glistening water of Lake Ontario, she had a distinct memory of being under the same clear blue sky, feeling the warmth of the sun on her back and the waves lapping gracefully at her feet. Before that, it happened in New York, when she entered a neighbourhood unknown to her. Although she felt lost and disorientated by her whereabouts, a part of her remembered the same tree-lined street, despite not being able to connect it to a time in her mind—the unsettled feeling faded quickly.

There were many other times throughout her life that she failed to recall, but she remembered the feeling and compared it to the one she felt at that moment. Looking down at her phone, she saw a picture of Megan. The picture had been taken earlier that morning and uploaded to all her social media platforms. She felt an irrepressible urge to smile as she observed the photo. Megan stood with a bunch of flowers in front of a VW truck. The photo was beautifully staged with perfect surrounding colours complimenting the flowers in the background. Then there was Megan; the Nashville summer sun beating down on her glowing skin, her eyes as pretty as the lotus petals in the background, her smile so wide the edges of her mouth crinkled, creating another set of dimples to accompany her already present ones. Ashley couldn't help but feel captivated by her beauty, a genuine smile that revealed her soul to the world. It was rare, that kind of irrefutable beauty that made you stare over and over again with no reason other than to admire the elegance on show.

That's when Ashley felt the fleeting sense of déjà vu. The picture seemed familiar; the way she posed with the flowers. Jason being present, offering Ashley another drink. Then when Jason spoke, it felt even more surreal.

"Why are you grinning like that?"

"Nothing."

"Is Madison sending you rude messages from the other room? I'll be having words with her." Jason walked towards the bedroom.

"Jason, that's not it at all. Don't go in there."

He raised his eyebrow inquisitively. "Not from Madison then?"

"I haven't received anything from anyone I was just smiling at a video."

Ashley was a terrible liar. She knew there was no way he'd believe her.

"Prove it." Ashley looked at her feet, any eye contact broken. "Megan?"

She nodded. No words were needed.

"Can't I smile at a photo now?" Ashley challenged.

"Sure. No judgement here."

Except he was judging, and Ashley could sense it.

"Have you ever felt a strong sense of déjà vu, but you're almost certain it hasn't happened before?"

"Of course, all the time. Do you feel that now?"

"Yes, weirdly."

"What do you think about it? Some people like to believe that you've been there in a previous life, others are more scientific."

"What's the scientific theory?"

"I looked it up once. It's described as a conflict in your mind between the sensation of familiarity and the awareness that the same familiarity is in fact incorrect."

"So your mind's playing tricks on you?"

"I guess you could say that. Apparently, as you get older, you don't experience it as much because your mind gets weaker."

"I think I'd prefer to believe in the fantasy version."

"Me too," Jason agreed. "Maybe you should write about that."

"What?"

"Déjà vu—people's beliefs and experiences."

"You think people would be interested in reading that?"

"I would."

"That explains a lot," Ashley joked.

"I need to tinkle so I'll leave you to stare at your imaginary girlfriend some more."

"It's not imaginary if they're a real person, you idiot," Ashley called. She got the middle finger in return.

Alone with her thoughts, she observed the picture one last time. Her finger hovered over the like button; back and forth across the screen went her thumb indecisively. That was the moment she realised there was more to her feelings than she'd anticipated. The inability to like a photo based solely on some warped idea of how she *should* act was the icing on the cake. The reality was she wouldn't have to think about liking it at all if they were purely *just friends*—she knew that.

Truth be told, none of it mattered. She'd already made up her mind and rarely did it change.

21

9 months later
Ashley

'Is it too soon?'

That was the question Ashley had asked herself every day since the beginning of February when she'd purchased the solitaire diamond ring. A whole three months' wages, that's what she'd spent, as directed by whoever came up with that stupid rule in the first place. She was thousands of dollars lighter and excruciatingly nervous. It did make her wonder whether she was cut out for such a feat—marriage. It hadn't ended well for her parents or the other 50% of Americans whose marriage ended in divorce. On the plus side, same-sex marriage had been legalised in the state of New York as of June 24, 2011—so that was one less concern.

The pressure had mounted throughout the winter months. Despite their short-lived romantic relationship, they'd known each other for an extensive period of time—eighteen years to be exact. Madison had been quick to accept Ashley's girlfriend proposal nine months prior. Since then, they'd been inseparable. The commitment was exactly what she needed; a stable loving partner with whom she could build a future. They wanted all the same things, they had the same morals, the same friendship circle, their families adored one another and most importantly, they lived in the same city and had done since they were kids.

All that being said, she felt uncertainty creep in from time to time. Was the choice to propose solely her own? Or had the pressure of friends and Madison's childhood dreams of getting married swayed her decision? All Ashley wanted was to make her happy—Madison deserved that. She was kind-hearted and naive to a degree. She needed that someone to sweep her off her feet and promise the rest of their lives. Ashley wanted to be that person for her; she had no doubt about that. *Then why the niggling self-doubt?*

She mumbled to herself, "Is it too soon?".

Emily's ears pricked up. "Is what too soon?"

"Nothing."

Emily wasn't aware of the ring or the proposal. On numerous occasions, Ashley had wanted to tell her, but instantly she would tell Jason and then they'd never let it slide. The added pressure would be too much. She accepted that Emily would be angry; she would deal with that afterwards.

Ashley went down the traditional route of asking for Madison's hand. She'd gone to the cemetery where her father lay to ask his permission. No thunder cloud appeared above her head and no strike of lightning, so she could only assume he would be happy for them.

The idea of marriage felt like more of an expectation than a desire. She wondered whether anyone else felt the same. There was an unwritten rule that said you will get married, you will have kids, you will have a stable job that contributes nicely towards your retirement fund, you will retire on time and live out the rest of your days playing with your grandkids and reading on your porch. Some people wanted that life—would die for that life— but Ashley questioned whether that was the life for her. *That's natural*, she told herself. Such a life-changing event brings out the deep, rumbling concerns we didn't know existed.

"You've been acting weird lately," Emily said.

"I have not."

"Yes, you definitely have."

"How?"

"You've been weird and secretive. You're up to something." Emily placed her hand on her hip.

"I am not up to anything."

"Right, well if I find out you are and you've lied to me, I'll be extremely upset."

"As if." Emily would forgive her one day—she hoped.

"Where are you going tonight? Madison said you guys are going out."

"The Campbell Bar."

"Is that the one at Grand Central?"

"That's the one."

New York was famous for a lot of things and marriage proposals were right up there. Who wouldn't want to get engaged in The Big Apple? Ashley had seen numerous proposals play out before her eyes. Low-key, simple settings like Central Park to grand public gestures in the centre of a crowded Times Square or at the top of the Empire State Building. The opportunities were endless, but for Ashley, the idea had come to her rather easily.

Grand Central Terminal, the place it all began. They'd arrived there on the 11:00 p.m. train five years earlier, with nothing but hopes and dreams of starting their life in the city. They'd spent the whole day loading the truck and ferrying their belongings up and down the stairs to their new apartment. They returned the truck to Ashley's cousin and took the train back into the city.

When they arrived like two giddy children on a school trip, they spun around in the middle of Grand Central station amongst the crowds without a care in the world, admiring the famous building for what it was—a landmark, a movie hotspot and the terminal of dreams. They'd gone for celebratory cocktails at The Campbell Bar that night—it was one of the best nights of her life. The start of her new life. And now, it felt like she had come full circle. Some might say she was about to start her life again.

"My plans fell through tonight. Can't I come?"

Emily's neediness had been at an all-time high since her recent break-up.

"Not really."

"Wow, thanks."

"I don't mean that in a nasty way. Mads and I just haven't had any time together lately. I want it to be special." Ashley cringed at the dishonesty.

"Fair enough."

"You're not mad, are you?"

"No, I get it."

"Pinky swear?"

"Yes, now leave me alone whilst I try and make other plans."

"Are you allergic to staying in on your own?" Ashley felt it was a genuine possibility.

"Maybe. It's lonely."

"Still can't stop thinking about Stephanie?"

"Something like that."

They'd broken up two weeks earlier. It was declared a mutual agreement, but the mutual was more of a wish than a fact on Emily's part.

"Have you tried talking to her about how you feel? Maybe she feels the same?"

"She won't answer my calls."

"Why?"

"I think I offended her."

"You think?"

Emily winced. "I definitely did."

"What did you do?" Ashley said, frowning.

"I accused her of moving on suspiciously fast. I basically said she must have been cheating on me when we were together," Emily cringed.

"Do you really believe that?"

"No, but now she won't talk to me."

"Were you drunk when you accused her of these things?" Ashley said.

"I was slightly intoxicated, yes. What's your point?"

"You're an idiot when you're drunk, everybody knows that. I'm surprised she's not just accepted it and forgiven you already."

"I've attempted to call her and text her a dozen times. No response." Emily sagged in the armchair, frustrated by her own lunacy.

"Okay, I can see it's bothering you and I don't want you sitting here all night on your own."

Emily perked up. "So?"

"So, you can be a part of the evening I have planned."

"Yay!" She jumped from her seat and threw her arms around Ashley. "Wait, what do you mean 'be a part of'?"

"There is a little more to the evening than just dinner at The Campbell Bar."

Emily's eyes lit up. "What do you mean?"

"If I tell you, you have to keep it a secret, and I mean it, you can't go acting all strange for the rest of the night."

"No to strange, got ya."

Ashley took a deep breath and prepared for the squeals. "Here we go," she mumbled.

***

The *'whispering gallery'* inside Grand Central Station, as it's referred to, was an acoustic oddity Ashley was yet to experience. She had only heard of the unusually perfect archways on the lower level that could carry the sound of your whisper. After asking around, it seemed to be true, but she was yet to test it herself.

"What are we doing?" Madison laughed.

"Trust me, I heard about this from some people at work. I want us to try it."

"Try standing against a wall? This isn't my idea of a date night."

"Very funny. Apparently, if you face the wall at that side of the archway and I do it at this side we should be able to hear each other."

Madison raised her eyebrow. "Have you gone mad?"

"Trust me. Face the wall," Ashley said as she made her way to the opposite side. Reluctantly, Madison turned to face the wall. She stood right in the corner of the arch between two parts of the wall that extended out.

Once Ashley reached the opposite side, she did the same. The smell of concrete filled her nostrils. *Here goes nothing*, she thought.

"Can you hear me?"

"Yes!" Madison giggled, "I can actually hear you."

"Crazy, right? I wasn't sure if it would work."

"It's so weird. I do feel a bit silly though," Madison confessed.

"Do you not remember when we first arrived in the city and we saw a couple doing this?"

"I don't think so."

"Course you do. We laughed uncontrollably for about five minutes because you pretended to be a teacher telling them off."

There was a delay in conversation as the soundwaves made their way across the arch. One or two words sounded muffled, but they managed to piece together the majority.

"Oh, of course! I'd put them in the naughty corner," Madison chuckled.

"We thought they were strange. Little did we know this was what they were doing."

"Okay?"

"You're wondering why I'm making you stand here, aren't you?"

"Kind of."

"I was curious to see if it worked, but I also wanted to try something."

"What?"

"Listen very carefully."

Ashley took a deep breath. *This was it*, she said to herself. The moment of truth. Without further ado, the words she'd been fearing all day left her lips.

"Will you marry me?"

Madison paused, her voice shaky, "What did you say?"

Ashley quickly went the length of the terminal to land behind where Madison stood. Dropping swiftly to one knee, she held the small black box in her hand, now open, revealing the gold-banded square solitaire diamond. She could feel the beat of her heart throughout her whole body, vibrating like a sound system cranked all the way up.

"I said…will you marry me?"

Madison spun around. "Oh…my…God," her hand flew to her mouth. "are you serious? Really? You want to marry me?"

Ashley noted the commuters who had stopped in their tracks, waiting for an answer to the most important question Ashley would ever ask.

"I wouldn't ask you if I didn't." She laughed. The silence was unbearable. "Well?"

"Yes, 100% yes. I will marry you."

Ashley placed the ring delicately onto Madison's finger.

"Wow, like wow. It's incredible."

"You like it?" Ashley grinned.

Madison held her hand towards the light, wiggling her fingers. The shine of the diamond like a star in the clear night sky. "I absolutely love it."

The commuters who'd taken the time to observe began to clap. Ashley pulled Madison closer. If there was one occasion fit for public displays of affection it was a proposal. They kissed softly, repeatedly, as the tears began to fall.

"I hope they're happy tears?" Ashley said.

Madison grinned. "The happiest tears anyone could cry."

***

The Campbell Bar was a historic architectural masterpiece with a contemporary twist. The hand-painted ceilings soared twenty-five feet above the ground and century-old lead glass windows were the backdrop for the contemporary gold and black bar. Every part of the room was so thoughtfully curated, from the bold brass finish to the green leather furnishings. They took a seat over by the grand stone fireplace. Their cocktails arrived promptly—a Moscow Mule along with an Old Fashioned.

Ashley raised her glass, "To us."

"And our future," Madison finished.

She took a sip of her drink. Thankfully, the nerves had subsided allowing her to enjoy the night.

"Thank you for indulging me."

"By dancing in the terminal?" Ashley nodded. "You buy me a ring like this and I'll dance naked in the middle of a crowded arena."

"You will not! I can't have everyone else seeing my fiancée naked."

"That sounds weird, being someone's fiancée."

Ashley shrugged indicating it wasn't that big of a deal. "I'm kidding. It's a huge deal." She winked.

"Is there a twenty-four-hour window where I can revoke my answer? Just in case." Madison teased.

"Nope, it's set in stone now. You're all mine forever and ever," Ashley laughed like a villain.

"Suppose people have had to deal with worse."

The strong smell of lime juice from her Moscow Mule filled her senses. "Do you know why I brought you here at this time?"

"No," Madison said, shaking her head.

"This is the time we arrived in New York City five years ago."

"Really? How do you remember things like that?"

"I only remember the important things."

"I did think it was a little late, you know. You were stalling at dinner earlier. Now it makes sense."

Ashley sat back in the chair and told the story. "We arrived at 11:00 p.m., we saw a couple at the whispering arch and then we came to this very bar and sat in these very seats. If you remember we were so annoyed because it shut at midnight."

"And the bartender let us stay whilst he cleared up!"

"Yes, he was great! I think I recall asking you to get his number." Ashley smirked, "Ah, the days when you weren't sure if you were ready to give up men for good."

"Well, there's no going back now is there." Madison flashed her diamond ring.

"The reason I brought you here is to see how we've come full circle; that was the start of our new life. At the time, we were best friends, but even so, you were still the person I wanted to explore life with. It's nostalgic in a way. Now, you're still the person I want to explore life with, except I want you to do it as my wife."

"You'll make me cry again." Madison dabbed the corner of her eyes with a napkin. "Thank you, for doing everything so perfectly." She reached across the table to intertwine her fingers with Ashley's.

"You deserve perfect."

"What I want to know is, did you have any help choosing this gorgeous ring?" Madison admired the rock on her finger once again.

"Nope. I'm your best friend as well, remember. I know what your ideal ring would be. You never stopped talking about it after we saw it in the window of Louis Martin."

"Is this the exact one?"

"Of course."

"Wow, I knew it looked similar, but I can't believe it's that ring. I saw that before we were together."

"I know. Luckily, they still stocked it."

"You're amazing, do you know that?"

"I try." Ashley winked.

Madison leaned across the table and delicately kissed Ashley on the lips. It was sweet and affectionate; a true sign of the love they had for one another.

"What about Em? Does she know?" Madison questioned.

She executed the poker face to perfection. "No."

"You didn't tell her? Oh, dear."

"You know she would have told you before I did. She's a nightmare. I'm sure she'll get over it." Little did Madison know that Emily and Jason were already planning the celebrations back home.

"Yeah, maybe by the time the wedding comes around. Shall I ring her and tell her?"

"No, wait until we get home. She'll be so excited in person she might forget I didn't tell her."

"Wishful thinking. Does my mom know?"

"Not quite."

Madison raised an inquisitive eyebrow. "What do you mean?"

"I didn't tell her."

"Oh."

"Your mom scares me. I figured it would be better coming from you."

"You're such a chicken. She loves you."

"Yeah, but does she love me enough to let me marry her daughter? Bearing in mind, three months ago, she asked you if you'd seen your childhood boyfriend whilst you were back in town."

"You know she didn't mean it like that. We stayed good friends."

"Either way, I'd prefer you to tell her."

She rolled her eyes. "I'll call her tomorrow."

"I did ask your dad, though." Ashley smiled sincerely.

"You went to his grave?"

"Yes, the last time I went to visit my mom. I remember going with you when we were growing up, but it's been a while. We had a good chat."

"I can't imagine he had much to say." Madison smiled softly. She was openly able to talk about her father's death. After almost fifteen years, it still felt surreal to her that he wasn't around, but she firmly believed he was always watching over her which allowed the trauma to fade over time.

"Well, this is how I interpreted the conversation."

"Here we go." Madison laughed.

"Basically, in a nutshell, he said I was the perfect person for his daughter—really kind, funny, polite, attractive—everything you could want really. He even went as far as to say that you would be absolutely insane to say no. He said as long as I look after his little girl, then I have his blessing."

"He said all that did he? Even the attractive part?"

"His words not mine." Ashley shrugged.

"Well, I totally agree with him."

The bartender arrived with two glasses of champagne. "We heard you just got engaged. Congratulations! This one's on us."

"Thank you so much."

"You were confident I'd say yes." Madison laughed.

The drinks must have been arranged by Emily or Jason because Ashley hadn't called ahead, but she played along.

"Well, I told them if we looked upset and in deep discussion to not bring them over."

"Good thinking. On a serious note, thank you for going to my dad's grave. That's really sweet. It means a lot."

"I knew it would. I left a bunch of flowers too."

"Thank you, baby."

Ashley raised her glass for the second time. The thought of actually getting married—walking down the aisle in front of all their friends and family—suddenly hit her. Until that point, it had been just the proposal, an act of love that displayed her long-term dedication to be with Madison. The planning of the wedding hadn't even occurred to her, which admittedly she knew was odd, but she'd always been a one-step-at-a-time kind of girl.

Then, like a high-speed train, Megan's face appeared in her mind. One second, she was there, the next gone. A flash, but it was enough to trigger an invasion of the calming, joyful aura she'd tried to portray all night. The flash was enough to consume her thoughts as she smiled, composed and in the moment, but her mind had wandered elsewhere. *How would Megan feel about the proposal?* They hadn't spoken in months, so did it really matter? The night was about Madison and her, about her proposal to the girl she loved. She knew better than to dwell once again on the past. Ashley determined that was easier said than done.

22

Megan

The applause from the crowd grew more intense with each second. The shot clock reset for the final time. The last possession, if run as planned, would leave just 0.8 seconds on the clock with no time-outs. The other team would have a very slim chance of taking it to overtime. Megan had been waiting for this moment for three years. Each long season came just shy of the ultimate prize, but not this time. She was determined to make sure she walked away a champion.

The season had been played flawlessly. Twenty out of twenty wins sent The Mets through to the play-offs with ease. After beating the 8th seed Nottingham Wildcats, they advanced to the semi-finals to beat the Essex Rebels 82–79. The game took everything Megan could summon. With a stat line of 36/7/8, she carried the team into their first ever finals appearance. Now, she stood in The 02 Arena in London with upward of 10,000 fans chanting, *'defence, defence, defence'*.

The Mets had been the underdogs coming in. Despite their first-place finish, they had barely any play-off experience. The newspapers spoke about how they would choke at the final hurdle, but Megan blocked out the negativity. Following in the shoes of some NBA players, she'd de-activated all her social media once they reached the play-offs. She allowed for no distractions, and up until now, it had paid off. They faced the team with the second-best record in the league and the defending champions—the London Lions. The advantage sat with them. It was their hometown and their fans outnumbered The Mets' by 2:1.

Coach Mayer gave the team their last words of encouragement.

"This is it, the biggest 24 seconds of your playing careers. Look how far you've come. Look at what you've achieved, but are you happy to stop here? Is just being a finalist good enough for you?"

"No!" cried the team.

"Exactly! You want to be champions. You deserve to be champions. This is your time! So, here's what we're going to do."

Coach Mayer demonstrated the play before the team, assigning each player an individual role that had to be carried out with fool proof precision. The buzzer sounded and Megan wandered towards centre court.

"They're here for you." Mayer pointed towards the WNBA scouts in the stand. "Show them what you've got, kid."

She nodded. "Yes, coach."

Megan was as ready as she'd ever been. Her body was conditioned and strengthened to the highest calibre. They'd run the play a thousand times in practice. It wasn't rocket science, but the pressure of the moment would weigh heavy. Megan channelled the crowd, remembering the words of her youth coach— *'Never let the crowd be your disadvantage. When you're playing away, make the crowd your crowd'*.

The score was 76–74 in favour of the Lions. The Lions had done their homework. After she hit her first two three-pointers they started closing her down on the perimeter with fierce urgency—showing her the respect she deserved. The best 3-point percentage in the league that year sat with her. The competitive edge within rose to the surface once again. All eyes were on Megan as she passed the ball to the point guard and moved towards the right side of the key. Instantly, a defender from the opposing team took an aggressive stance, blocking her path to the rim. When the small forward cut off the screen set by the centre and the power forward, Megan baseline cut to the middle of the key.

The clock was ticking; 12 seconds remained. Immediately after setting the screen for Megan to cut, they set an elevator screen to allow Megan to break through to the top of the key—4 seconds remained. Megan planted her feet. A bead of sweat gathered on the tip of her nose; the roar of the crowd silenced; the pulse in her neck throbbed; the play had been run and the final shot fell to her for the biggest catch and shoot three of her career.

She'd run the play a thousand times in practice. She'd run it a thousand more at home, but nothing compared to that in-game feeling. It was do or die, win or lose. The hopes and dreams of her teammates sat firmly on her shoulders. In that moment, she couldn't rely on her record-breaking 48% average that season. When it came down to it, that meant nothing.

She glanced to the left; her parents stood, frozen to the spot. Beside them was Cheryl, and two seats down sat three WNBA scouts. Cheryl had pre-warned of their arrival. They were there to watch Megan and two girls from the London Lions. Three of a potential six scouts had turned up, she wasn't sure which teams they represented. When she turned back to the shot clock it read 3.1 seconds. She caught the ball. With no time to adjust her grip, she pulled up for the three. The opposing defender had been quick to recover from the screen and launched herself forward to attempt the block.

Megan was already in full motion. The release felt off, her technique affected by the extended arm of the Lions centre-forward. The ball soared through the air, spinning toward the rim. Megan fell backwards as she landed on the defender's foot below. The shot clock expired as the ball hit the inner left side of the rim and went through the net.

Megan, with all the adrenaline, quickly jumped to her feet and tracked back for the final 0.8 seconds. She'd just hit the biggest shot of her career, but the game wasn't over. The Lion's centre launched a quarterback-style pass from one end of the floor to the other. As the ball landed in the hands of their shooting guard, the buzzer sounded. Megan fell to the floor, head in hands as her teammates swarmed her. The bench and coaching staff stormed the floor pulling Megan to her feet.

"I knew you could do it."

"What a shot, Meg."

"Amazing shot, Megan!"

The feeling was like no other. She thought she knew what to expect. The overwhelming happiness, relief and adrenaline all mixed into one, but it was so much more than that. The years of disappointment faded and the taste of glory at that moment brought an excitement that she felt would last a lifetime. She was on top of the world with the belief that she could achieve anything in life if she continued to work hard. The faces of Megan's teammates as they smiled and hugged one another; the crowd as they clapped and chanted her name, and the confetti falling all around was a mental picture she hoped to dream about.

The official statistician for the game handed Coach Mayer a piece of paper.

"How does it feel to be a champion?"

"It feels incredible, coach."

"You finished with 33 points, 2 steals, 6 rebounds and 7 assists tonight. Not to mention the winning shot. You killed it." He wafted the paper in the air proudly. "I think those WNBA scouts over there ought to see this, what do you think?"

"Do you think I have a chance?"

"I think they'd be darn stupid not to recruit you."

"Thanks, coach, for everything you've done for me over the past three years."

"I didn't do anything. My job is to make you believe in your own ability. I just unlocked the door, now it's time for you to walk on through it and become the player I know you can be."

"Do you think it's a little late in the day?"

Coach Mayer's eyes bulged. "Don't be ridiculous. You're twenty-five, Megan, not thirty-five. You have a good ten years left in you to make an impact in the WNBA."

"Yeah, you're right."

"Trust me."

"Thanks, coach."

He placed his hand on her shoulder. "Now, go celebrate with your teammates. These nights don't come around too often."

***

Cheryl shouted across the arena to Megan. "I want you to meet someone."

She excused herself from the celebrations with her parents and wandered over to the crowded courtside.

"Megan, this is Steve from Phoenix Mercury."

Megan shook his hand. "Great game out there. That final shot was the thing of dreams, right?"

"Thank you, yes it was. Unless you miss then it's the thing of nightmares."

He laughed, which eased her nerves.

"Agreed. We have been keeping a close eye on you over the last few months and we're impressed. You went to Stanford?"

"Yes, sir." She nodded.

"I will be having words with our American scout. I'm not quite sure how we let you slip through the net when you graduated."

"Don't worry, I get it, my 3-point average was roughly 10% less than it is now." She smiled.

"Best in the league last season. Incredible work."

"Thank you."

"Who's your inspiration? Do you model your game after anyone in particular?"

"A lot of my influence has come from my dad over the years, but in terms of the type of player I want to be, it has to be Steph Curry."

"Solid choice, arguably the best 3-point shooter to ever play the game. Is that what you aspire to be in the women's game?"

Megan considered her response carefully, she could tell him what he expected to hear, the quick version, but the champions t-shirt she currently wore gave her a newfound confidence.

"I aspire to be a great teammate and a champion. Personal accolades are great, but that's not what drives me. I want to be a part of a team that wants to win, a team that will stick together and dig deep when it really matters. I will put my body on the line every single night to be the best I can be and I would expect the same from my teammates. I hold very high standards for myself, so I will always aim to be better than I was the day before. I believe in my game and my work ethic and what that amounts to on the court will reflect that."

Steve's veneers glistened, showing the ultimate Hollywood smile. "Speaking like a true champion and a leader."

"Thank you."

"I won't keep you much longer. It's been great to chat with you. Once I get back to Phoenix, I will be in touch."

Cheryl arranged an exchange with each of the remaining two scouts. One flew in from Chicago and the other from New York, the home of the New York Liberty and the place she longed to be again. The roster at Liberty already had two stand-out shooting guards. Being a fan of the game in general, she watched as many of the WNBA games as she could, often comparing herself, analysing what each player brought to the game and how she could better improve it or make herself more desirable. They did lack in the point guard position though. *Could she switch roles?* The ability was there. She believed in her facilitating game. Her dribbling and offence intelligence was top-notch, but she hadn't played that position since high school.

"Cheryl, how do you think it went?"

"Really great. They loved you."

"Chicago didn't love me." Megan rolled her eyes.

"She's always like that, believe me. I have dealt with her before so don't take it personally. She likes to play her cards close to her chest."

"Okay, what about Liberty?"

"I think she was impressed. Liberty won't be easy, probably the most difficult of the three, but you held your own well. Your game speaks for itself, Megan. I will be expecting three offers on my desk Monday morning."

Megan grinned. "You think that's possible?"

"I know it's possible. Just leave it with me."

"Oh, one more thing. Can you tell Liberty that I'd be willing to switch roles?"

"What do you mean?"

"I know their roster and I know they don't need another shooting guard."

"Unless one of them leaves," Cheryl pointed out.

"This is true, but if they don't, I'd be willing to play the point."

"Okay, I'll make sure I tell them that. So, you're set on New York, huh?"

"It's my home. I miss it. If I could go anywhere, it would be there."

"Then I will focus all my energy on getting you there. You've done the hard part, now let me get you the deal you deserve."

"Thank you, Cheryl, I don't know what I'd do without you."

"You'd succeed anyway, it's in your nature. Now, go enjoy your night." She nodded toward the centre of the arena where the trophy now took pride of place.

Megan ran towards her parents and embraced them both once again. "Thank you for being here."

"Do you think we'd ever miss this?" Michael said. "What did Cheryl say?"

"It's looking good. All three scouts are looking likely to come back with a deal next week," Megan beamed.

"That's amazing, baby girl, I'm so proud of you."

Amanda Davis reached out to stroke away the strand of hair from her face. Proudly admiring her daughter.

"Mom, stop."

"What? I'm just so proud of you."

"I know, but I'm sweaty."

"I don't care, come here." They embraced once again. This time, Megan didn't pull away. The bond she had with her parents would outlast any time constraints society put on her. So what if they made her feel like she was still sixteen years old, they loved her and that was all that mattered. The tears in her mom's eyes counteracted the happiness shown on her face. If everything went to plan, Megan would be thousands of miles away once again and she knew that would be hard for her mom.

"I need to go. They're going to present the trophy."

"Okay, sweetheart, have fun. Congratulations again."

"Thank you, love you."

Megan joined her teammates. The announcer called out across the arena.

"And now for the presentation of the 2017 WBBL finals trophy and the WBBL finals MVP award. Please welcome league commissioner, Lynne Randel."

A woman in her late 40s with shoulder-length brown hair took centre stage.

"Thank you for what has been such an entertaining season. Finally, after what was a dramatic and hard-fought final game, we get to crown a champion. First of all, I'd like to say congratulations to the Lions on a fantastic season." The 10,000-strong crowd applauded the Lions' efforts. "Now for the trophy, please welcome your 2017 WBBL champions, the Manchester Met Mystics."

Lynne Randel handed the trophy to the point guard and captain of the team, Brittney Miller. Megan watched in awe as the crowd erupted and the canons fired red and blue confetti into the atmosphere. Then suddenly, it was as if the celebrations of her teammates and the crowd sounded from a million miles away, fading slowly into the background. When her triumph was being recognised and the glory felt staggering, all that she pictured in the subdued silence was Ashley. The realisation that Ashley wasn't present for the biggest moment of her life felt wrong. Despite the complexity of their relationship, Megan felt a hole. She couldn't help but consider how different she'd be feeling if Ashley was there, standing on the courtside with her parents. *What if they'd found a way to be more than friends? How different would her life be?*

The announcer eventually broke the trance that consumed Megan. "Now to present the finals MVP award, once again, Lynne Randel."

"With a dominant performance, scoring 92 points in three games, averaging 30 points a game in these finals, close to 7 assists and 3 steals, the unanimous MVP vote goes to…Megan Davies."

Lynne handed Megan the small glass trophy. Once the applause settled, she continued.

"Megan, first of all, congratulations. How does it feel to be the WBBL champions?"

"It's incredible. This group of girls have played their hearts out this season. We left nothing on the table. 20/20 in the regular season all the way through to the finals to now be crowned champions, it's been an unbelievable run and something we are all incredibly proud of."

"You led the league in scoring and 3-point shooting this year, what did you do differently with your game to get to this point now as opposed to the previous two seasons?"

"I don't cheat the game of basketball. Every single day I work hard. I get up early, I stay late. I train every hour I possibly can, I always have. I think sometimes things just click. You have to trust in your ability and the shots will fall. My team has helped me immensely. I wouldn't be scoring if it wasn't for the precision passing of my teammates, or the incredible plays drawn up by the coach. We all play a part in being able to succeed so I owe it all to them. Oh, and my dad, of course, I can't forget him." Her father winked from the front row, amused.

"Do you have any thoughts on your future? Will you remain in England? There are reports the WNBA is knocking at your door?"

"I can't comment on that. I just want to enjoy this moment right here, celebrate with my teammates and we will see what next season brings."

"Thank you for your time. That's it folks. The finals MVP and your 2017 WBBL champions. Give them a round of applause."

***

The celebrations continued back in the locker room. Megan took phone calls from Nancy and Julie. She had over twenty messages from family and friends as well as fellow basketball players. Much to her disappointment, there was no message from Ashley amongst them. *Maybe she wasn't aware?* Megan hadn't used social media since the play-offs began, so unless Ashley followed the games she wouldn't know—wishful thinking. *Maybe she just didn't care*, Megan thought, *why should she?*

Megan felt like a bitter cliché. She wanted what she couldn't have, or more accurately, she wanted the idea of what she thought she couldn't have.

The thoughts of Ashley consumed her, so much so she reactivated her social media purely to make her aware. Gone were the days when we as humans would straightforwardly process our emotions, which now felt unimaginable. Instead, she would post on social media and wait patiently for people to like it, so that she could scrutinise every like that appeared until she found one in particular, the one that would give her the validation she needed. Maybe it would spark a conversation. Even a simple 'congratulations' would suffice, anything at all. She just wanted to be acknowledged. Megan wanted to know if, after three years, Ashley still thought about her; still wished or hoped that they could one day be in each other's lives—like she did.

Then she saw a photo, the first one that appeared before her eyes—the algorithm knew. The heavy interaction with said photo put it at the top of Megan's feed. There was no un-seeing it. No way to misinterpret exactly what the photo represented.

Megan slumped back on the bench as the celebrations continued around her. The noise levels drowned out the whispered disbelief that escaped her lips, "She's engaged".

The realisation hit her hard. A lump formed in her throat as she tried to swallow down her emotions. The truth had been revealed for the world to see. The assured elation of her earlier championship win had given her hope, a reason to believe that anything was possible.

Naively, she'd allowed herself to dream, even just for a fading moment, that had been enough.

The truth hurt. "She loves Madison, not me."

23

Ashley

"How you feeling?" Madison leant over the back of the sofa and kissed Ashley on the top of the head.

"Not great," she grumbled in a hoarse voice.

"Coffee?"

Ashley held out her empty cup. "Yes, please."

"What are you watching?"

The computer sat on her lap streaming the WBBL final.

"It's the women's basketball final. The one Megan's playing in." Ashley avoided looking in Madison's direction.

"Oh, so that's why you got up so early. How's it going? Are they winning?"

The time difference forced Ashley to wake at eleven in the morning. After a heavy night of celebrations and a house party that went on until five that morning, it took a significant amount of effort.

"I think Nancy might tell me off if I don't watch. It's going good, it's close though they're up 3 in the third quarter."

Ashley kept her tone detached, after all, it wasn't a big deal—or so she told herself. Nancy was the one who mentioned Megan reaching the play-offs. Nancy was the one who told her the time and date of the final—yes, she did already check online just to be sure, but that was beside the point. Waking early after a night celebrating your engagement to watch someone you dated once in a basketball final was normal. It was completely and utterly natural; it was a show of support, that's all.

Ashley's internal debate with herself lasted the whole time that Madison made coffee. The roar of the crowd and the commentary from the game filled the awkward silence as Madison didn't respond right away.

"Here." Madison handed her the coffee.

"Thank you."

"Have you spoken to her recently?"

Ashley knew exactly who she meant, but raised her eyebrows curiously, hoping her unruffled attitude might ease any tension. "Who?"

"Megan."

"No. Not for a while."

"Interesting."

"What?"

"I'm just surprised, that's all. You wanted to be friends, yet you don't speak."

"It is what it is. Kind of hard to be friends with someone who lives in England." Ashley shrugged.

"True." Madison wasn't satisfied with the outcome; her head tilted slightly and her eyes looked unengaged. She had never been certain of Ashley's emotional intention towards Megan and this time was no different. "Anyway, I'm going back to bed. Oh, before I forget, something came in the post for you yesterday." Madison flicked through the wicker basket on the kitchen side that held an accumulation of letters.

"Here it is." She tossed it in Ashley's direction.

"Thank you, Mads, love you."

"I love you too. Don't be loud." She scowled as she returned to the bedroom.

"Huh, maybe the ring has special powers," Ashley whispered under her breath.

Moments later, she was screaming, "Yes, Megan!" as another picture-perfect 3-point shot fell through the hoop. It felt odd for Ashley, essentially watching Megan on TV like some sort of *'fan-girl'* vying for her attention. Watching as people cheered her name, asked for her autograph before the game and fought for even a small bit of attention. To Ashley, she was just Megan.

***

"Did you get the invite?" Nancy said.

"What invite?"

"I sent them out a couple of days ago, you should have received it."

"Oh wait, what did I do with that?" Ashley searched the living area and found the invitation on the cluttered coffee table.

"Ahh, here it is. I was too busy watching Megan's win yesterday. I forgot all about it." Ashley placed the phone on the kitchen side and proceeded to open the little cream envelope.

"I'm so glad you watched it. She played great, didn't she?"

"Amazing. Well-deserved MVP."

"I agree. She was so happy when I called yesterday. It was heart-warming to hear."

"I bet." Ashley's text had still gone unanswered, which wasn't like Megan. It left her with an uneasy feeling.

"Wait, you're getting married? You're already married."

"It's a vow renewal, you silly thing."

She glanced again at the invite, "Oh, of course." Ashley laughed.

"It's our twenty-year anniversary in December. We wanted to do something special to celebrate. Might be the last big anniversary we celebrate."

"Don't say that!" Ashley warned. "You're going to live until you're at least a hundred, so we will remember this conversation at your Ruby anniversary. That is forty years, isn't it? Or is it Pearl?"

"It's Ruby, and I hope so."

Nancy and Christopher were both in their late seventies. Neither of them had any serious ailments, they still worked over thirty hours a week at the bar and walked around Central Park almost every day.

"I know so. You're fitter than me."

Nancy sniggered. "So, are you coming?"

Ashley didn't hesitate, "Of course, I wouldn't miss it for the world."

The little white card inside had silver writing that read, *'We still do'*, with a photo of Christopher kissing Nancy on the forehead lovingly—a wedding day shot that gave her shivers.

"I knew you'd come. Will you bring Madison?"

"Yes, if that's okay?"

"Of course, darling. I just need to know for numbers, so I'll put you down with a plus one."

Ashley thought about asking if Megan would be there, but that was a stupid question.

"Where are you thinking for the venue?"

The card was a save the date style, but the venue was TBC.

"Well, Christopher suggested hiring out a venue, but I don't want it to be extravagant. It's not about that, so I was thinking Central Park, by the bench. What do you think?"

"I think that sounds like an incredible idea. There is so much sentiment behind that bench, that's what people absolutely adored about your story. I think it's perfect. Maybe back to Nancy's for the reception?"

"I agree. I asked Julie if she would officiate for us."

"That's great."

"That brings me to my next question," Nancy paused. "There is absolutely no obligation, so feel free to say no, but I was hoping maybe you could say something?"

"At the ceremony?"

"Well, at the reception. The ceremony will be pretty quick I would imagine. A lot of people strolling by, etc. so I thought maybe the speeches could be done at the reception afterwards."

"Okay, obviously I would be delighted to, but what would you like me to say?"

"I'll leave that to you. You're amazing, I know you'll come up with something."

"No pressure, then." Ashley laughed. "Who else is speaking? I want to know my competition."

"Probably just my son, Michael. He spoke at the wedding, so I think he'd like to and Christopher of course."

"And then me?" The request took her by surprise.

"Why do you sound so shocked?"

"I don't know. It's a big deal, isn't it? It's such an intimate setting with all the people that know you the best and I just feel…" Ashley searched for the right words, "…probably a little inadequate."

Nancy sighed. "How long have I known you now?"

"Three years I think."

"How often have I seen you in those three years?"

"A lot."

"Exactly. Probably more than my children, my grandchildren and my friends. People come into our lives for a reason. You came into mine unexpectedly and brought me so much joy from the words you wrote. After that, you continued to bring me joy, day in day out, sitting in the bar, writing away. To this day you always call, you help out at the bar when we're struggling and you never ever forget a special date. You, my dear, have become family and that makes you anything but inadequate."

Ashley's eyes glazed over. She dabbed underneath her eyes to stop the tears from falling. The kindness displayed by Nancy since the first day they'd met still amazed her.

"I'm so glad I met you. Thank you for allowing me to speak at your ceremony. I am honestly so honoured."

"The pleasure is all mine."

***

Three days passed before Ashley received a reply from Megan. A simple message that read:

Thank you for watching the game. Your support means more than you know. Congratulations on the engagement by the way! The photo was beautiful and that ring, WOW! Madison is a lucky girl. I'm glad you're happy, you deserve it.

That clarified what Ashley assumed. Megan had seen the photo. She'd known about the engagement prior to the message of congratulations and chose not to reply. That hurt Ashley, but deep down raised a lot of questions about the complexity of their relationship. While Megan remained on a different continent, their ability to be friends diminished with every passing day.

There was a reason the two met, on that day, in that bar. She firmly believed that. There was a reason Megan introduced Ashley to Nancy, making their lives forever intertwined.

Ashley continued tapping away at the keys on her laptop. The evening had disappeared into night. It was midnight and she was no closer to sleep. The room was dark, she'd switched off all the lights and the TV to sit and think in silence. The distractions she couldn't bear, not when writing. Madison had retired to bed after a long day at work, but Ashley couldn't shake the story within; her imagination going wild as it often did.

She'd been at *The New York Times* for almost a year. In that time, she'd learned more than she ever thought possible. The fundamentals around news judgment, style, tone of voice and perspective were all key things she could see improving in her articles. She had worked on countless daily news articles, as well as learning graphics and the depth and detail that is needed for special projects. The newsroom was always bustling with reporters, journalists, editors and producers all scrambling to get the next big story. The team of people behind the Anchor or behind the Newspaper was immense and Ashley loved being a part of it.

There was a certain hierarchy to the newsroom and she was firmly at the bottom of the food chain, but that only made her strive to be better. The one thing she had in her favour prior to getting the job was her already established freelance writing. There was rarely time to write her own articles in her current role, but she still tried to write at least one a month, whenever the inspiration hit. Each article she would drop onto Bryan's or Sonia's desk and wait for the green light. It didn't always come. Some of her work wasn't quite what they wanted at that moment, but they often took the time to recommend another publication.

The moments of inspiration came almost always at night. The moonlight shone through the window like the softest of flashlights, leaving a window frame silhouette on the living room floor.

The words came naturally.

It's me again, here with another instalment of all things controversial. Today I want to talk to you about the "One That Got Away'—the dreaded phrase, we've all been there, right? You crossed paths and connected with someone on a magical level and now you cling to the idea of that person and what could have been.

You often remember all the scenarios you invented, all with a blissfully happy ending (even if that was not the case). In our mind, we know it's not healthy to obsess over the "What If", but it's almost impossible to shake the feeling.

It goes back to the age-old cliché—right person, wrong time. A cliché is a cliché for a reason, despite it being so overused and losing its original meaning, we must remember that primarily it was based on truth. Someone can be your right person at the wrong time, period. Naturally though, there can be an array of different reasons. Maybe it was distance, emotional unavailability, withholding commitments or maybe it actually turned into a significant relationship, but ended for all the innumerable reasons relationships cease to exist.

Now, if you're still following my train of thought, then you've also (more than likely) compared said person to other partners. You've probably wondered, on numerous occasions, what it would be like to see them again. Wished for a change in circumstance that would allow the world to spin perfectly on its axis once again, freeing you from the mundane Groundhog Day effect your mind plays on repeat.

However, this is where I open your eyes to reality. There is no "One That Got Away". That would mean there is only one person on this whole entire planet made for us—similar to my soulmate controversy in my earlier articles. The concept that we are meant for only one person is distressing. That essentially means if you're not with that "one" person, then you will search your whole life comparing, pining and hoping for them— causing every other relationship to perish in a cloud of smoke.

Have I convinced you yet? No, I thought not. The romanticised version of the "One That Got Away" will always prevail. Our minds won't allow otherwise until we have explored the possibility. Explore it—go ahead, find out. What's the harm in that?

But before you do, just think about your current partner. Maybe you're their "One That DIDN'T Get Away"...

24

December 2017
Ashley

Ashley raced into the bedroom. "Madison, have you seen my speech?"

"It was on your desk yesterday."

"I can't find it." Frantically searching, she brushed off some old articles; stationery fell to the floor, there was no sign of her speech. "We literally need to leave in five minutes."

"Where have you looked?"

"Everywhere," Ashley snapped.

"You made some tweaks to it last night, didn't you? While you were sat on the sofa—check there."

Ashley raced towards the living room. She launched one cushion after another from the sofa. There it was scrunched in the corner. "Thank God."

"Got it?" Madison called.

"Yes, thank you."

"Good." Madison kissed Ashley on the forehead. "Just breathe. I know you've been worrying about this speech, but you'll be amazing."

"My heart is racing. I don't think I have ever had to make a speech."

"I know, but I believe in you." They shared another tender kiss.

"You look amazing, by the way." Madison grinned.

"Thank you, baby. You're not so bad yourself." She winked.

Ashley wore a slim-fit grey suit with white cowboy ankle boots and a white tee; her large wool overcoat sat comfortably on her shoulders to combat the plummeting temperature that now firmly sat in the 30s. The snow had fallen in recent days—just enough to cover the ground—Nancy's wish had been granted. When asked what her picture-perfect vow renewal would be, she said, 'a snowy Central Park'.

The thought of seeing Megan triggered a lot of anxiety. The fleeting relationship—if you could call it that—still left a significant impact on Ashley, causing her to accept that she never quite got closure from their affinity with one another. The fear of the unknown caused the nauseous feeling in her stomach. The day was supposed to be all about Nancy and Christopher. A day to celebrate the undying love they shared for one another, but Ashley was distracted with questions. *How will Megan act towards me? What should I say? Will she have a plus one? How do we interact as friends in the company of my fiancée?*

The last one troubled her the most. *The first step to conquering a fear is embracing it*, she told herself repeatedly. It was time to face the awkward encounter in the hopes that the catastrophic sequence in her head was merely an over-exaggerated scenario she'd concocted in her mind and nothing like what she was about to experience.

"Have you heard from Nancy this morning?"

"No."

"Did she confirm Megan was coming?" *Had she not told Madison?* Ashley questioned herself. Megan had been doubtful to attend the vow renewal due to some personal reasons that Ashley didn't query further with Nancy, but after a brief conversation the day before Nancy confirmed her attendance.

"Apparently so. She was supposedly flying in yesterday."

"That's good, then. I know how happy that will make Nancy."

Ashley gulped. "Are you okay with it?"

"Sure I am."

"You sure?"

"As you said, you spent one night together. It wasn't a big deal. You chose to remain friends afterwards and that's all it's been ever since. As long as she feels that way as well then there will be no objections on my behalf."

Ashley felt guilty for withholding the truth, despite her own understanding of the truth being foggy.

"Thank you for being so understanding."

"Well, I am the one with the big rock on my finger."

"That is true."

***

The cab dropped them off at the corner of West 72nd. From there, they took the familiar route to the Lake. The bench had been the place she first discovered Nancy and Christopher's love story; it had since become the place she went for inspiration.

The branches of the pine trees bowed under the weight of the snow. The wide-open meadows saw cross-country skiers create an array of zigzag lines on the powdery white surface below. The sweet and refreshing smell of the pine trees reminded Ashley of a fruity cocktail she used to make at Analogue. The harsh blizzard-like snow predicted for the week ahead stayed out of sight. The idea of wearing two pairs of socks, two pairs of pants, heavy-duty winter coats and fur-lined boots to a wedding felt like fashion suicide, so they were both grateful for the weather temporarily withholding the inevitable. Like any normal day, the paths were overflowing with dog walkers, tourists and locals alike. As they crossed Bow Bridge, the lake below was frozen solid.

Ashley felt Madison's grasp tighten around her hand as they approached the party of guests who'd already arrived. The park grew quieter the nearer they got to the bench. Christopher had chosen the perfect spot all those years ago. From a distance, she didn't see Nancy, but she recognised the woman blowing ferociously on her hands as Julie.

One man towered above the rest. With a short grey buzz cut and a slim athletic build, Ashley assumed he was military. It wasn't until he turned to the right and she had a clear view of his face that she recognised him. It was Nancy's son—aka Megan's father.

Ashley closed in on the group, her eyes darting from one face to the next. No Nancy and no Megan.

"Where's Nancy?" Madison said.

"I'm not sure."

The guests gathered around the bench in no particular order. Julie stood at the front talking with Christopher. Ashley and Madison tucked themselves away at the back of the crowd. The chatter faded as people split off one by one creating a natural pathway through the middle.

Then she saw Nancy, her arm linked tenderly with Megan's as they gingerly made their way across the snowy pathway. Ashley noticed the original wedding gown from the photo in her article. The minimalist crepe fabric and delicate back still looked as elegant as it did twenty years earlier. She wrapped a faux fur shrug tightly around her shoulders to partially keep out the cold.

When Nancy glanced her way she mouthed, *you look beautiful*. Nancy winked in response. Megan remained to Nancy's side, hiding her from Ashley's view. As she leaned forward to adjust the strand of hair falling loose from Nancy's chignon hairstyle, she spotted her.

Their eyes said all that needed to be said. Megan softly parted her lips to reveal a knowing smile. Ashley could have sworn the slightest blush appeared on her olive-skinned cheeks. There was something so safe inside her eyes. Instantly, the cold air that had made her skin icy to the touch felt no more—it was replaced by a warmth she'd only ever felt in Megan's presence. Her elegance and grace matched Nancy's and Ashley imagined her walking down the aisle at her own wedding one day, picturing how she would be the epitome of beauty.

Were they ever strangers? The first day Ashley saw her, there was some pull that she still struggled to understand. That same pull was stronger now. Over the three years they'd known each other, they had formed a bond that was forged in the timeline of their lives.

In that moment, Nancy should have been the only focus, but as though Nancy was somehow a ghost, Ashley saw straight through her, maintaining a steady gaze as Megan guided her grandma into Christopher's arms.

Throughout the ceremony, Ashley's eyes met Megan's with each softly spoken vow. She tried to look away, but unaware of the time she had left in her presence she felt compelled to admire her.

***

After the ceremony finished, Ashley got a cab along with Madison and three other members of Nancy's family—none of which she recognised. The short twenty-minute ceremony had been a beautifully meaningful show of their love and their willingness to recommit to each other once again. The celebration afterwards was at Nancy's bar—that was the part Ashley feared. She was yet to make any contact with Megan that didn't solely involve their eyes.

Nancy's had been closed off to the public for the day, meaning the forty people in attendance were all guests of the happy couple. A large white balloon arch towered over the entrance as the main feature and smaller balloon arrangements were dotted around the room. A make-shift stage had been assembled beside the bar where the DJ finished setting up.

Ashley found Nancy by the bar after a few minutes.

"You honestly look unbelievable." Ashley beamed.

"Thank you, darling." Nancy leaned forward and air-kissed both cheeks—La Bise-style.

"Were you nervous?"

"You don't get nervous at my age, sweetheart. At this stage, there is nothing I haven't already experienced."

"That is a good point. Can you feel your hands again though?"

"Just about. I think the complimentary gloves were a good idea."

"Agreed."

"Have you met my son yet?"

"No, he's the tall one over by the bar?"

"Yes, how did you know?"

"Aside from the fact he's the tallest here and he used to play basketball? It was a no-brainer. You have shown me pictures though."

"And Megan? Where is my granddaughter hiding?" Nancy searched the room, head on a swivel. "She was here a minute ago."

Ashley felt Madison tense up. Her hand slipped from her arm.

"I'm not sure, I'll catch up with her soon though." Ashley attempted to change the subject. "What time do the speeches start?"

"We are going to give it an hour for everyone to get here and settle in then we can start. I'm looking forward to yours the most, just don't tell Michael."

Ashley used her index finger to make a symbolic cross over her chest. "Promise."

"Are Emily and Jason still coming?"

"They said so. I imagine they'll be here any minute."

"Good, the more the merrier."

Nancy had extended the invitation to Emily and Jason for the after-party. They spent many days and evenings at the bar with Ashley, so Nancy felt it was only right. That relieved the pressure from a social standpoint as Madison didn't know anyone other than Nancy and Christopher. That had been playing in the back of Ashley's mind, especially if she was to speak with Megan for a prolonged period of time.

As if the universe predicted it, Emily walked through the entrance. Seconds later, Megan appeared from the restroom and made her way towards Nancy and Ashley.

"I'll go and say hi to Emily," Madison said. She kissed her delicately on the cheek and departed.

Megan strutted confidently, stopping beside Nancy. Their eyes never left each other, apart from a quick glance at their colour co-ordinated outfits—another coincidence. Megan wore a light grey figure-hugging dress that stopped just below the knee. The neck was high—a clever choice considering the weather—and covering her shoulders was a dark grey faux fur coat.

"Hi." Megan smiled.

"Hey." Ashley leaned in and kissed both cheeks just as Nancy had done, ultimately trying to ease the tension. As she did that, Megan's hand—strategically or not—cupped underneath Ashley's chin; the touch felt intimate, which sent a shiver down her spine that lingered long after she removed it.

"I can see Christopher wants me so I will leave you two to catch up." Nancy clinked their champagne glasses together before she left. "I'll call you over for the speech shortly, my dear."

"A speech huh? Look at you, you're like the second granddaughter she never had," Megan teased.

"Are you jealous because I'm her new favourite?"

"Oh yeah, super jealous."

"On a serious note, I was shocked when she asked me."

Megan sipped her champagne. "I wasn't."

"Really?"

"She never stops talking about you. It's quite annoying actually. 'Ashley worked this shift for me', 'Ashley helped me with this', 'Ashley's going to pick me up a few bits from the store', 'I went for a walk through the park with Ashley today'." Megan rolled her eyes whilst laughing. "It's sweet though. I'm happy that you created that bond with her. Her family is spread all over the place and I know she finds that hard sometimes. So yeah, I wasn't surprised she asked you."

"I just hope I do it justice."

"I have read all your articles. It will be amazing."

"All of them?" Ashley raised her eyebrows; the surprise was obvious.

"Yes, why so shocked?"

"I don't know."

"Do you think I could get away with not reading them when my gram tells me every single time and then asks me for my thoughts the week after? It feels like a test."

"Is that the only reason then? You're basically coerced into it?" Ashley chuckled.

"Between me and you, I would read them regardless."

"Thank you."

"Well, I know you watch my games. So, it's the least I can do."

"I only watch them for that pretty blonde woman on your team. What's she called again?"

Megan smirked behind her glass. "Oh, I see. Speaking of women, where is your fiancée?"

"She's chatting with Emily and Jason." Ashley looked around. All three of them turned their heads rapidly.

"It seems we are being watched," Megan said.

"Looks that way doesn't it." Ashley was now well aware of the eyes burning a hole in the side of her head. She wondered what her friends would make of the encounter. *Did it seem flirtatious?* She was wary of her body language and not being too inviting, but they continued to hold each other's gaze for a second too long.

"What about you anyway? How does it feel to be a champion?" Ashley said.

"It's everything I thought it would be. Magical at first, life-changing, but it's fleeting, and as soon as the moment passes you want to feel it again. The motivation within me is ten times stronger than it was before. I have had a taste of the glory now and it makes me want more. It's an addiction, probably similar to your writing."

"I can understand that. It was great to see, your game was insane. You must have had the scouts lining up at the door?"

"I had a few options, but they fell through. It's been a nightmare few months trying to figure out my next move."

"Will you be staying in England?"

Megan hesitated. "No, I thought that was the case at one point as they offered me a crazy deal to stay."

"But?"

"But eventually the offer I wanted came through."

"Is that why you only flew in yesterday? Nancy said you might not make it at one stage."

"I wouldn't have missed it for the world, but I had to tie up a few loose ends first."

"So?"

"What?" Megan laughed.

"Are you going to keep me in suspense? Where are you taking your talents to next? France? Germany? California?"

"It's a little closer to home than that."

"Oh, I thought you weren't staying in England?"

"Not that home, stupid."

"New York?"

Megan nodded. "I got an offer from New York Liberty."

"The WNBA?" Ashley froze in place, becoming suddenly aware of her own heartbeat.

"Yes."

"So, you're coming back to New York? For good?"

Megan leaned into the conversation. One arm hugged her body, the other held the champagne glass lightly with the tips of her fingers. Their gaze didn't break once. "I hope so."

***

Michael's speech was a heart-warming encounter of the first time he'd seen Nancy and Christopher together. In his words, *it all made sense after that, the world had brought back together two people meant for one another.*

The guests raised a glass to the happy couple and then Michael introduced Ashley. "Next, we have Ashley. Many of you will remember the beautiful words she wrote about my mom and Christopher in *The New York Times* newspaper article, and that's how their relationship started. Since then, she has become a big part of their life and an extended member of our family. Come up here, Ashley."

Michael had a sweet smile. She could tell he was a kind man. He passed her the microphone and whispered, "It's nice to finally meet you. Don't show me up, will you?" He winked and walked off stage to join Megan and her mom.

If there was ever a time Ashley wanted the room to swallow her whole, it was now. The nerves reminded her of the first time she'd pitched her idea to a room full of editors. The same nauseating feeling ate her up inside. The microphone felt sticky in her hand; her palms were sweaty. Forty people stared her way, expecting words that would evoke unimaginable emotion.

Except in that moment, the crowd of people didn't matter. She looked out and saw Madison, the girl she loved, her best friend, her confidant and the keeper of secrets, stood proudly admiring her from afar. Ashley glanced in the other direction. To the left of the room stood Megan, who smiled reassuringly.

Suddenly, she had a moment of striking realisation—a true moment of clarity. Just before the point of no return, she realised she'd been incredibly naive. Firstly, to think that she had everything under control, and secondly, in thinking that the speech she was about to make wasn't someway, somehow connected to Megan.

She loved her. In what capacity, she didn't understand, but she loved her without knowing how or when it happened. She had been out of sight and out of mind (to a degree) for three years and now she was back—for good. The feelings Ashley tried to bury time and time again rose to the surface revealing her vulnerability. Megan's eyes watched intently; her brow raised.

There was no time to dwell on the unknown, the guests had settled to complete silence as the final glass clinked.

Ashley raised the microphone to her lips, a little voice in her mind said, *here goes nothing.*

Sometimes in life, there are significant moments of clarity. A realisation that someone or something was always meant for you…

TO BE CONTINUED

Spring 2022

Thank you for reading *If We Meet Again.* I hope you enjoyed it.

Want to stay updated with news about my books?

Follow me on Instagram : **@nss_writings**

Like me on Facebook : **NicoleSpencerSkillen**

And if you have a moment please take the time to review *If We Meet Again.* I would be eternally grateful.

Thank you once more for your support, and I hope we meet again between the pages of another book.

ABOUT THE AUTHOR

Nicole Spencer-Skillen is a best-selling author of Sapphic Romance novels and a die-hard LA Lakers fan. She is incredibly passionate about writing novels with relatable, funny and emotionally compelling LGBT+ characters.

Born and raised in Lancashire, England, she has aspirations of surfing rooftop bars and ice-skating in Central Park, whilst living out her dream career in New York City.

Printed in Great Britain
by Amazon

19977637R00185